"Ye are truly

"Not quite."

"If there is no betrothal, then 'tis nae binding." Studying her thoughtfully, he added, "I dinna care if ye are no longer a virgin."

"How dare you?" Outrage filled her, an emotion she was grateful for, since it helped burn away some of the raw need inside her.

"'Tis a natural assumption." He reached to straighten the collar of her surcoat, his fingers brushing lightly over her neck.

Rosalind swore that scant touch made her feel faint. Weak. She'd had no right to kiss him, let alone thrill to his every caress.

* * *

The Laird's Lady
Harlequin Historical #769—September 2005

Ch   Br

Praise for Joanne Rock

"Charming characters, a passionate sexual
relationship and an engaging story—it's all here."
—*Romantic Times* on *Girl's Guide to Hunting & Kissing*

"Joanne Rock's talent for writing passionate
scenes and vivid characters really sizzles in this story.
Even the hot secondary romance has chemistry!"
—*Romantic Times* on *Wild and Wicked*

"*The Wedding Knight* is guaranteed to please!
Joanne Rock brings a fresh, vibrant
voice to this charming tale."
—*New York Times* bestselling author Teresa Medeiros

"A highly readable medieval romance with an
entertaining touch of the paranormal...."
—*Romantic Times* on *The Knight's Redemption*

The Laird's Lady

Joanne Rock

HARLEQUIN®

TORONTO • NEW YORK • LONDON
AMSTERDAM • PARIS • SYDNEY • HAMBURG
STOCKHOLM • ATHENS • TOKYO • MILAN • MADRID
PRAGUE • WARSAW • BUDAPEST • AUCKLAND

ISBN 0-373-29369-0

THE LAIRD'S LADY

Copyright © 2005 by Joanna Rock

www.eHarlequin.com

Printed in U.S.A.

Available from Harlequin Historical and
JOANNE ROCK

The Wedding Knight #694
The Knight's Redemption #720
The Betrothal #749
"Highland Handfast"
My Lady's Favor #758
The Laird's Lady #769

Please address questions and book requests to:
Harlequin Reader Service
U.S.: 3010 Walden Ave., P.O. Box 1325, Buffalo, NY 14269
Canadian: P.O. Box 609, Fort Erie, Ont. L2A 5X3

For Joyce Soule, thank you for encouraging me and
for reading my earliest attempts at writing this book.
And to Catherine Mann, who read a few other versions
of Rosalind and Malcolm's tale on its journey to
publication. Thank you, my friends!

Finally, from *Braveheart* to *Rob Roy* and
The Highlander, my hat's off to Hollywood for the
tales of Scotland that have made those misty moors
such an intriguing setting for my imagination.

Chapter One

August 1307

Married women never had these problems.

Barbarians swarmed at Beaumont's gate, and the unwed daughter of the house was the only person who could lift a finger to stop them. Rosalind of Beaumont pounded her fist in frustration, causing all the miniature flower-filled urns on her worktable to jump.

Where was Gregory Evandale and his promise of marriage when she needed a man to lead her people to battle?

Rosalind's steward burst into the solar, scattering her thoughts. John's sprint across the rushes belied his fifty years as he skidded to a halt a scant step from her. "The brutes demand to speak with the lord of Beaumont, my lady."

"Too bad Beaumont Keep has no lord." Rosalind massaged her throbbing temple, willing an idea to manifest. It was a well-kept secret that the ruler of Beaumont was not a son, but a daughter. After the fire that had devastated their lands three short years ago, Rosalind's loyal people had helped her perpetuate the notion that her brother had not perished in the blaze along with their parents. The guise had been a matter of safety until she could one day petition the king to wed her father's former squire, and all would be well again.

Now this.

To compound her troubles, she had awoken this morning plague-ridden with a fever and headache.

"We have nigh twenty knights within the walls," John reminded her. He leaned over her table to right an urn that had fallen over when she'd banged the table.

"Knights?" Rosalind scoffed. "Most of those untried men you call knights have never seen battle. And what good are twenty knights, when the heathens at my door have—how many men would you say?"

"Over one hundred, my lady." He mopped up a small puddle of water from the spilled flowers with his tunic.

"—when the Scots have over *one hundred* men?" She turned to her audience, which had grown from John to half her household in a matter of moments. The people of Beaumont had been attacked by Scots before, and all were terrified of another massacre. Saints protect her, she could not allow them to suffer again.

John cleared his throat. "Who will speak with the invaders?"

A single answer came to Rosalind's mind. Only one person could talk to the Scots savages in lieu of the lord.

She sighed to think of Gregory, far away when she needed him desperately. The son of a neighboring lord, Gregory had been like a brother to her during the years he'd served her father. In the weeks following the fire that had claimed her family, Gregory had vowed to wed her as soon as he could procure the king's blessing so they might one day restore Beaumont. Until then, he had joined King Edward's wars, and they had agreed to allow the world to believe her brother still lived, a fiction that protected Beaumont from a harsh lord of the king's choosing. The story hadn't been all that difficult to perpetuate, given the king's preoccupation with battles throughout Scotland, followed by his recent death.

Still, Rosalind longed for the security of marriage to Gregory after three years of sorrow and fear. Why wasn't her champion here now to defend her people from this threat? She grew so weary of fighting all her battles alone. Until she could get word to him, she needed to protect the keep herself. She had not safeguarded her father's beloved holding this long only to lose it to the scourge of the north that had nearly burned the whole keep around her ears a few scant summers ago.

"Gerta, attend me in my father's bedchamber." She called to the maid warming her hands by a dwindling blaze in the hearth. "John, accompany us and wait outside the door for consultation."

"But—" John and Gerta began.

"*I* shall speak with the Scots savages as the lord of Beaumont." Rosalind silenced their mutual protest with a meaningful glare. Her raised chin defied any to argue with her.

Her confidence failed several minutes later when she climbed to the windy battlements of the outer bailey, dressed in her father's aged garb. Assailed by doubts, Rosalind wondered how she could disguise her voice when she shouted down to the enemy. Perhaps her hoarse and scratchy throat would prove useful on this one occasion at least.

What if the leader demanded they meet face-to-face? Her ruse might work from afar, but she could never pass for a man at close range. Her father's garments hung from her pitifully, and even when she concealed her long hair under the collar of the tunic, her smooth complexion made her look like a young boy.

It did not help that Rosalind shivered with alternating chills and fever.

"My lady, it is not too late to get someone else to play this role," John hissed in her ear, for the third time since she'd donned her father's raiments.

Rosalind shook her head, having already dismissed that idea. She couldn't risk this confrontation going awry. She must be the one to speak for her people.

Grudgingly, John extended his hand to lift her up to the outer ward wall atop the gatehouse. Their positions were far enough above the Scotsmen to keep them safe, but close enough to be heard.

"Is there any way I can look down first, without

showing myself?" Rosalind whispered, her voice betraying her trepidation.

John nodded. "Chances are they won't have their eyes trained up here anyway. Just stay low."

Gingerly, she raised herself up and peeked over the smooth, lime-washed stones of the parapet.

"Oh." She gasped at the spectacle below. Cold fear swept through her, chilling her far more than her illness's icy grip. John had said there were over one hundred men, but Rosalind would have guessed there to be twice that many.

Scots warriors congregated en masse at Beaumont Keep's front gate. Many of them bore blue-painted faces, a tradition passed down through their fearsome Pictish bloodlines. Even from Rosalind's high perch, the men looked monstrously big. *The brutes,* she amended, recalling the devastating fire the rebels had set.

She shook her head to clear her mind of the haunting visions. No time for that now.

On more careful inspection, Rosalind decided there were indeed just over one hundred Scotsmen. Their size, along with the war paint and animal skins they wore, enhanced their savage aspect.

Although most of the combatants seemed to blur into a sea of blue faces, one man caught Rosalind's attention. Dark hair brushed his shoulders, the black locks as unrestrained as Rosalind's own tresses. Broad shoulders supported a long leather cape that was clamped about his throat with a silver brooch.

Flanked by two warriors wearing similar devices,

the man in the center stood a bit shorter than the hulking giant to his left, a bit taller than the more refined knight to his right. All three possessed a proud nobility amid the hectic siege preliminaries, but Rosalind's gaze repeatedly fell upon the Scotsman in the middle. He wore a mantle of authority as easily as his cloak, and something about him called forth a trembling sensation in the very core of her being.

Fear. He could be the man responsible for this siege.

Forcing her eyes from the dark warrior, Rosalind concentrated on measuring the might of the gathered force on the sunny fields surrounding the keep. They didn't have many horses, but then again, neither did Beaumont. The Scots had a huge battering ram, though, and Rosalind had no doubt the weapon could shatter their portcullis with a few of the immense invaders wielding it.

Slipping behind the shelter of the wall again, she sank down beside John.

"It is the battering ram I fear most," she confided, picking at loose pebbles along the stone partition. "If not for that, we might be able to stave them off until they run out of rations."

"What if we were to concentrate our efforts over the portcullis? The men could shoot flaming arrows, and the women could haul boiling water and whatever else we can find to dump on their heathen heads."

If she hadn't been scared senseless, she might have smiled at the notion. Her people would relish the opportunity to finally deal retribution. When the warmongering Scots had come, they'd attacked in the dead of night and retreated as the fire waged their battle for them.

"Do we have many rocks stored up here that the younger boys might throw?"

"Of course." John nodded eagerly. "That is one of our few well-maintained defenses. Gerta often sends boys to gather stones for throwing over the battlements. It is a chore mischief-making children relish."

"Hmm…" Rosalind considered their choices as time ran out. She would have to speak with the invaders at any moment. Should she begin preparing her people for battle, risking their lives to protect her home? Or should she relinquish her keep quietly and mayhap risk more lives to the Scots' famed brutality?

She glanced in John's direction, wondering what his advice would be. His grim expression told her all she needed to know. He'd lost his wife to the fire. He knew the same fears as Rosalind.

And the same determination to live in spite of them.

She took a deep breath, steeling herself for a fight she'd prayed she would never have to face. At least not alone. "I will try to discourage them, but failing that, we fight."

John nodded and scrambled down the wall faster than many men half his age could have done. Rosalind looked after him, thinking how much she had grown to love him like a father. All the survivors of the Beaumont fire were family to her now. She could not bear to lose any of them.

She swallowed hard and whispered a hasty prayer. At least today she had an option of fighting. Struggling to stand in spite of the headache that threatened her balance, she drew herself up to her full height and faced the invaders.

Malcolm McNair scanned the parapets of the borderlands keep, searching for weaknesses with the practiced eye of an experienced battle tactician. He'd traveled far to secure the Beaumont holding—both for his king and for more personal reasons. If the need arose for a siege, he would be ready.

He'd long dreamed of a holding of his own. A lofty goal for a second son of a Highland laird who possessed more might than wealth. Still, the dream had not left him, especially since Robert the Bruce had hinted Malcolm was due for some recognition by the crown. Perhaps Malcolm could start a family here, escape from the endless violence of war and extend the reach of his clan's power.

Now Malcolm sat tall in the saddle, bracketed by his brothers as he had been at birth. His McNair kin had accompanied him on this siege—Ian to escape the memories of his dead wife and Jamie to quench his thirst for adventure. After ten years away from his family seat, Malcolm had proved useful to his family. His battles gave his brothers a place to belong until they sorted out their lives.

Ian McNair, the burly oldest of the trio, nodded in the direction of the keep, where a slight man had appeared on the battlement. "It seems the rat has emerged from his hole. He looks as the Bruce thought he might—an inexperienced wee lordling."

Malcolm narrowed his gaze in the sunlight to see the young lord positioned between the squat towers of the northern gatehouse. A small head swam above ridiculously large robes. The man's features were indistinct from this distance, but the face looked to be that of a boy, smooth and pale.

Beaumont was held by a young son who had come into the holding upon the death of his father. Ever the clever strategist, the Scots king had known the sprawling stone fortification would be an easy target.

Malcolm expected no fight from the border keep.

"Aye. This should be an easy day," he agreed, striding forward against a mild summer wind to speak for the Scots. The McNair banners snapped in the brisk breeze, while his men quieted to wait for the confrontation.

"I am Malcolm McNair," he shouted. "I come to claim Beaumont in the name of my king, Robert the Bruce." The yard became still as the antagonists faced one another, the silence broken only by the occasional snort of a horse.

Finally, a response tripped down from the parapets.

"I am William, Lord of Beaumont, and I do not recognize this king you claim." Though he shouted in a voice scarcely beyond puberty, the lad stood tall against the relentless chill of the wind, his stance defiant. "Scotland and England share but one sovereign, Edward II, and your presence here is an insult to his royal highness."

"And I tell ye, young sir, we willna leave until Beaumont is held in the name of Robert the Bruce."

Malcolm pressed his claim with calm authority, convinced his cause was just. If the English king possessed a shred of common sense, he would never have left a prize such as Beaumont to be guarded alone by this wee lordling. "If ye surrender to us peacefully now, ye have my solemn oath that none of yer people will be harmed."

The young man's face twisted. Was it anger? Fear?

"No harm will come to my people?" His voice rasped, more high-pitched and charged with feeling. "And I am to take *your* solemn oath on that fact?" His tone dripped with disdain. "I trust the word of no Scotsman, least of all one who would camp uninvited at my gate in direct defiance of our king."

The raw emotion in the lord of Beaumont's voice did naught to sway Malcolm's resolve. He would hold Beaumont within the sennight, whether the young man said yea or nay.

"I have explained to ye that I dinna share yer king. And ye might question yer own loyalty to a sovereign who would abandon his people at a time of such great unrest. Yer young King Edward willna be here to help ye anytime soon, as he has made it clear that folk of the borderlands will have to fend for themselves until spring."

There was a pause from above, and Malcolm hoped maybe his words swayed the lad.

"I do not believe it will be so long until our new king comes to settle this dispute," the Beaumont lord finally replied. "But it does not matter, because one way or another, you will leave my grounds."

Damn. Malcolm did not particularly wish to cross

swords with an opponent scarcely older than a squire. After ten years of battle, Malcolm craved peace. But he would do whatever he must to secure the holding for his king and his clan.

"I have made it abundantly clear that I willna, sir, and I am afraid I canna afford to give ye more than a quarter of an hour to change yer mind, or ye will feel the brunt of our convictions in this matter."

There was another pause.

"Then I accept that time, sir, to confer with my people in regard to your proposal." The younger man disappeared once again, leaving Malcolm confident as to what the outcome would be.

He might have lost his taste for battle, but he had yet to lose a fight.

Rosalind hadn't fought a battle before, but it seemed she needed to win one today.

In one breath she cursed Gregory Evandale for deserting her, and in the next prayed he would come back soon. Why hadn't he married her before joining King Edward's wars? He'd claimed he needed to acquire loyal men and the king's approval for their marriage. Hadn't he done so by now?

After descending the outer walls, she flew across the courtyard, the thin soles of her decorative slippers providing little protection from the hard stones. Men and women, young and old, busied themselves making preparations to defend the keep. Several large fires were already lit to heat cauldrons of water. Men hauled rocks up the walls with pulleys, along with garbage from the kitchens and, Rosalind guessed, the contents of the chamber pots. Beaumont's crude knights moved stealthily up the walls, positioning themselves with arrows to shoot at a moment's notice.

Looking about her, Rosalind knew they were make-shift efforts, but that could not quell the immense pride she experienced to see their hard work. She was almost to the keep when John intercepted her.

"Well?"

"We have a quarter of an hour in which to confer." Rosalind snorted in disgust, her heart still slamming erratically in her chest after her confrontation with the enemy warrior. "The arrogant Scot thinks we will give in to him and his band of heathens without a fight."

"Your father would be proud of you today, Rosalind. I know it with every old bone in my body." John clapped a reassuring hand on her shoulder before hastening off to continue preparations.

A wealth of emotion squeezed her insides, the familiar ache of loss accompanied by fear. Hope. Desperation. Heaven help her, she wanted to make her father proud. And her mother. And dear William, whom she'd adored…. Praying for strength, Rosalind darted inside to help Gerta in spite of the chills that wracked her weakened body. In all likelihood, their defense of the outer walls would not last long, maybe not even through the night. But the inner bailey and keep were much stronger and built to withstand a long siege.

Yet…

Something bothered her. She tried to push aside the pain in her pounding head long enough to think clearly. To plan her strategy and plot for all possibilities. She could not shake the sinking feeling she'd overlooked something.

For the life of her, she could not remember what. Cursing her illness and muddled thoughts, she hurried to the great hall to see Gerta barking orders to everyone in sight.

"We have less than a quarter of an hour until we must defend ourselves," Rosalind shouted over the din of villagers scurrying to carry crates of harvest fruits and root crops into the keep. Gerta hesitated for only a moment upon hearing the message, then redoubled her efforts to move foodstuffs and other provisions inside the inner walls.

Scrambling up the stairs to her chamber, Rosalind dispensed with the last of her father's robes as she sailed through the door. Throwing open the chest at the foot of her bed, she rummaged through her few treasured possessions—a gown of her mother's, a poem Gregory had penned for her long ago, her box of herbs—and finally found her father's jeweled dagger.

Although she doubted she would ever have use for a weapon meant for hand-to-hand combat, Rosalind felt more protected with Lord William Beaumont's blade on her person. Perhaps she might gain a bit of her sire's strength today when she needed it so desperately.

Glancing briefly into a small looking glass, Rosalind blinked in surprise at the banner of bright flaxen hair swirling about her shoulders. Since her parents' death, she had worn her locks in a severe fashion, pulled tightly back in an intricate knot of braids. Even in her sleep, she'd kept the waist-length tresses plaited.

Her neatly dressed locks had not fit under her father's head covering, however, so she'd unfastened them. Now it was rather disconcerting to see the abundance of hair floating around her body like a veil. For a moment, she almost resembled the girl she had once been before marauding Scots had robbed her of so much.

But she was that gentle girl no longer. The amethysts on the hilt of her father's knife shone in the dull glass, reminding her how far she would go to protect her people. The fever that weakened her body gave her cheeks deceptively healthy color. Rosalind's luminescent green gown shone none the less for being crammed beneath her father's heavy houppelande and outer robe. She remembered her mother's lesson that in order to command respect, your demeanor must warrant it. And although her hair floated recklessly about, all else about her person befitted her station.

Beaumont might not have a lord in place this day, but she remained mistress of the holding. As lady of the keep, she would not hesitate to take up arms to defend all that was left of her father's dreams for his family and his people.

Thus armed with his blade, Rosalind prepared to lead her people into battle.

Chapter Two

"Ready? On three. One…" Wiping the sweat from his eyes two hours later, Malcolm shouted above the noise of battle. The cursed castle folk were fighting with the desperation of the damned. Scorched fur on his cloak and a smear of rotted quinces on his forearm only stirred his anger.

Devil take young Will Beaumont for risking lives in a battle he had no prayer of winning.

"Two…" With the last surge of the battering ram, his men would break through the outer ward and then the people of Beaumont would be trapped inside the keep, at Malcolm's mercy.

"Three!" Twelve men, with Malcolm at the lead, hefted the battering ram on their shoulders and ran at the portcullis once again.

This time the shuddering crack reverberated through Malcolm's bones as the stubborn oak gate relented. Victory teased him, close enough to taste. Beaumont was a mix of old and new fortifications, the four round outer towers strong and stalwart, but the northern gate a weak spot with its wooden reinforcements.

Now, Malcolm's warriors poured through the freshly made breach into the outer courtyard, their boots pounding over the stones so heavily that the earth trembled with their weight.

They were close now. Beaumont would be a jewel in the crown of the Scots' defenses along the borderlands, and Malcolm would make it impregnable. The keep had not been well maintained, with signs of old battles evident along the outer walls. Now that he was inside the village, he could see well-tended gardens between the crofters' cottages. Underneath the stench of rotting kitchen remains tossed down on his men from the outer walls, he could still smell fresh hay from the nearby stables. Beaumont was indeed a prize.

Forcing his thoughts back to the victory now well within his grasp, Malcolm directed his men to imprison the enemy knights who scurried across the ward to the keep. Malcolm's were faster, and more than a little angry that the English had fought them with flaming arrows, boiling water and worst of all, the contents of the castle chamber pots. His younger brother was still railing at having his garments soiled in such ignominious fashion.

But the Scots took their vengeance now. Fifteen of the nearly thirty men who defended the outer walls were quickly taken prisoner. Judging by the look of the captives, a mixture of old and young, the Beaumont defenses were on their last legs. No true warrior fought among them. Malcolm allowed himself a moment of satisfaction, knowing this siege would not last much longer.

His gratification vanished as an arrow sailed past his head, a mere hairbreadth from his ear.

"Christ's bones," he muttered as a fresh slew of arrows rained down upon the heads of his men.

Shouting orders to take cover, he sought the protection of a slender sapling, the outer ward of Beaumont boasting few trees or bushes. He slapped his helm back into place over his eyes, but the shower of arrows halted as quickly as it had begun.

No doubt such desperate men sought to use their arrow supply judiciously. Even so, two of the Scots were struck in the most recent onslaught, and six other of his men had been either killed or seriously wounded in the battle at the outer walls. A needless waste of life. He lay the loss of his comrades at Will Beaumont's feet.

The cursed fool. Apparently Lord Beaumont possessed enough bravery to order a hopeless battle against his conquerors, but lacked the grit to participate in the skirmish himself.

"What say ye now, Malcolm?" Jamie McNair shouted from his position behind a small stone well. "Shall we poison their water?"

Malcolm stifled a chuckle, mentally thanking Jamie for diverting his dark thoughts. "Still a bit out of sorts about yer fine garments, I see. Ye're not usually so bloodthirsty."

Jamie plucked at the sodden fur lining his leather

houppelande, his dark eyes narrowing. "'Tis ruined, brother, and well ye know it. Damn foot-licking English." He glanced up at the walls of Beaumont and then back to Malcolm. "How do ye plan to get inside their keep?"

"We'll explore the outside." This was the part of battle Malcolm enjoyed the most—the tactical preparation, the search for a chink in the defenses. Once he ruled his own lands, he would use the knowledge he'd gained at war to maintain peace. "I'll meet ye around the back of the keep and we'll see what we've found."

Beaumont Keep was hardly a feat of fresh construction with its low towers laced with centuries-old Roman bricks. Yet the four-rectangular-tower layout had proven solidly defendable when well manned and Malcolm had no doubt that with a bit of effort the keep could be impenetrable.

Not today, however.

"Och. Ye would bring down more pox-bitten English arrows on yer flesh and blood?"

Malcolm grinned as he prepared to bolt to the next tree, more than twenty yards away. "Stay low."

He could hear Jamie muttering even as he started to run, until the unmistakable hiss of an arrow whizzing through the sky reached Malcolm's ears. Resisting the urge to raise his small wooden shield above his head, Malcolm put all of his effort into reaching the tree before him. The hissing grew louder, forcing him to dive headfirst for the shelter of the thick walnut.

Thwack!

The force of the arrow roared through him as it

struck the shield still clutched in his hand. Bemused, he stared as the flaming arrowhead ignited the shield with lightning speed. The heat of the burning wood finally penetrated his dulled wits, and Malcolm withdrew his grip from the rapidly disintegrating armor. Although not an heirloom, the shield had been crafted by Laird McNair for his son. Malcolm was disappointed to see it ruined, but it had served its purpose today, protecting him from what would no doubt have been a mortal blow.

From the stout defense of the walnut tree, he peered up to the northern watchtower, from whence the missile had come. He blinked to clear his vision, knowing his eyes must deceive him.

Yet there she was.

A woman.

Standing defiantly on the crenellated parapet, she did not even bother to duck behind the safety of the wall now that she had discharged her deadly shot. She lowered her crossbow, her gaze never leaving her intended victim.

Briefly, Malcolm wondered why none of his men were firing upon such an exposed target, but a quick look around the bailey showed him those few who spotted her now gawked in disbelief.

The fey creature was no kitchen maid. She reeked of nobility. Her green-yellow gown shimmered with the precise hue of newly unfurled spring leaves, and even from Malcolm's considerable distance, he could see the voluminous folds and rich color conveyed wealth. A golden girdle sparkled around her hips in the sinking sunlight.

And her hair…

The woman's hair outshone her adornments. It floated in a halo about her head and shoulders, rippling clear down to her waist. Loose flaxen strands caught by the breeze gave the impression of gentle disarray. She looked like a pagan sacrifice to the ancient gods of spring. Her appearance bespoke purity, yet her stance remained insolent and proud, her eyes trained on her quarry with the instincts of a natural predator.

His blood surged hotly through him—part lust and part fury—as he watched the noble beauty turn away and descend from her post. Who the hell was she to be up on the keep walls, practicing her archery skills on his head?

Cursed she-demon.

Distancing himself from the undeniable temptation the woman presented, he turned to his task of surveying Beaumont Keep. The mystery of the green-gowned siren would wait until later.

"Malcolm McNair, 'tis mighty slow ye're moving." A familiar voice hissed at him from the cover of a few bushes nearby.

"Ye canna tell me ye made it all the way around the keep, Jamie." But there was his younger brother, hidden behind a tall hedge, now on the other side of Malcolm.

"Aye. And what has taken ye so long? Could it be ye were beset by a fairy from above, to be still standing there, gaping upward?"

Malcolm made a mental note that he owed his brother a pounding. "Nay, ye quarrelsome wretch, merely a crossbow-wielding strumpet who wished to incinerate me with a flaming arrow." No matter that she'd tried to torch his arse, Malcolm had to admit he admired her skills with a bow. "What did ye find?"

Jamie leaned close, heavy eyebrows waggling with good tidings. "I found a southern tower half in ruins and plenty of options to gain entry. But we best wait until night falls to cover our activities."

The news negated the pounding he owed Jamie. Malcolm grinned at his brother, reminded of his good fortune to be a McNair.

"Well done." He gestured toward the setting sun, mere inches above the horizon. "We willna have long to tarry. Come explain to us all at once."

Stealthily, they moved back to the front of the keep to rejoin Ian and make their plans for wresting Beaumont from its unfortunate lord. And although Malcolm knew his thoughts should be fixed on his impending victory, he couldn't stop an unwelcome surge of lust over the prospect of meeting the she-devil up close.

Rosalind had kept her gaze trained out the narrow slit in her solar for the past two hours, to no avail. All she had to show for her effort was a headache grown steadily worse. The sky loomed black as pitch under the new moon, and she perceived no movement of any kind in the outer bailey.

"Perhaps they have camped outside our walls for the night," John suggested. He perched beside her, as nervous and restless as his liege lady.

"Perhaps." *But don't rely upon it.* Something was definitely afoot. Rosalind could sense it in the deep chill that had taken hold of her bones. Where could the invaders have disappeared?

The inner keep of Beaumont was secure enough....

Or was it?

A thought hit her with all the force of a Scots battering ram as Rosalind realized what had been niggling at her all day. "John, did we post men around the south tower?"

Color drained from the steward's face. "I never thought—"

Rosalind pushed past him and tore through the keep, the foursquare plan of the fortification mirroring the design of the outer walls on a smaller scale. She raced down the stairs from her living chambers, across the great hall and through the southern chapel to the crumbling staircase that led to her parents' former rooms. At first she thought his footsteps followed behind her, echoing her own. But by the time she reached the abandoned old tower, she realized he must have been waylaid for she was well and truly alone. Unease tickled her spine.

The narrow southern tower, built of timber and rock, had been completely destroyed in the fire. The wood had burned out from underneath the stone, leaving the tower a crumbling heap of rubble. Under Gregory's guidance, Rosalind's tenants had helped her wall off the tower from the rest of the keep, and now no one ever cared to go there. The past was better left forgotten in that heap of stone.

Until today.

Why hadn't she recalled the weaknesses of the southern end of the keep? It was the illness, she knew, that made her fuzzy-headed. She never would have overlooked such a thing if she had been well. The wall the serfs had built stood strong considering the un-skilled workmanship that had fashioned it, but lacked the solidity of the rest of the structure. The makeshift barrier wasn't as high as the watchtower bastions on the other three corners of the keep, nor was it as thick.

Fear twisted her gut as she finally beheld the wall with her own eyes. But there were no savage Scotsmen in the southern tower. No sledgehammers chipping away at the stones.

All was well.

Weak with relief, Rosalind turned on her heel to fetch sentries for the southern wing, but was yanked back by two strong arms.

A yelp of fear rose in her throat, squelched when a large palm covered her mouth. The arms around her were thick as tree trunks, crushing her against a heavily muscled chest.

Rosalind's heart pounded until the beating deaf-ened her.

"What a surprise." Though her captor's words were a hoarse whisper against her ear, Rosalind detected the lilt of Scotland in his speech.

Her blood chilled in her veins.

"The coldhearted siren is a living, breathing woman, after all. But I warn ye, dinna make a sound." The huge palm edged away from her mouth.

She remained pressed to the hard wall of his chest, and although she could not see her enemy, his chin hovering over her head attested to his intimidating height. Some barbaric fur that he wore tickled her neck, the scorched scent of the cloak intensifying her fears. He wouldn't be pleased with her just now, after their resistance.

Rosalind fought the terror that filled her by remembering the people of Beaumont who counted on her for protection. She must remain calm. Steady. Seeking her voice, she forced herself to edge words from her lips.

"Are you the only one who has made it inside?" Perhaps if she screamed, her people would arrive before the rest of the Scottish slime oozed through the cracks.

"Aye, but dinna doubt there will be others any moment."

At her sharp intake of breath, his hand clamped tightly over her mouth once again. "I warned ye, lass, 'twill go the worse for ye if ye call out."

True to his words, a soft thump sounded nearby in the darkened corridor. From the shadows, another Scots voice echoed over the stones.

"'Tis the lass from the watchtower," a blue-painted beast of a man observed as he dropped softly to the floor beside them. "She's no phantom, but a wee fair maid."

"Aye, fair of face and a fair shot, too," another Scots voice chimed as a third blue savage appeared, climbing down a rope she spied dangling along the wall. The third warrior was not quite so massive as the other two, but still a head taller than Rosalind. The newcomer wore a silver broach of a mythical griffin, the same device she had spotted on the warlord's cloak earlier. "'Twas yer head she was aiming for, Malcolm. If ye were a damn sight slower she might have taken it."

Malcolm.

She knew whose broad arms now held her fast— the dark-haired warrior who had drawn her eye earlier. The same Scots knight who had called up to her from the battlements.

Her whole body trembled with fear, with memories of the Scots' wrath the last time they had visited her borderlands keep. The hulking giant stood to one side of her, the more refined knight to the other. As a cold sweat broke over her brow, still more of the blue-painted knights materialized, dropping down one by one from the rope slung over the southern edifice.

All Rosalind's preparations for a siege were for naught because she had never given the crumbling tower a second thought. The people of Beaumont would suffer for her oversight.

She had to find a way to warn them.

"I am going to remove my hand from yer mouth and ye will direct me to the hall, wench." Her captor's voice, low and threatening, turned Rosalind's skin to goose-flesh.

Thinking she might be able to aid her captor to her own advantage, she nodded.

"Out this door." A plan took shape in her mind, a desperate measure for a desperate time.

Replacing his hand on her trembling lips, the warrior headed the direction she pointed, while his men spread out behind him. Rosalind waited for her chance, leading the Scots closer to the main hall. There would be but one opportunity to scream. She must be heard.

Her captor opened the chapel door and peered inside. The scents of pinewood and sweet incense reached her nose, the fragrances she'd long associated with comfort giving her little succor now. His hand slid from her mouth again, as if he expected her to instruct him. Rosalind saw her chance.

Gripping the hilt of her father's small dagger for whatever courage the weapon might lend, she let loose a scream to raise the rafters.

The Scotsman's cold blade pressed to her neck halted her cries. Her hand flexed around her own weapon in turn.

"Demon wench, I warned—" The man's words died in his throat as Rosalind's jeweled dagger sank into his side.

Horrified by the sticky warmth that covered her hand, she fought the roll of her belly. Her cause might be noble, but she did not mean to actually kill a man.

A roar of fury erupted behind them, and Rosalind fled from the slackened grasp of the captor. She launched herself forward through the cover of darkness, leaving the stunned invaders in a turmoil of oaths and shouts behind her. Knees quaking, she shot through the door and into the hall, where her people scurried about in confused response to her shriek. A young maid dropped a heavy decanter on the stone floor, the clang of the silver urn echoing through the huge room as Rosalind struggled to speak.

"Scots…within the walls." She gasped for breath, still recoiling from the memory of her act.

The people of Beaumont needed no further urging, for the pounding of the enemies' footsteps in the corridor emphasized her words. A wave of shrieks greeted her ears, accompanying a mass exodus toward the far door.

"Halt!"

A deep voice boomed throughout the hall, amplified by the echoing stone walls.

Even in their terror, many of the fleeing English turned at the commanding voice. An eerie silence grew as the residents of Beaumont fixed their gazes behind Rosalind, where she knew the blue-painted Scots must be arriving.

"No one leaves this hall."

Rosalind froze at the familiar sound of the speaker's voice behind her. It couldn't be. Turning, she looked over her shoulder. It was *him*. The man she had just plunged her dagger clear through. Rosalind glanced down at her hands, as if to assure herself his blood still stained them.

"Fear not, wench, yer blade dinna miss." The warrior before her bled profusely down his side, staining the rushes red. Yet any pain from the wound remained absent from his livid visage.

Do not let him take out his wrath on my people.

Rosalind trembled as she faced him. He was enormous. She had known that before, when he'd held her from behind, yet in the darkness she had not fully realized his size. He was the most intimidating man she had ever seen, and right now his expression was nothing less than ferocious.

"Ian, take ten men about the keep and round up whoever is missing. I would have all of Beaumont before me." The Scot's gaze never left her as he barked orders. "Jamie, head outside and see if anyone escaped. Angus, ferret out my squire to tend this damn bleeding gut of mine."

He stepped closer to Rosalind, and a collective gasp rose among the English as he glowered down at her, his expression hard and cruel. "Where is the young lordling, Will Beaumont, and who in Hades are ye?"

Rosalind felt the anger radiate from him in waves, but fought to face him boldly. She could not allow her people to see her falter. Not when they counted on her to be strong. "Lord William left the keep hours ago to fetch the king and bring us aid. I am his sister, Rosalind."

"Yer lack-witted brother started a war with hostile invaders, then left his sister to fight his battle while he trots off to London to find yer hedonistic king?" One heavy black eyebrow lifted in disbelief.

She gulped for air, as if the brute who cornered her had somehow robbed her of that, too. Glaring back at the Scots heathen, she merely tilted her chin in defiance.

"Tell me, Lady Rosalind, does it not shame ye to have such a coward for a brother?" He glared down at her from his intimidating height. At such close range, Rosalind noticed patches of bronzed skin under his blue paint. Dark hair brushed his broad shoulders. Heavy black brows perched over angular features slashed in a fearsome scowl.

She bristled under his criticism, but knew her lies did indeed make the man sound like a coward. "He did what he felt necessary, knowing we were outnumbered by barbarians."

"Ye call *us* barbarians, lass?" A sudden stillness came over the Scotsman. "We, who sought to shed no blood in the inevitable conquering of yer keep?"

"You have no right to Beaumont," Rosalind retorted, her loathing of the invaders pouring fresh through her veins. "We have previously experienced the Scots' brutal notion of war and will not be misled by your claims of no killing. We have lost too much at your people's hands to blindly give over our home to bloodthirsty marauders."

"I will address yer slander of my people at a later date. For now, I suggest ye keep yer venomous tongue in check lest ye find yerself cooling yer temper in the dungeon."

A soft exclamation echoed among the English that their lady would be threatened so cruelly.

John Steward stepped forward. "We mean no offense, sir, but my lady has lost—"

"*Yer* lady? And who might ye be to speak for her?" The Scot moved toward John.

Rosalind stepped between the men, willing herself to remain calm. There was nothing she could do to change the past, but she could try to negotiate with the barbarian to guard against any more deaths.

"Please, I will speak for myself and endeavor to do so in a more subdued manner." She nodded to John, silently assuring him she would be more reasonable. When she turned to the Scotsman, smug satisfaction marked his stark features.

But she could not afford to be proud at a time like this. Lives might depend on how humbly Rosalind could beg the warlord for mercy. "I would speak with you in private, sir."

His laugh boomed, dark and echoing to the high ceiling. "And give ye an opportunity to thrust yer dagger more deeply into my gut? I think nae, but 'tis an amusing suggestion."

"You have my word that I will do nothing of the sort." Panic swirled through her. What if he killed them all in retribution for fighting? "I merely wish to discuss a peaceful shift of power from me to you."

"Yer word means naught to me, as ye have attempted to kill me twice already today." In spite of his words, he did not look the least bit frightened for himself. In fact, he grinned down at her now, as if her words were a great jest.

A Scots voice called out across the hall. "We found the stragglers, Malcolm."

Both Rosalind and the wounded warrior turned to see the remaining Beaumont folk being ushered in, along with the Scotsmen who had gathered them together.

"Aye. And ye'll have my thanks for it. Take some sort of count so we can keep track of them in the days ahead." He turned back to Rosalind, good humor still playing about his lips despite the gaping hole in his side. "Ian, do ye see who has asked me for a private audience to discuss a peaceful shift of power?"

"Ye dinna say?" The man called Ian eyed Rosalind carefully, his gaze detached. "'Tis the lass with the crossbow…the same one who raised her dagger to ye."

"Aye. Think ye I should grant her this boon?"

They attempted to shame her by discussing her as if she were not present. She itched to rail at them all, but to do so would be but a selfish indulgence of her temper. Instead, she settled for hoping the warlord would collapse from blood loss as quickly as possible.

"I think there are nae many men who would refuse such a fair maid a private audience." Another man, younger and more mischievous looking than the others, spoke up.

Embarrassment spread like wildfire through Rosalind's veins. Her virtue meant naught to such men. If anything, her maidenly status could be one more thing for brutes like these to plunder. What would Gregory think to find his bride defiled by savage Scots?

Surely her cheeks flamed with the heat of her discomfiture. Then again, her cheeks had been flaming all day with the bout of fever that had taken hold of her.

The Scots leader laughed again. "Jamie lad, that is why I will live a good many years beyond ye. 'Tis not wise to think with yer manhood." The jesting ended when he turned back to Rosalind, his face devoid of expression.

She prayed his words meant her virtue was safe.

"I will grant ye a meeting, lady, all in good time. For now, however, I must keep ye safe from harm and from interfering in my business. Understand, I do this because I can see ye would not allow me to take over Beaumont peacefully, yet that is what I want above all things."

His blue eyes glittered, icy and merciless. Rosalind shivered, both with fear and the chills of her illness, as she waited for his pronouncement. Vaguely, she wondered how a man so outwardly attractive could be so cruel inside.

"Ye will stay in the dungeon until I have yer holding well in hand, and then I will give ye a private audience in which ye can defend yer actions today."

The English people gasped at the sentence.

Rosalind's head swam with images of what might happen while she was locked in her own dungeon. An outright massacre because of her foolish actions. Why had she bothered to put up a fight against such a strong invading force? All of Beaumont would pay for her rash decision.

Every death would be on her hands.

Her fears got the better of her as her knees went weak at the thought. Dizziness assailed her. And her hated enemy's face became a blur as she sank heavily to the floor at his feet.

Chapter Three

Rosalind could not remember ever being so cold. Shivering under her quilt, she pulled it more tightly about her shoulders. Why wasn't the fire lit? Just as she started to call out for Gerta or her maid, Josephine, she remembered what had happened.

She was in her own dungeon.

Rosalind groaned aloud as she recalled the damning words of the Scotsman responsible.

Malcolm McNair. The formidable Scot had consigned her to the dungeon until things were "well in hand" at Beaumont.

Blinking away the fog of sleep, she peered around her quarters. Food had been left for her, but the bread and cheese held no appeal. She even slept on a pallet instead of the cold floor, so her lot was not too bad. Yet all she could think of was the brutality the Scots could be inflicting on all the people who looked to her for protection.

Steady streams of tears rolled unchecked down

Rosalind's cheeks. Reaching blindly in the dark for a chamber pot, she retched as terror knotted her belly.

She envisioned the huge heathen setting fire to the keep, locking everyone she loved inside so they might burn with it. Just as they had before.

Stomach empty, she collapsed in a heap, too weary to move. She fell into nightmarish sleep, with one breath cursing Malcolm McNair for stealing her home, and with the next, cursing Gregory Evandale for allowing him to do so.

The next morning Malcolm knew his endeavor must be blessed. The people of Beaumont were not welcoming, but they had not revolted, either. They made the best of an unhappy situation, which was all he could reasonably expect.

Since his arrival the day before, everything had moved according to plan. He controlled the keep, thanks to his brothers' help. Soon the south tower would be rebuilt, not as a comfortable living space, but as part of the defense fortifications.

Now he broke his fast in silence in the Beaumont great hall. A few of his men still slept on the floor of the hall near the keep's hounds, their snores mingling with the crackle of a low flame in the hearth. The sun had not fully risen, a purple haze penetrating the chamber's high windows.

He frowned as he bit into a quince and thought of his first task for the day—retrieve the former mistress of Beaumont from the dungeon. He could not regret his decision to lock her up, since her defiance could have cost lives. The wench had shot a flaming arrow at his head.

And yet how could he blame her? He'd attacked her home, after all. Perhaps he'd locked her up because her strong-willed determination reminded him too much of his faithless Isabel. She had teased him with the notion of marriage until she'd found a wealthier lord to share her bed.

Now that he could think clearly, Malcolm decided Will Beaumont deserved the dungeon far more than his sister. The bastard had stupidly chosen to fight a battle he must have known he had no hope of winning, and six of Malcolm's men had paid for his foolishness with their lives. His thumb smashed the quince he held, his grip tightening as he recalled the men he'd buried.

How could the English knight have gambled so carelessly with his own men? Beaumont could not have known the invaders would refrain from killing anyone seized in battle. Indeed, it ranked as highly unusual for a conqueror to take prisoners in the midst of warfare. Beaumont had been willing to sacrifice everyone at his outer bailey wall.

Malcolm itched to face the fainthearted Beaumont lord and tear the coward limb from limb to avenge the six men he'd lost, but the former ruler was nowhere to be found. The only target for his vengeance had been Will's fierce sister. Her skills with a crossbow would have made any Highland father proud. Malcolm did not want to reward Rosalind's bravery with a stay in the dungeon, but he could see from the pride in her eyes that she would never sit idly by while he took over her home.

Safer for everyone if she were locked out of harm's way.

But now that things were well in hand, Malcolm finished his quince, left the table with the hound at his heels and descended into the dungeon.

"Lachlan Gordon!" he shouted in the sleeping jailer's ear when he located the door to the keep's bowels.

The wiry old man jumped, jangling the keys at his waist. "Yes, sir, she is locked away safe and sound."

"Then let me in, my good man. We canna leave the lady of the keep locked up all week." Malcolm grinned at the aged Highlander guarding the door. He had not wanted to bring Lachlan on a siege with him, but the old man had been too cantankerous to deny. The McNair lands had been safe for so long under Ian's rule that some of the men itched to leave solely for the sake of adventure.

Malcolm could only hope he would one day have the chance to be as strong a laird as his brother.

"We canna?" Lachlan rubbed his beard and seemed to consider that news. "'Tis sorry I'm being then, for I fear I have nae given the prisoner much care."

"What do ye mean?" Malcolm stood very still, digesting the old man's words.

"Well, she hasna been fed, and I only let her little maid in for a few moments. I dinna know I was to be treating her different than any other captive."

Unease crept through Malcolm at the thought of

how Lady Rosalind might have fared. He tried to re-call the image of Beaumont's mistress up on the bat-tlements. She was a strong lass and a fearless one at that. She would not be frightened by imprisonment. Then another memory entered his mind: of Rosalind crumpling to the floor when he'd announced she would stay in the dungeon.

"Open the door *now*."

Lachlan fumbled with the keys, but managed to turn the rusted lock.

Grabbing a torch as he brushed past the jailer, Malcolm raced down the stairs, cursing himself for entrusting the keep's mistress to a failing old man. He peered around the dank stone walls. There were several cells, but he could see no movement in any of them.

A sneeze emanated from the farthest chamber.

Hastening toward the sound, Malcolm shoved open the door to the last cell. *Hell and damnation.*

Curled into a tight ball and tangled in threadbare blankets slept the former lady of Beaumont, now look-ing more like an urchin straight off Edinburgh's streets.

Kneeling beside her pallet, he scooped her into his arms. She still wore the green gown he'd last seen her in, though its radiant spring hue had faded beneath a layer of grime. Her body radiated feverish warmth against him, yet she shivered violently. As he headed for the stairs, her eyelashes fluttered.

"They are dead," she whispered, her gaze glassy and unfocused as she stared at him. "All of them…" Her eyes closed once again, and in the growing light Malcolm discerned heavy purple shadows beneath them.

· "Find Gerta, the busybody nurse," Malcolm shouted to Lachlan as he emerged from the dungeon.

"Aye." Though the old man hurried off, Malcolm did not miss the distraught look upon his weathered face.

Traversing the steps to the main living quarters, Malcolm puzzled over Rosalind's words. Who had died?

Guilt pricked him as he peered down at her weary form, his fingers sinking into soft feminine curves he would rather not notice. The McNair men had been taught to cherish women. Malcolm knew firsthand how frail they could be. Ian's young wife had died in childbirth last winter, too gentle for the harsh demands of life in the Highlands.

Not all women possessed the resilience of Scottish thistle and a heart of stone like the woman he'd once planned to wed.

Malcolm searched Lady Rosalind's face, struck anew at how young and slight she appeared, her body sweetly warming his where he held her. Was this the same lass who just yesterday had boldly fought off a small army and slid her dagger into her enemy's gut? She did not look capable.

Yet she had done these things and more, he reminded himself, ignoring the way her cheek settled softly against his arm as he carried her. He must not be foolish enough to soften toward her because she was a woman. She had tried to kill him twice in one day. Heaven knew, the English felt no such sympathies for the women of their enemies.

Tamping down any compassion he might have felt, Malcolm deposited his delicate burden in a chamber at the top of the stairs and strode out the door without a backward glance. He nearly knocked over Gerta in his haste.

"She's in there," he barked, leaving the old woman to nurse the Beaumont she-demon back to her former good health.

Rosalind awoke to a light so bright she feared she had passed into the hereafter.

"You awake, love?" asked a familiar feminine voice.

An angel?

"You are awake, I can tell. Open your eyes, Rosalind Beaumont, and cease this nonsense."

No angel. It was most certainly Gerta.

Rosalind peeked out blearily to see her childhood nurse frowning at her. Sunlight filtered in through a small window high above her. The normal courtyard sounds of carts rolling and crofters shouting drifted on the cool breeze, while a fire burned merrily at the foot of her bed.

"I knew 'tweren't nothing wrong with you that a bit of sleep would not cure." Gerta smiled, a rare display for the perpetually irritable elder woman.

Rosalind marveled how the change in expression transformed her wrinkled face. Gerta was a fair woman yet.

"Everyone has been fretting about you, but old Gerta knew you were too stubborn to let the dungeon get the best of you for long."

The dungeon. Memories of the cold, endless night assailed Rosalind.

"Is everyone…" Her belly roiled again. She could not finish the question, but she had to know if anyone still lived after the Scots invasion.

"You thought those Scotsmen would slaughter the lot of us, didn't you, my poor little lamb?" Gerta squeezed her mistress's hand in her own. "I had a feeling that is what worsened your health these past days—fear for the rest of us and none for yourself."

"How long has it been since the siege?"

"Three days. One in the keep's underbelly for you, two up here convalescing."

For Rosalind, time had been a blur. "What did they do to me?" Had they beaten her? She honestly couldn't remember much.

"They did naught to you, sweeting, but neither did they take very good care of you. I let that old goat Lachlan Gordon know what I thought about his neglect, you can be sure." Gerta's gray coronet bobbed in time with her emphatic words. "Treating the lady of Beaumont like a common prisoner of war. But at least Lord Malcolm remembered to go fetch you out."

"Who, pray tell, is *Lord* Malcolm?"

"No offense to you, but the McNair does run the keep now. The servants did not know how else to call him."

Rosalind pondered this, appeased but not pleased.

She could hardly ask Gerta to purposely bait a barbaric Scotsman.

"At any rate, it has been two days since he brought you upstairs and asked me to care for you."

"The same man who locked me in my own dungeon to start with?" The thought of herself in Malcolm McNair's arms disturbed her.

"Aye. But at least we have not lost any lives. A bloody miracle, considering the fight we put up."

Rosalind's annoyance fled. Had she heard properly?

"It is true," Gerta continued, as if sensing her disbelief. "All of the prisoners they took in battle were spared if they would but give the Scots their allegiance."

"They did what?" Rosalind shot upright, anger pulsing through her even though her head swam at the quick movement.

"Not to the Scottish cause." Gerta patted her shoulder. "Just a promise not to turn on the new lord."

"It is the same thing." Rosalind threw aside her covers and slid out of bed. "You mean to tell me all of Beaumont has sworn loyalty to these Scots?" She yanked a surcoat out of the closet, snagging the fabric in her haste.

"I knew you would be upset, but—"

"Upset does not begin to describe my feeling on the matter." Rosalind pulled the torn surcoat over her kirtle. "My whole household has given loyalty to the same people who only a few years ago burned half of Beaumont to the ground? The same murderous lot who took all my kin?"

Tears glistened in the old woman's eyes. "John Steward refused to swear loyalty. He was banished."

"Banished?" Rosalind croaked, pausing for a moment in her battle with her garters. "What will he do?"

"The rest of us did not have the courage to defy them. I could never be banished from Beaumont, my lady." Gerta dabbed her eyes with a worn scrap of linen from her cuff.

Rosalind's heart softened. "Did John say anything to you about his plans or where he was headed?"

"I do not know, but John mentioned he hoped to get word to Lord Evandale."

An enormous weight seemed to slide from her shoulders. Gregory would come. He would come if only to save her, she knew, but as her betrothed he had another interest in expelling the Scots—Beaumont would be his once they wed with the king's approval.

"Perhaps all is not lost." Smiling, Rosalind squeezed the older woman's shoulders. "If Gregory comes, he will rid us of these barbarians."

"In the meantime, will you try not to rile the new Scots lord at every turn? Sometimes you can learn much more if you are smart enough to go along with things." Gerta fiddled absently with the hem of her sleeve as she rose from the bed. "Shall I call Josephine for you? It would seem you need help getting dressed."

Rosalind glanced down at her wrinkled gown. The tear in her seam glared from her surcoat. Her kirtle was crooked. One garter already slid sadly to the floor. Knowing she would never be able to conduct a rebellion if she wasn't at least properly garbed, she nodded.

Two hours later, she was glad she had listened to Gerta even if she hadn't been allowed to leave her chamber. An aging Scots warrior loomed outside her gate, his thick brogue almost unintelligible, but his refusal to let her pass into the hall had been clear enough. She was as much a prisoner in her chamber as she'd been in the dungeon, but at least here she could be comfortable enough to think and plan. To recover her health. To plot against her captors.

Now, she sat in an unforgiving chair draped with a weathered tapestry, her supper on a tray beside her. Picking at a bit of stuffed pigeon to help regain the strength she'd lost to her illness, she barely tasted the food. As much as she resented Malcolm McNair's arrival, she counted her blessings that he had spared so many lives. Most conquerors would not be so generous.

Malcolm. The very name roused anger and…curiosity. Although she bitterly resented his invasion of her home, she could not deny that his war tactics had surprised her. Who was this warmongering Scot who spared English lives? And had he truly spared them, or was he merely biding his time to wrest hard labor from her people?

Savoring a sip of mulled wine, she recalled the strange sensation that had assailed her from the first time she'd looked at the man. She could appreciate his warrior's might even if she despised him as her enemy. In the time that Gregory had been away, Rosalind had come to long for a man's strength at her side. Life would be so much easier with a powerful lord as a

mate. Surely the fact that she noticed Malcolm Mc-
Nair's capabilities as a warrior only underscored how
much she missed Gregory.

Satisfied that she'd uncovered the source of her
strange response to Beaumont's unwanted visitor, she
returned her knife to the trencher as a knock sounded
at her door.

"Come in, Josephine, your timing is perfect." She
pushed away her half-eaten meal.

The door opened, and a cool gust of air blew into
the solar as a heavy footstep crossed the threshold. "I
fear 'tis nae Josephine, but I hope ye find my timing
equally pleasing."

Rosalind did not need to look over her shoulder to
know who had just entered the chamber. The man's
presence radiated from a league away.

"I am afraid I find *your* timing deplorable. I would
have you depart my chambers immediately." Rosalind's hand shook as she replaced her cup on the tray.
Had he come here to dislodge her from the master
chamber, to oust her from what small domain she still
held?

"Can ye be forgetting so soon that ye wished a private audience with me? I am merely fulfilling yer
wish."

She refused to turn around and look at him. Instead
she stared fixedly at a silver Celtic cross mounted
upon her wall. How could he sound so lighthearted and
full of good humor when her whole world had crashed
around her ears, her future destroyed by the Scots'
quest for domination?

"My wish," she ground out through clenched teeth, "was greeted with smug hostility. You threw me in the dungeon rather than listen to me. I have no desire to say anything to you now."

The heathen did not reply, but Rosalind could hear his footsteps as he moved to the sideboard, followed by the splash of wine into a cup.

"Perhaps ye need another drink, lady. Ye look rather…tense."

A huge hand reached around her to take her cup from the tray. Rosalind stiffened at his sudden nearness, but still declined to look at him.

When he returned with her drink in hand, however, she had no choice but to do so. He sank onto a low footstool as if he belonged there.

"Here's to yer health, lass, and to yer very successful recovery." He clanked his cup heavily against hers and drank the contents down in one gulp.

What did he think he was doing here, making himself at home in her solar, drinking her wine, smiling like a cat that just swallowed the first spring robin? The insolent Scotsman looked a far sight more grand than the last time she'd seen him. When he had ordered her to the dungeon, he had been the very image of a barbarian with his leather cape askew and his blue war paint.

Now he appeared more refined. And surprisingly clean for a heathen. In fact, Rosalind could detect the scent of Gerta's soap about him. His tunic boasted a fine weave of silk, though the garment had not been decorated after the fashion of noblemen.

His hair shone with cleanliness, as well, falling to his broad shoulders and tied neatly at his nape. Black as sin, the locks seemed indicative of his character. Thick sable brows sheltered eyes that were a clear and vivid blue, perhaps a sign of Nordic ancestry. They should have been raven's wing dark, too. 'Twould be more reflective of his soul. Still, fine creases around his eyes suggested he was no stranger to laughter. A straight and somewhat prominent nose hinted at pride or mayhap intelligence.

Overall, he was rather pleasing to the eye for a war-mongering miscreant. But a fair countenance did not change the fact that he was still a conqueror. And above all, Rosalind craved peace. This was a man to be wary of, no matter what lighthearted jests issued from his mouth.

He seemed to be studying her as intently as she perused him. Attempting to quiet her jittery fears, Rosalind raised her cup to her lips and drank.

"'Tis no Scotch mead, of course," he commented, his gaze steady upon her, "but 'twill do on a warm eve like this one. Would ye care for some fresh air, perhaps?"

"No," Rosalind lied, refusing to be affable to a man who'd robbed her of her keep. In truth, she longed to tell him she was not sorry she'd stabbed him, that she would do it again in a heartbeat.

Concern for her people forced her to hold her tongue, along with a healthy dose of good sense that told her not to enrage this man and risk being thrown onto her back and defiled. He might seem trustworthy in that respect, but she could not afford to let her guard down. It was fortunate no lives had been taken in the siege. She would not risk any more by provoking the Scots leader.

"Then we will talk here." He stood abruptly and paced the length of the solar, his quick gait betraying no sign of the wound she'd given him, which surely must pain him even as it healed.

Her feminine chamber, draped with rich tapestries and gossamer silks, seemed an odd backdrop for a warrior who exuded such maleness. Did he mean to take her chamber for his own and displace her? For a fleeting moment, she envisioned his muscular body reclined on the dark coverlet that graced her bed.

Regrettably, the image was not as absurd as she anticipated. A very clear picture came to mind, burning her cheeks as hotly as if she'd spoken the thought aloud.

"We need to come to some agreement." His solemn manner assured her he had not somehow divined her misplaced thoughts. "When last we met ye mentioned a 'peaceful shift of power' from ye to me. I want to discuss this transition. But first I want to know why this shift of power would come from ye, and nae yer brother, William. Does he hold no authority at Beaumont?" He sat again, waiting for an answer. His eyes never left hers.

She longed to stand, to walk away from him and the peculiar stirring he seemed to arouse in her, but to do so would make her appear intimidated. Her bout of illness had left her too weak to walk steadily, and his presence only made her knees more unsteady.

She found him as disconcerting as his pointed questions. Had he guessed the secret of her brother's disappearance? "In my brother's absence, I speak for Beaumont."

"Tell me again about this strange departure of his." Malcolm's hand strayed toward her leg. Startled, Rosalind flinched, but he only picked up the pomander that dangled from a chain at her waist, careful not to actually touch her person. "None of my men saw him leave. How is it possible he escaped our notice?"

Distracted by his keen interest in the keepsake from her mother, Rosalind watched Malcolm as he carefully traced his callused finger over the intricate pattern of Celtic carvings.

She shivered despite the warmth of her room, and warded off the sensation by snapping at him. "Think you I will give away all of our secrets? Perhaps there are ways to and from the keep that you have not discovered."

"I will discover them all, ye can be sure. No keep of mine will be wrested out from under me." Allowing the pomander to fall from his fingers, Malcolm rested his elbows on his sprawled thighs. The gesture put his face disturbingly close to her own.

Unwillingly, Rosalind absorbed the warmth of his presence, the heat of his body.

"Ye would do well to learn this now, Lady Rosalind."

"You must know I do not consider this your keep, therefore when it is wrested out from under you, I will only be regaining what is rightfully mine." Burrowing her backbone farther into her chair, she created as much distance between them as possible. Not that he scared her, but he definitely unsettled her. She'd begun to trust that he wasn't here to make a grab for her, or else he would have done so by now.

"Ye mean yer brother will be regaining what is rightfully his, do ye not, lass?" A half smile twitched his lips.

"Beaumont is mine in his absence." She cringed inwardly at her own blunder and at the laughter in his voice. Cursing her flustered weakness, she vowed to be more careful around him.

"A position ye seem at home with." He looked around the master chamber meaningfully. "Would ye care for more wine?" One heavy black brow rose with the question.

Rosalind shook her head. Did he suspect her lies? She watched him covertly as he poured himself another cup. The man was completely out of place in her solar with its dried flowers and romantic notions. She guessed him to be a few inches above Gregory's imposing height. Malcolm's broad shoulders spanned a vast width, and the muscles at his calves bunched as he walked. A small knife fit into a sheath at his waist.

A warrior to his toes. It occurred to her that he did not look like the sort of craven churl to set fire to a keep and then disappear into the night. She had learned from their conversation that Malcolm liked to keep what he took, for one thing, which an anonymous raider could not do. Just by looking at him she ascertained he was a man accustomed to fighting—something the gutless torch-wielders were not, since they had set blaze to Beaumont and then disappeared into the night.

Thus Malcolm McNair was probably not responsible for the murder of her parents. He still represented the savages who committed the deed, of course, and his conquest of her keep was reason enough to despise him. Just not quite so much as she would have if she had remotely suspected him of the Beaumont fire.

"Getting back to this peaceful shift of power." He finished his drink and sat before her once again. "I know ye must care for your people, else ye wouldna have been at the parapets wielding a crossbow."

Rosalind lifted her chin. Did he think to make her feel guilty?

"I find such loyalty admirable," he continued, surprising her completely. "I understand it was nae yer fault yer brother led ye into a pointless battle. I lay the blame on him for the needless loss of lives in this siege."

Rosalind was grateful Malcolm glanced away, else he would have seen the guilty flush steal over her features. Given her own losses, she should not mourn the loss of her enemy's men. Yet guilt pricked her to think men had died because of her actions.

"Because I know ye care for the tenants and servants, I know ye will want to ease their adjustment to my presence."

Perhaps sensing a protest, he raised his hand to silence her. "I know ye dinna want to face the reality that yer dreaded enemy now rules Beaumont, but 'tis a fact. Ye will only cause distress and mixed allegiances among the people if ye decry me. Would ye honestly want yer tenants to revolt and risk their lives against trained knights of war to preserve ye as their ruler? And dinna mistake me, 'twould be risking their lives."

"You brute." Rosalind rose from her seat so that she might look down at him. "How dare you threaten these good people when they have already done everything but kiss your bloody Scottish boot soles."

He could have stood, as well, and intimidated her, but he remained seated, as if unperturbed by her outburst. Or was he perhaps still feeling some of the sting of the wound she'd given him three days before?

"'Tis well ye know I threatened no one. 'Tis my way of asking ye to lend me yer support and nae rile all yer household. If only ye will allow yerself to be reasonable in this, ye will see the truth of my words."

"Be reasonable?" Anger churned through her. "I am being more than reasonable allowing you into my chamber. I am being reasonable every moment I do not spit in your face. It is completely *un*reasonable of you to ever think I will submit like an obedient little maid to a hostile enemy, just because you have the advantage over me at the moment."

"Ye will risk the people of Beaumont to bolster yer wounded pride?" His voice rumbled with restrained anger and his fingers flexed tightly around his drinking chalice.

"I will not risk my people, heathen." It occurred to her that at some point during their conversation she had realized she could rail at this man without fearing for the Beaumont folk. Although the warlord might seize her home, he would not vent his annoyance on her people. How odd to think, in this small way, she had already come to trust him. "I shall be rid of you before long. If the king will not come to our aid, Will has other allies to turn to."

They glared at each other, brilliant blue eyes locked with hers, as the two of them reached an impasse.

"I think our talk is at an end," Rosalind said finally, spinning away.

Malcolm rose, returning his cup to the tray with a clank. "Nay, Rosalind."

The low rumble of his voice, the supreme confidence with which he contradicted her, gave her pause. Her heartbeat faltered.

He strode to her and, before she knew what he was about, clamped her shoulders in his heavy palms and held her a scant foot in front of him.

The heat of his hands permeated her thin summer kirtle. His touch confused her, for, although it was hardly gentle, neither was it threatening.

"If our talk was more successful, I would see no need for this." A look akin to regret crossed his face. "But as it stands, ye will have to be confined to yer chambers until we can come to a more favorable understanding."

Her heartbeat thrummed in her ears. "Favorable for who?"

His grin was slow and deliberate. "For me, of course. Sooner or later ye'll be coming around."

He actually winked at her before striding out of the solar.

Rosalind picked up a pillow from her chair and threw it at the door. The gesture helped vent her frustration, but did not take away the tingling she still felt where he'd touched her.

Chapter Four

"If the steward remained with us, he could have bloody well handled the harvest." Malcolm squinted out over Beaumont's fields, which were ripe with grain. His brothers stood beside him.

Beaumont had been his for a mere seven days, and already problems arose from all sides—disputes among the tenants, angry whispers among the servants about his treatment of Lady Rosalind, who remained confined to her chambers. Still there had been no news from Robert the Bruce. And now the obstacle of organizing the harvest.

Usually, Malcolm could count on his family to help him with most any crisis, but even the three McNairs together couldn't seem to solve Beaumont's current dilemma. Experience in battle did not prepare a man for the demands of the land, it seemed.

Malcolm nudged his younger brother as he leaned back against the low rock partition separating the wheat fields from a cow pasture just outside the keep's walls. "Ye dinna know *anything* about bringing in crops, Jamie?"

"I never took an interest in such things. I was meant for more lofty pursuits from the time I was the smallest of lads." Jamie plucked a cherry from a nearby tree and took a tentative taste.

Ian laughed, a deep rumble that fairly rattled the low branches. "More like ye were afraid to soil yer hands."

"I didna ever see *you* helping with the harvest at Tyrran." Jamie snatched another fistful of cherries, popping them into his mouth in quick succession. Ever the well-bred McNair, he topped his brothers in refinement, but he ranked as fierce a warrior as the elder two.

"Too busy making war," Ian returned, a shadow crossing his features as he reached to try the sun-warmed fruit, as well. "And then last year, Mary was in her confinement…." He looked into the distance before the flash of sorrow in his eyes dissolved into a scowl.

Malcolm clapped his brother on the shoulder, powerless to alleviate his grief. Although Ian had left Tyrran, their family seat, to join his brothers on the Beaumont campaign, Malcolm knew that Ian's late wife still claimed his thoughts.

Given Ian's darkened mood, Malcolm welcomed the interruption of a stout female trundling out of the keep with a basket in hand. "I hope you are saving some cherries for the rest of Beaumont, my lords. Cook uses the fruit in dishes more tasty and refined than any of the crude fare you'd find in the north."

Malcolm stood back to make way for the nurse, who seemed to preside over the household with Rosalind. "Ye're speaking heresy to a Scot's ears, woman. Perhaps ye need to pay a visit to a Highland keep to change yer mind."

"You seem to have brought the Highlands to Beaumont in spite of my lady's most fervent hopes, haven't you?" Still grumbling, Gerta worked to fill her basket with fruit, her weathered hands moving over the branches with quick efficiency. "And even your own Lachlan Gordon admits the superior flavor of Beaumont's dishes, or he would not have begged me to gather more cherries for the cook. But then, I should not have been surprised he could not pick his own cherries, when even the mighty McNairs seem to be flummoxed by the matter of the coming harvest."

Jamie straightened, looking offended enough for all of them, but Malcolm elbowed him before he could quarrel with the presumptuous old nurse.

"The McNairs are warriors, not farmers, as ye well know." Malcolm would allow Gerta to have her moment to gloat. The elder woman had been practical enough to see the merits of submitting to his rule as soon as he'd arrived in Beaumont's great hall, after all. "Do ye know how the work is orchestrated?"

Cackling, Gerta shooed away a bird intent on stealing from her basket. "Nay, my lord, but Lady Rosalind can tell you all about it."

Malcolm heard Ian mutter beneath his breath at the mention of Rosalind's name. No doubt he and

Jamie were still disgusted with her for stabbing him. Loyalties ran deep in their clan.

As for Malcolm, he had found forgiveness for the blade in his thigh easily enough, even if the wound still ached like the devil. Years of battle had taught him to ignore physical pain. If only he could ward off the unwelcome desire for her so simply.

"Dinna jest with me." He took his responsibilities to Beaumont seriously, since Robert wanted the keep in good working order. For that matter, Malcolm had a very personal interest in maintaining the lands if there was a chance the Bruce would grant them to him. "I may nae know much about reaping a harvest, but I know the work is done by men, nae noble maidens."

"Begging your pardon—" Gerta bristled visibly "—but Lady Rosalind organized the work after her father's death. She needed her steward's guidance the first year, but she can do it on her own now."

"Ye lie," Ian accused, whistling to the same birds Gerta tried to wave away. "Her brother would have been taken under the steward's wing, no matter how young he was at the time. Why would the steward bother with a female who would have no use for such learning? Ye insult us with yer tales." He swiped a few cherries from Gerta's basket and grinned. "Ye grow excellent fruit, however."

"I do not lie, Ian McNair," she huffed, yanking the basket out of his reach. "You may choose not to believe me, but do not call me a liar before you have tested the truth of my words. Ask Lady Rosalind what she knows about the harvest and she could well weary your ears till dawn." Gerta scurried away as quickly as her aging legs would take her, muttering about the lack of manners in arrogant Scots.

Ian watched her depart for a moment before he exchanged a wink with Jamie. "I am thinking Malcolm would rather enjoy the opportunity to listen to the fair Rosalind till dawn."

Malcolm glowered at them, frustration building every day he spent holding a keep that he didn't know how to run effectively. "Lady Rosalind is a coldhearted English noblewoman, nae some pleasing Highland wench to pass a night with."

"'Tis nae only the English who are coldhearted, McNair. Yer Isabel has been wed nigh on four years. Ye shouldna let yer bitterness over her prevent ye from enjoying the warmth of another's arms."

"I havena spared her a thought since her unfortunate marriage." The conversational turn made Malcolm remember one of the few reasons he sometimes preferred wartime to peace. Running hell-bent for your life to keep an arrow out of your arse ensured there would be no discussion of women.

Ian jabbed Malcolm in the ribs with a brotherly shove. "I suppose ye were nae thinking of her when ye risked yer neck to free her from her English cage?"

"I am sworn to protect our people from the English fury." Refusing to think about his failed attempt to free Isabel, Malcolm banged his boot against the rock wall to loosen caked soil from the sole. "I feel nothing for Isabel anymore except admiration for her courage and pity for her captivity. But as I know her well, I dinna fear for her. She will find a way to be free of the English king whether her blackguard husband helps her or nae."

Malcolm had done all he could as a warrior to save her, but since the woman remained in English hands, he'd found it difficult to come to peace with his efforts. Hellfire. He'd grown as morbid as Ian of late, and without half as good a reason.

"Think ye there is any truth to Gerta's words?" he asked, eager to leave behind all talk of Isabel. Perhaps speaking to Rosalind would cheer him. She might be as ruthlessly ambitious as Isabel, but Malcolm took perverse comfort from knowing that at least Rosalind was safe under his watch. "Might the good lady of Beaumont know something of the harvest?"

"Very likely." Ian laid out a row of cherries on the rock wall, enticing a little bird to hop closer and closer to him.

"Then ye were cruel to call her a liar," Malcolm admonished, wondering how Ian could be patient enough to let wild creatures come to him.

"Aye, but riling her surely yielded some useful insights."

Grudgingly, he had to admit Ian could be very wise at times. Malcolm only hoped *he* could maintain some of the family wits about him tonight when he confronted Rosalind. He would need to be clever if he wanted to extract information from the stubborn former mistress of Beaumont.

* * *

Malcolm finally sought Rosalind's solar some hours later, hoping he had not delayed the task so long she would be abed.

Rosalind engaged his thoughts all too often this past sennight. He had almost enjoyed his last visit with her, though he knew *she* had not. She was practically hissing by the time he departed.

It was unfortunate they were on opposite sides of the Scots-English dispute, for he had to admit she would be an admirable ally. She was a fierce fighter, a loyal kinswoman and, if Gerta were to be believed, exceedingly sharp.

But those same reasons kept her his opponent. She would never forsake her English heritage to swear loyalty to him, he realized. He could lock her upstairs until doomsday and she would not relent.

Candlelight shone from under her solar door when he reached it. Anticipation gripped him as tightly as he clenched the master key in his hand when he inserted it into the lock and turned.

A tempting vision greeted his eyes. All traces of the bow-wielding warrioress vanished, Rosalind now stood in the center of her private chamber surrounded by flowers of every hue. Like a forest sprite with only nature to adorn her, she presented a charming picture.

She held delicate blue flowers—damned if he knew one clump of petals from another—in one hand as she arranged another bunch of spiky red blooms in a tall vase. A basket of pale yellow blossoms sat at her feet. Other containers, already filled and arranged, were perched on every available table and chest. The room smelled heady and sweet, like a hothouse at midsummer.

This gentle creature was his ambitious, blade-wielding enemy? He could scarcely reconcile this woman with the Rosalind who'd cursed and railed at him the week before.

For a long moment, she did not hear him, absorbed as she was in her task. The flowers, the scents, the feminine chamber—even the lady herself—fit into his recurring dream of a home.

Home.

His heart ached with longing for the domestic pleasures a woman could gift a family with. Rosalind's slippered feet tread on sweet-smelling rushes, her cutting knife moving deftly from one stem to the next. He could not see the whole of her face from the side, but he could tell she bit her lip as she worked, seemingly caught in thought.

She trimmed the stem from a long rose before plunging it into a hammered silver urn, then looked up. If he'd surprised her, she hid it well.

"Good evening, heathen." She smiled charmingly before returning to her work.

She wished to pretend his arrival was of no consequence to her? Point one for the lady. She'd managed to rile him already.

"Ye've stuffed yer rooms full of greenery with nae a holy day in sight." For that matter, even on holy days, he'd never seen a chamber so lavishly appointed with nature's bounty. "What are ye up to?"

"Because you have seen fit to lock me indoors, I have brought the outdoors inside where I can enjoy them."

"Where did ye find all these?" Malcolm asked, wandering around the room to study the blooms. There were at least a dozen shades and shapes of wild-flowers and roses.

"My mother's garden."

"I have seen no blooming garden. Ouch." He sucked a drop of blood from his finger. "Yer foliage is danger-ous."

"I must choose my opportunities to inflict a small measure of pain upon you where I can." The wench grinned unabashedly. "The garden is surrounded by one of the crumbling walls of the south tower."

"We will begin rebuilding the walls on the south-ern side tomorrow." He joined her at the plank table where she worked.

"So I have heard. That is why I have chosen to pick as many flowers as I could before your men trample my plants."

"How do ye know our plans?" Malcolm plucked the small shears from her hand, preferring to leave the unpredictable maiden unarmed. "And who picked all of these?" He knew very well she had not left her chambers all week. Her door remained guarded.

"I told you at your last visit, McNair, there is much you do not know about the keep." Arching a brow, she peered at him over a vase of spotted yellow lilies. Lilies? Hell, they could have been some kind of fancy herb and he wouldn't know the difference. "I picked these myself and I heard your men talking about their plans to fortify the southern walls."

"Ye lie," Malcolm told her, employing Ian's tactic.

She merely smiled.

He tossed up his hands in disgust, lacking his brother's patience. "I refuse to get trapped in a discussion of petty nonsense. Ye will sit and talk to me reasonably." He seated himself on a stone bench and gestured to the chair beside him.

Rosalind did not move. "As you can see, I still have a great deal of work to be done, so if you do not mind—"

"I do mind." She thought she had work to do? He had a field bursting with grain and no clue how to secure it for the winter. He wouldn't take any chances with the harvest lest the people of Beaumont starve, proving once and for all he did not deserve a keep of his own. "Come and sit down."

Sighing, Rosalind laid her plants back in their basket. She paused at the sideboard before joining him. "I seem to recall you have need of spirits when we talk. May I pour you some wine?"

"How pleasing ye can be when ye choose." He wondered what it would be like to lead the kind of domestic life in which a woman brought him wine at the end of the day. A damn sight nicer than consigning himself to some bedroll on the cold ground on a battlefield. Especially if the shared cup of wine led to even more relaxing pursuits. "I can think of nothing I would like better."

He watched her take her time filling the cups and seating herself. She looked radiant despite having been locked in the dungeon, then confined to her rooms all week. Perhaps she really had strolled out in the walled garden today. It would explain why she looked so fetching.

Malcolm shook his head to clear it of wayward thoughts. More than likely the scent of all the damn flowers had gone to his head.

He sipped his wine, in no hurry to talk just yet. Rosalind drank hers slowly, too, he noted. Probably plotting her strategy to keep him off balance. He allowed himself a moment to absorb the sight of her, hoping maybe if he studied her more carefully he would discover the secret of her attraction and, in turn, find a way to better arm himself against her appeal.

Her kirtle and surcoat were two shades of purple—the kirtle a pale lavender, the surcoat a rich plum. The sleeves and bodice fit closely, revealing a softly curving, altogether pleasing form beneath. And he thought this closer investigation of her would somehow help?

Shifting in his seat, he gulped the rest of his wine in an attempt to cool the fire within. Forcing his gaze to safer terrain, he noted the brightly colored gems glittering about her wrist, and a cluster of amethysts shining at her waist identified the hilt of a dagger. He winced at the memory of that particular blade and wondered why he had not taken it from her earlier.

Flaxen hair still hung loose about her shoulders, brushed to a fine glimmer that caught the candlelight as she moved. One thin braid, wound with silver thread, dangled amid the tresses falling to her waist.

She glanced up suddenly and turned brilliant eyes upon him, perhaps waiting for him to speak. Why had he never noticed the color of her eyes before? They were exactly the shade of heather, the small flower that grew rampant throughout the Highlands.

"I have much work to do yet tonight." If she meant to prod him out the door with her words, she would be disappointed. He had no intention of leaving here without the information he sought.

But first, he would unsettle her. Rattle her just a little. Perhaps then she'd be all too glad to give him the answers he wanted so she could send him on his way.

"So ye have said, lass." Setting his empty cup aside, he edged closer to her. Not obnoxiously close. Just near enough to catch a hint of her soft scent. "I was wracking my brain, I was, to name the color of those eyes."

A flush crept into her cheeks, although she did not seem quite worldly enough to fear the carnal direction of his thoughts. She shook her head and made no reply, her face the picture of innocent confusion.

"Rest easy, darlin', I have solved the problem, for ye have eyes the color of heather."

"Heather?" She wrinkled her nose. "Truly you know naught of flowers, McNair. The blooms you speak of are a generous shade of purple, while my eyes are distinctly gray."

"Heather." He'd never been the kind of man to wax poetic about a lass's beauty before, but then waging war didn't require as much tactical planning as catching Rosalind Beaumont off guard. He needed to press any advantage he could, and strangely enough, it proved all too easy to flatter the bold, brave lady of the keep. "But dinna fash, lass, I have come here for yer expertise on another matter."

Predictably, she appeared relieved, her shoulders relaxing by slow degrees as some of the hectic color faded from her cheeks.

If he were not a man of honor, it would be all too tempting to seduce prickly Rosalind. But that was not his objective. "The fields will be ready for harvest next week."

"A fine harvest it will be," she observed, sipping her wine with more caution than he had. "The weather has smiled favorably upon our crops for once."

"On yer flowers, too, 'twould seem."

"I have been fortunate that Mother Nature saw fit to cooperate with me this year." She twirled her cup between restless fingers, her gaze settling upon anything in the chamber but him. "Two years ago it rained so heavily all summer, I feared the roots would rot right out from under the stems. But the plants are hardy, no matter how delicate they might look."

"The same might be said for their mistress." Malcolm did not miss the pleasure in her eyes as she spoke of her garden. He struggled to recall she was his enemy and not a tempting maid, because no matter how fair she looked among her flowers, Rosalind was as determined and ruthlessly practical as his faithless Isabel had been. Any wench who fought off her enemy with a crossbow was bound to be trouble.

"There is naught delicate left within me, I fear." Her unexpected remark seemed to be spoken to herself more than him before she downed the rest of her wine in a hearty swig. "Life in the borderlands has a way of stomping out the softness inside us, doesn't it?"

Ah, hell. He could not be taken in by the blatant hurt he spied in her gaze. To soften toward her now would be a fool's folly.

"I want to make a deal with ye." He rose from the bench to slowly pace the solar floor. Sitting close to her seemed to distract him far more than it rattled her. "But first, ye must tell me what ye know of bringing in a harvest."

Rosalind plucked one of the roses from the basket at her feet and inhaled its fragrance. "If I told you, I would have nothing left to bargain with."

As if his hands had a will of their own, Malcolm found himself drawing her from her seat to hold her in front of him. Unwise, he knew. Yet he could not resist the urge to touch her again, to find out for himself if she was as soft as he remembered.

"If ye dinna tell me something to demonstrate yer knowledge of the subject, I willna believe ye are capable of this task."

She stared at him in breathless silence, but did not pull away. Her eyes widened and grew dark in surprise. Malcolm flexed his fingers around her upper arms, gently pressing the soft flesh beneath the delicate linen of her kirtle. When had he last held a woman?

He could see her pulse throb in a slender blue vein at her neck. He fancied he could feel her heart pound right through his fingers. The scent of roses seemed to radiate from her.

Swiftly he set her away from him, wondering what had possessed him to touch her in the first place. "Do ye ken, Lady Rosalind?"

He was gratified to see her sway on her feet for a moment before she smoothed her skirts and seemed to collect herself.

"Very well, then. The barley must be cut before anything else, as that will be the ripest, followed by the wheat. I can tell you how many serfs should be allotted to each field, and which serfs are better at cutting and which excel at threshing. Then, of course, there is the matter of the rents. I know who is entitled to what portion of the crops and how much must be given back in rent." Rosalind crossed her arms and glared at him. "Do *you* ken?"

"I can consult the account books to determine the rents." He did not wish her to know she'd surprised him. "I hardly need yer help in that."

"Even if you can read, heathen, you do not know where my steward keeps his books." She circled around him like a seasoned warrior sizing up her opponent.

"This ye will tell me." How had he lost control of the situation, when he'd been so sure he could distract her?

Apparently, he'd seriously overestimated his charm.

"In exchange for my freedom, McNair, and not a moment before."

Cunning wench. Still, he knew when to cut his losses. "Yer freedom will have its limitations, but ye may leave these chambers and join us for meals if ye share yer knowledge with me."

"My freedom will have no limitations and I will be respected as the mistress of Beaumont," she countered, stepping forward to press her advantage.

If he was not a chivalrous man…bloody hell, didn't she know better than to step so close to a man?

"And have ye incite the serfs to riot by nightfall tomorrow?" The lass must think him lack-witted. He had fought battles with more success than arguing with Rosalind Beaumont. "I dinna think so."

"I will have access to a horse when it pleases me."

"Ye may ride out with me when I allow ye to." Malcolm felt his blood heating with a combination of frustration and the damnable attraction he seemed to have developed for her.

"I will give the orders to my people at crop gathering time." She crossed her arms over her chest.

Malcolm tried valiantly not to notice the way the gesture only enhanced already-delectable curves. He tugged at the collar of his tunic, impatient with the close atmosphere of her floral bower. "Ye may stand beside me when I do so."

Rosalind stamped her foot in frustration. "I will be given my keys back!"

He was unable to suppress a grin. "Done. Do we have a deal then, ye intractable wench?"

"That's 'my lady' to you, heathen," she reminded him as she headed for her chamber door.

He hastened to block her path, and laid one hand over the knob. "Where do ye think ye are going at this hour?"

"For a walk in the garden." She reached past him for the handle, anyway.

"Well, ye are not going out alone." When he saw the swift intake of her breath and sensed a protest, he covered her lips with his fingers.

"Ye owe me a great deal of information, *Lady* Rosalind. I would have ye make good on yer promise."

She nodded, but glared at him until he lowered his hand.

"You need not impose your touch upon me. It is not a civilized practice to grasp a woman about her shoulders or seal her lips with your fingers when you wish to make a point."

"I have found sometimes 'tis the only way to make a stubborn lass listen." He opened the door in an exaggerated gesture of gallantry.

"That is because you are an ill-bred knave. I do not care to be manhandled so that you may get your point across."

Watching the gentle sway of her hips as she hurried down the corridor made Malcolm think he would not mind manhandling Rosalind, though not in the sense she thought. She was too tempting by half.

He caught up with her, easily matching his pace to hers. "How will ye see anything at night?"

"There is a moon."

They crossed the great hall, drawing several inquisitive glances from late-night revelers as they passed. Rosalind led him through the southern chapel to the makeshift wall the Scots had breached to invade the keep. Abruptly, she turned to the right and pushed open a small door. He had to duck to enter the narrow passage, which looked more like a crawl space, but he followed silently. The passage led down some steps, around a sharp corner and then up more stairs. At the end of the passage, she shoved at another door and led them out into the garden.

Floral scents washed over them with the tangible force of a strong breeze off the nearby mountains. The air hung rich and humid in the closed space despite the cool night. White rocks lined the pathway to the center of the sanctuary, where clusters of young fruit trees stood guard over wrought-iron benches. The stones practically glowed in the moonlight.

Rosalind perched on one of the benches and absorbed the scene around her with obvious pleasure. Unwilling to disturb her reverie, Malcolm took his time joining her.

"Have you ever seen nature so beautiful?" she queried, a wistful note in her voice.

"I have." He sat close enough to converse, but far enough away to discourage himself from touching her again. Perhaps the fresh air would help cool his overheated thoughts.

"Where?" Her skeptical tone suggested he'd offended her.

"A rolling Scottish hillside, so vividly green ye

think there has never been a color so pure." He closed his eyes, recalling the home he had not seen in years. "There are patches of heather at the crest, snow-covered blue mountains behind ye and a thrashing sea in front of ye." The memory filled him with nostalgia for more peaceful days and a home of his own.

"My father thought the Scottish countryside was splendid, I recall. He traveled there often to trade before the trouble started along the border."

"Aye. If only Scotland could have chosen her own king without calling upon the sly King Edward I to decide the matter, all would be well today."

Rosalind shook her head. "My father said King Edward would have engaged the Scots either way."

"Aye, because he was a greedy old bastard who didna know when to mind his own lands. Yer father had the right of it."

She raised her chin. "It was not King Edward who made reaving a popular pastime in the north. Had you all remained on your own side of the border, our sovereign would not have been so anxious to have a hand in ruling your thieving nation."

His disgust with the English, never far beneath the surface, surged through him. Isabel, for all her faults, did not deserve the torture of the cage King Edward had placed her in. "'Tis unwise for us to discuss affairs of state, lady. Let us think only about a successful harvest."

She sighed, her own frustration ill disguised. "Fine. We will discuss your seizure of my crops. You must call a meeting among the tenants tomorrow so you can share your plans with them. They will need to commit all their time, except for Sundays, to the harvest for the next three weeks."

Malcolm became distracted as he watched Rosalind's lips move while she spoke. She began listing the endless tasks involved with the harvest, and all he could think about was how much time he would be forced to spend in her company.

One evening in her presence and he was already exhausted from the continual effort to control his misplaced desire for her.

How the hell would he get through the next three weeks?

Chapter Five

A fortnight later, Rosalind watched the progress of the harvest from the shelter of a shady oak tree and forced her gaze not to linger on the arrogant Scot who fancied himself lord of her keep.

After too many days spent in his presence these last two weeks, she could no longer tell herself that the lingering looks she cast his way were merely an attempt to gauge her enemy. Nay, she'd taken her measure of him long ago and found him a formidable opponent and, if truth be told, an intriguing man.

Now she poured several cups of ale for the hot workers who toiled in Beaumont's fields, her role in the harvest much the same as it had always been when her father had ruled the lands. She provided food and drink for the villeins, hauling mead and ale to the fields during the heat of the day and ensuring a feast for all at twilight. Malcolm kept watch over the workers, but she noticed he wasn't above picking up a scythe now and then to help.

When Gregory had helped her recover from the

fire, she'd never seen him labor in the fields. He'd been an effective taskmaster, finding duties for every man, woman and child inhabiting Beaumont lands, but he'd never participated in the toil himself. Rosalind couldn't deny a strange warmth of feeling as she watched Malcolm share a jest with the crofters while they worked, the broad expanse of his back clearly outlined by his tunic in the heat. The strength in his arms was all too apparent as he swung a blade at the stalks of grain, making quick work of the fields.

Preoccupied in her observation of Malcolm, she didn't notice one of her tenants approaching until he spoke.

"It is the best crop of barley I have seen in all of my days." Thomas Cole, a respected man as Beaumont's miller, tossed down a cup of ale and handed the empty horn back to Rosalind. He mopped the sweat from his brow and checked the position of the sun.

Wrenching her gaze from the Scots lord—or laird, as his brothers referred to him—Rosalind cursed her unwanted interest in the enemy.

"Aye. I only wish we did not have to hand it all over to the Scots brutes." She could complain to Thomas, a longtime friend of her father's, though she was careful not to grumble before the serfs in general. She did not want them to rebel against Malcolm and cause more bloodshed on her behalf.

"It hurts me, too, my lady, but only because you deserve to reap the benefit from this good harvest. McNair is not such a bad lord for a Scot, but he has not shouldered the burden of responsibilities these last three years the way you have." He greedily drank down a second cup of the cold ale Rosalind offered him.

The fields were hot and the barley itchy to work with, but Gerta and Rosalind kept a steady stream of beverages available for the laborers. They had harvested for nearly a sennight now, and would finish with the barley by nightfall.

"And Gregory oversaw the planting that first year," she reminded him. He might not have helped much after those first few months, but in all fairness, he had been concerned with making himself useful to the king so he could gain permission to wed Rosalind. "He will most certainly drive out the Scots when he hears of this."

Although she had to admit she did not understand why he had not appeared at the gates long before now. She'd watched and waited for him for months before the Scots arrived, knowing he loved Beaumont as much as she did. Indeed, he seemed to think of the lands as his legacy, an inheritance due to him as much as her, since they'd promised to wed. It seemed only fair that Gregory rule Beaumont after he'd worked so hard to oversee the rebuilding of the keep.

"Maybe so." Thomas did not look so certain of Gregory's arrival, his attention quickly shifting back to the fields at the mention of Rosalind's future husband. "But for the serfs it matters not who receives their tribute, only that they can pay their rent and stockpile grain for the winter. So you needn't worry for us." Thomas wiped his mouth on his sleeve and replaced the cup on the table before trudging back to his work.

There could be no denying it. The people of Beaumont liked Malcolm. Even those who'd witnessed the fire liked him, possibly more than they had Gregory. How could her people be so fickle?

Discouraged, Rosalind climbed up the hill to the keep, leaving Gerta to finish distributing ale while she supervised dinner preparations. Meals were a huge affair during harvest time, and this year those raucous evening meals were presided over by the new lord, not Rosalind.

When would Gregory come? No matter how genial Malcolm and his brothers had become over the last two weeks, the thought was never far from her mind these days. She would rid Beaumont of the Scots in the near future, but in the meantime it seemed most prudent to appear compliant with McNair's wishes.

In truth, it was not terribly difficult, only damaging to her pride. Aside from her flustered confusion over his nearness that night alone in her chamber, Malcolm had been easy enough to get along with. Though she suspected he was only being agreeable to fulfill his greedy expectations for his newly acquired lands.

The heathen.

A thousand chores awaited her attention in the kitchen, but as she passed the lone entrance to her mother's walled garden from outside the keep, Rosalind could not resist venturing closer for a peek. She had not visited those grounds since Malcolm had instructed Ian to begin work on the south tower, but since all seemed quiet within, she decided to assess the damage done to the plants. Pushing open the tall,

rusted gate hidden among several ancient rhododen-
dron bushes, she stepped inside the empty retreat.

She did not realize she held her breath until it all
came out in a sighing rush of relief. Her flowers grew
lush and fragrant, as beautiful as ever. The roses still
climbed their trellises in peace. The herbs were un-
touched. If anything, they only begged to be trimmed
after a sennight of neglect.

A scaffold stood against the wall of the keep, but
its legs were carefully placed so as to avoid any plants.
The rocks were not piled on top of her flowers, as
she'd envisioned, but neatly stacked on various levels
of the scaffold.

Not quite believing her eyes, she bent to touch the
petals of a sprig of lavender to test the truth of her vision. This small plot had been her way of keeping her
family alive, their memories carefully preserved in
each thriving stem.

Even Gregory had not understood that, since he
had unknowingly hurt her the day he took his leave
from Beaumont a year ago. Rosalind recalled how she
had carefully plucked him a perfect lily the day he'd
departed, yet her future husband had carelessly
dropped her sentimental offering over the side of his
retreating boat into the waves of Solway Firth.

Touched by this small kindness now, she headed to
the kitchen, pondering why Beaumont's conqueror
had allowed her garden to be spared. She did not wish
to feel gratitude toward the McNair laird, yet there
could be no other name for the relief she'd experienced
upon seeing her mother's private sanctuary unharmed.

The kitchen lay only a few steps ahead of her when the pounding of a horse's hooves across the courtyard made her turn. A familiar silhouette filled her vision, the strong lines of Malcolm's broad shoulders swaying in time with his horse's step until he swung off his mount and hailed her with a wave.

"Yer barley crop could feed yer people twice over this winter, Rosalind." His long stride brought him too close to her before she could think to back up. "To celebrate, I thought we might toast the bounty of a fine harvest long into the night and make tomorrow a day of rest."

"That would be…nice." She licked her lips, not sure what else to say to a man she could not afford to befriend. "Thank you for sparing my flowers."

Maybe speaking those words aloud would put her on an easier footing with him. Rosalind did not feel that she owed this man a debt, but her sense of honor prompted her to at least be grateful for his thoughtfulness.

"Ye're quite welcome." He stared down at her a long moment, as if unsure how to read her. "I saw ye leave the fields and thought I would see if ye needed help with anything."

For a breathless space of time, Rosalind saw him as a man instead of a conqueror. A handsome, attractive man paying flattering attention to her. The sun shone warmly about them, and other voices in the courtyard—a handful of village boys playing with a small hound, serving girls from the kitchen retrieving water from the well—faded to nothing. And in those few seconds, Rosalind could see where she might have felt very differently about Malcolm had they met under other circumstances.

His blue eyes narrowed, darkened. She got the impression that he looked so far inside her he could see her quickened heartbeat, her twitchy discomfiture with the attraction she felt for him. What was it about him that called her to stare at him as though she'd never seen a man before? As if those muscular arms and narrow hips were so different from every other male's?

Confused, she considered turning her back on him and simply retreating to the kitchen, but just then he filched a strand of her hair blowing around her shoulder, smoothing the lock between his thumb and forefinger.

"Rosalind." Her name lingered on his lips, drawn out into a musical sound.

Heaven help her, she could have fallen right into that dark gaze of his. Right into those powerful arms…

"I don't need any help." She shoved the words from her mouth and stepped back, knowing she needed to insert more space between them lest she give in to the ridiculous urges of her treacherous thoughts. "I must see to the meal."

Gently, he replaced the wayward strand of hair behind her back with the rest. "Aye. Ye'll take yer place beside me at sup tonight. 'Tis yer crop we celebrate."

Nodding, she backed away from him and the potent pull of his eyes. She was grateful to finally feel the hard wood of the kitchen door behind her and to escape the turmoil of her thoughts.

Only when she was safely inside did she recall that the crops were not hers alone to celebrate. She'd promised Beaumont, herself and the reward of good harvests to another, whose face became more indistinct in her mind's eye with each passing day.

Angry voices assailed Rosalind's ears a few moments later, giving her little time to recover.

"You whoring slut, Moira!" a feminine voice shrieked. "You knew he was mine." An awful crash sounded as something broke.

"Can I help if he prefers me?" a sultry voice purred.

"How can you say he prefers you? You thought Lord Evandale preferred you, too, and he could not overthrow you fast enough once—"

They spoke of Gregory? Rosalind strode into the fray, heedless of flying dishes as she thrust all thoughts of Malcolm from her mind. "Lower your voices this instant or I shall turn you out."

Helga, the flustered cook, rushed forward. "My lady, I tried to keep them under control, but they began to say such wicked things—"

"Enough." Raising her hand to halt the torrent of words, she walked toward the two combatants, determined not to ask outright what they meant about Gregory. Even if it ate away at her not to know, she would not sacrifice her pride. "Explain yourselves."

A dairymaid named Deirdre stepped forward and curtsied, adjusting her skewed cap. "I am sorry, my lady, 'twas me and Moira that fought."

The other young woman, a serving girl who had often lavished much attention on Gregory when he'd been in residence, looked unruffled.

Deirdre hurried on. "I tol' everyone that I had my heart set on one of the Scotsmen. Real handsome, too. And then, day 'afore yesterday he winked at me, real nice like. But 'afore I got a chance to talk to him last night, Moira throws herself right in his lap like the slut she is!" Her face flushed with anger. She was a tall, attractive girl, but young enough to be a bit gangly and awkward.

"Moira, is this what happened?" Rosalind reserved judgment until she heard both sides. She'd grown up with these young women, the lines between noble and commoner blurred in a household that had been forced to pull together for the past few years. But now that she thought about it, she did recall that she'd caught Gregory talking with Moira in quiet corners of the keep a time or two.

The server smiled languidly, not bothering to look up from a careful inspection of her nails. "I imagine so."

"Do you think your actions were fair toward Deirdre?" Frustration tickled along nerves already stretched thin from the demands of the harvest and her encounter with Malcolm.

"I think Deirdre is too young to do more than dream about a real man. If he wanted her, he would have gone to her one of the many times she set her big cow eyes on him."

Deirdre's face grew mottled with rage. Rosalind vowed never to grow so enthused about the attentions of a man that she would resort to this sort of childish behavior.

"Moira." Rosalind ground her teeth, determined to hang on to the last vestiges of her authority. "You will conduct yourself with more restraint."

"Maybe Deirdre ought to just grow up instead. Besides," the server purred, turning insolent eyes on Rosalind, "I take orders from the new lord, not the deposed lady."

A collective gasp sounded. All waited to see what Rosalind would do as she weighed her options.

"I may be the new laird," rumbled Malcolm as he descended on them like an ominous cloud, blue eyes flashing cold fire as he took in the scene before him. "But ye better learn well that Rosalind is still yer lady. Ye will obey her in all things, knowing she speaks with my authority."

He turned to Rosalind. "I hope ye punish her suitably for her impudence." Staring at her for a long moment, he seemed to pay no attention to anyone else in the room. "I came to tell ye that it now rains. We will sup in the hall." Without another word, he stalked from the kitchen, leaving a wake of stunned expressions.

Not bothering to question Malcolm's decision to give her some of her former power, Rosalind looked to the arguing women.

"I do not want to hear another word about this mishap." Her mother had taught her the importance of maintaining authority. If she let hers slip now she might never regain it. "Consider the matter finished unless you give me reason to address it in the future. Moira, you will pay half the expense of the bowl Deirdre broke."

Both girls nodded. Rosalind could not help the momentary satisfaction she felt at seeing the ashen cast in Moira's cheeks.

"We will have to set tables in the entryway and double the trestles in the hall," Rosalind explained to the clerk of the kitchen. "I will send you help to move them."

Hurrying out of the kitchen to cross the courtyard in the rain, Rosalind gave orders as she went. She dispatched Gerta to help Helga. Jamie McNair promised to help with the tables. Another Scotsman agreed to entertain the waiting serfs with a tune on his lute.

She was seeking her chamber after she'd finished dispensing directions when Malcolm stepped from the shadows in the corridor.

"Everything is under control?" The unnatural darkness of the narrow hallway shrouded them in intimacy.

"Well enough. Harvest time is always busy." Actually, nothing was under control, but she would not share that with him. She still needed to dress for the evening meal, and now her hair was wet from the rain. The revelation in the rose garden and then Malcolm's strange pronouncement in the kitchen had unsettled her. Rosalind wondered if she'd ever feel in control of anything in her life again.

"I have been known to put the fear of the devil into men's hearts when I have a mind to." He leaned against a wall as rough-hewn as himself. "I hope it worked with yer little lasses, too."

"They seem duly chastened." Shouldering past him, Rosalind stopped when his hands reached out to halt her.

"That is all ye have to say on the matter?" He released her slowly, opening the door to her solar with his other hand at the same time. "No rant about my interfering with yer household?"

She eyed the entrance to her chamber, wondering if he meant to lure her inside and then... Her skin heated by slow increments to think about what a man like Malcolm might want with a woman who ranked as more a captive than an enemy. At least a low fire blazed in her hearth, while the darkened corridor had become much too interesting with his gaze fixed steadily upon her.

No question, she'd risk the privacy of her lighted solar over the intimacy of the shadows.

"I thought you'd be pleased that I am submitting so nicely to your grand plans for my household." She vainly sought to give her words a sharp edge, as she moved into the chamber, snatching up a length of dry linen from a nearby bench. It seemed she'd gone far too soft inside where the heathen Scot was concerned.

"I dinna know what to make of such civil responses from ye, Rosalind Beaumont. Are ye feeling well?" He followed her right into the room, oblivious that decorum dictated a man should never do so without an invitation.

Just what did he intend to do with her here in her chamber? She whirled to face him, unaware he was already directly behind her. He loomed so near her skirts brushed him as she turned.

"I am fine. I only wish to ready myself to sup." She backed farther away from him as she dried her damp hair with the linen, scrubbing fiercely in the hope she would generate some sense in her muddled head.

"Are ye sure ye are not ill, lass?" His voice full of sudden concern, Malcolm moved toward her, bringing them even closer than when she'd initially stepped away from him. He touched her cheek with callus-roughened fingers. "Ye look flushed."

He was much too near now. Rosalind's skin pricked with the awareness of his warmth, his strength, his utter maleness. His fingers skimmed down her neck to sift through her hair, tilting her head, angling her toward him. Heaven help her, she was so caught up in him she was surely no better than her errant kitchen maids.

Still, she could not tear her gaze from his. His blue eyes held her more captive than his arms ever had, searching out her secrets, dismantling her barriers against him. She opened her mouth to speak—to stop him? To call him closer? She did not know, could not call forth any words before his mouth descended on hers, sealing her to him with a burning, singeing, delicious kiss.

Her heart hammered with a mix of fear and hunger, desire for things she knew were forbidden to her. Dangerous. And yet, she did not push him away, did not dream of halting something that seemed to call to her at the most elemental level of understanding. Instead, she remained perfectly still, allowing him to show her what he wanted. What she wanted? She hardly knew. His hand—strong, large, sure of its course—moved to the small of her back, pressing her subtly forward. His lips met hers gently, soothing her into compliance with warm manipulation. Her startled gasp at the contact only eased his effort to deepen the kiss.

The taste of him—dark and complex, like no wine she'd ever sampled—flowed over her, through her. Pleasure swirled through her, weakening her knees and causing her to sink into him, his body every bit as solid as she'd imagined.

And then she felt it, exactly as one of her maids had once described the effect of a true lover's kiss—a fiery trail of sensation tingling inside her.

Oh, no.

She pushed at his shoulders, determined to break free of the seductive spell he wove around her. He released her instantly, jerking away as if burned. He looked surprised for a moment, as if he only just then realized who was on the receiving end of his kisses. But Rosalind was furious.

With him.

With herself.

With Gregory for never making her feel such things.

"You are angry." Malcolm's roughened voice still held a note of intimacy. The rich timbre reverberated right through her.

Rosalind did not trust herself to speak, unable to believe she'd just stood there and let him kiss her. As if they were not enemies. As if they were betrothed. And worse, she had enjoyed it. Could still feel the remnants of hot pleasure streaking through her.

"I dinna mean to upset ye, Rosalind." He brushed

a thumb over her cheek. "Ye quite took my breath away."

"Get out." She turned away from him, too shamed to meet his gaze and far too affected by his touch.

"'Twas just a kiss. Ye canna be that mad."

"I assure you, I am." She prayed he did not hear the tremor in her voice. And if he thought that was "just" a kiss, she wondered what he would offer a woman he wished to bed. "Get out!"

She sensed Malcolm's stare of disbelief, though she rigidly kept her back turned.

"Ye're showing yer English today, lass. Cold as a stone." Rosalind waited until she heard his steps retreat and the door close before she collapsed into a chair.

If only he were right.

Chapter Six

What the hell had he been thinking to kiss the feisty she-demon?

With Rosalind's kiss still warming his lips, Malcolm stalked through the long corridors of Beaumont to his chambers in another tower. He had only meant to speak to her for a moment before the meal, needing to reassure himself that she had resolved matters with the kitchen staff to her satisfaction. Somehow he'd wound up drowning in her unusual eyes, pulling her into his arms as if she were an agreeable maid instead of a prickly English noblewoman.

He might have more success forgetting the incident if her willowy body had not brushed against his, inciting every heated impulse a man could entertain. In that brief moment, the feel of her had somehow scorched itself into his skin. Malcolm knew he would recall the shape and texture of Rosalind's form as long as he walked the earth.

Slowly he attired himself for the meal, in no hurry

to see her again tonight. How would he get through a feast at her side when even now his palms itched to settle into her soft curves again? Hell and damnation, but she was a noblewoman, and that meant no one touched her without a bridal contract.

An image of Beaumont's fiery mistress garbed in wedding finery pierced his brain with sudden clarity. He blinked rapidly, forcing away the image. What was the matter with him? He wanted a wife who understood the pleasures of home and hearth, a woman who would take joy in her family. Rosalind preferred a crossbow to a babe in her arms, a fact that rendered her exactly the kind of woman he'd promised himself he would never pursue again.

Still, he could not help but admire her loyalty to her family holding. She could organize a harvest. She worked hard to help her people instead of watching them toil from the safety of some lofty tower. For that matter, her willingness to enter the battle fray the day of his siege might have been foolish, but in doing so, she proved she embodied the McNair motto, Family Above All, as much as his own kin.

Scrubbing his face clean with fresh water from a basin near the hearth, Malcolm wondered if such a strong woman might make a better wife for a man who wanted that kind of fearlessness. Ian swore he would wed such a lass if ever he married again. And as the McNair heir to Tyrran Keep, Ian had no choice but to wed one day. Would Ian want Rosalind for his own?

Heaven knew, she deserved the protection of a powerful man, one who could be worthy of her strength and intelligence. Yet even as Malcolm could see the logic of such a plan, his gut clenched in protest at the thought of Rosalind in another man's arms.

The evening meal ranked as the longest of Rosalind's life.

She supped at the high table beside Malcolm, aware of his every move, his every gesture. He sat in a place of authority, recognized as laird, yet Rosalind maintained her honor in being seated beside him. The position might have appeased her wounded pride at being displaced in her home, except that tonight thoughts of their kiss plagued her.

Did he find her presence as unsettling as she found his? It shamed her to think that Gregory's embraces—few though they were—had not inspired half the heated sensations Malcolm's did. Perhaps at seventeen years old she just had not been ready to be kissed, whereas now she had come into her full womanhood. That had to be it.

Rosalind certainly could not credit the possibility that Malcolm's touch left her breathless and wanting. The notion seemed ludicrous. Impossible. Above all, it struck her as supremely disloyal to her family, who'd died at his countrymen's hands. Saints forgive her for her weakness.

Tonight's harvest feast was the most festive yet this season. Ale flowed freely and platters were brought around several times, laden with lampreys and capons, stuffed pig and venison. Moira served the head table, but Malcolm seemed not to recognize her. Rosalind smiled at her, but the girl merely nodded. It occurred to Rosalind that she perhaps should not have let the server off so lightly, and made a mental note to watch over the recalcitrant maid.

Satisfied the feast had been a success, Rosalind was preparing to excuse herself when Malcolm beat his knife against his goblet for attention.

"My good friends," he shouted, gaining notice when he lifted his goblet to propose a toast. The hall quieted as others reached for their cups. "Yer honored lady has favored me with a walk in her garden this evening."

Rosalind moved to interrupt him, but he pulled her hand into his own. Squeezed. She kept silent, her anguish growing as several people shouted their approval.

Malcolm stood, drawing Rosalind to her feet with polished, courtly manners she had not seen from him before. "We leave ye to yer revelry and welcome ye to enjoy the fruits of yer hard labor. May God grant us many a harvest as rich and blessed as this one has been."

Offering her his arm, he used his other hand to raise his cup higher amid mixed calls of "Amen" and "Hear! Hear!" as all of Beaumont toasted a prosperous future.

Rosalind saw no choice but to accompany him from the hall, unwilling to create a spectacle for gossip-hungry watchers. The heat of Malcolm's hand penetrated her gown as surely as if he caressed her bare skin. A shiver tripped through her in response. As soon as they were out of sight of the revelers, she snatched her arm from his.

"I don't know what you thought that kiss meant, Malcolm McNair, but I swear you will regret making free with my person if you continue to haul me about at your whim."

He swung on her in the torch-lit corridor, startling her with a scowl that set his brows in a forbidding slash. "Save yer remonstrations until we are well away from any chance meetings. We will speak directly."

Pulling her through the chapel and into the walled garden, he slammed the door shut behind them. Rosalind was surprised he already knew the keep so well. Even more surprised and annoyed that he would bring her here, to her favorite place, in order to chastise her.

He continued his purposeful gait until he'd led her to a bench beneath the fruit trees, sat her down and faced her as if she were naught but a hapless maid. "What happened after I left the kitchen today?"

"That, you heathen beast, was no fault of mine. Had I known what you were about, I would never have allowed you to kiss me."

"Hellfire." His scowl eased for a moment. "Not that, Rosalind. What happened with the serving girl who sought to defy ye?"

He had not meant the kiss. She was grateful for the shadows of the moonlight as hot color rose in her cheeks. "You mean with Moira?"

"I dinna know the girl's name." He waved his hand in a mute gesture of disgust. "What punishment did ye settle upon her?"

Rosalind lifted her chin defensively. "She will pay for half the broken bowl."

"And?"

"And nothing. I told both girls we would let the matter drop if they would cause no further disturbance."

"That is all?" His raised voice reverberated through the garden, bouncing off the stone walls.

"There is no need to shout." She lowered her own voice, sincerely worried her flowers might be adversely affected by Malcolm's angry tone. Hadn't she lovingly nurtured them back to health with soft crooning after the fire?

"There is every reason to shout about it. Ye didna see the look she gave ye at supper this eve? Ye didna see the lass is sorely in need of discipline to know her place? Did yer brother see to the punishment of such insolence before I arrived?"

Rosalind forgot about her flowers, surprised he'd noticed her brief interchange with the maid. "Honestly, Malcolm, you make much of nothing. I saw no need to beat the girl. She merely stole the love of another girl's heart."

Malcolm gripped her chin in one huge hand. "Think ye I concern myself with the nature of two silly lasses' argument? I only care that the wench spoke to ye with open disrespect. If her arrogance goes unpunished, she'll spread ideas to others, and before ye know it ye willna be able to run yer own household." He shook his head as he dropped her chin. "Ye are a noble lady. Why do ye not know this?"

Sliding from her seat, she stood to more easily meet

his eyes. "Excuse me if I do not know my role here anymore. If my judgment in this matter was poor, it is because you have given me reason to doubt my authority. You made certain everyone at Beaumont knew who was lord here when you threw me in my own dungeon and later locked me in my chamber. It is no wonder my word is disrespected."

"I made it perfectly clear to everyone in the kitchen, including ye, that yer word has authority, backed by me." His tone was now cool and detached.

"You see? I have power only because you say so. It is nothing. I know it. You know it. And Moira knows it."

They stared at one another in the damp garden. The air was clear and cool now that the storm had passed. The roses bent heavily to the ground, petals beaded with fresh rain.

"And now," she continued, "you have undermined me further by insinuating some sort of liaison between us in the course of your toast just now."

"Nay." He pushed on her shoulders until she sat back on the bench, then lowered himself next to her. As he talked, he removed his surcoat and draped it around her shoulders to ward off the growing chill of night. "I have demonstrated my regard for ye. If ye will not hold firmly to yer authority here, then ye force me to help ye take it. The Moiras of Beaumont will learn to keep their peace once they understand I honor ye."

He reached beneath the collar of his surcoat to retrieve the long tresses he'd trapped beneath it. Gently, he pulled her locks free and arranged them outside the garment. The intimate act called to mind the kiss they'd shared. The warm brush of his hands sent ribbons of pleasure through her limbs.

Angry that his touch had such an effect on her, she jerked away from him. "What does it matter to you whether or not my position is honored? You are lord here now."

"Beaumont will become a greater burden for me if 'tis run ineffectually. If there is discontent here, the property becomes less prosperous and more difficult to manage. 'Tis far easier to keep a smoothly sailing vessel running than to repair a sinking craft. Ye ken?"

"You are using me." Rosalind focused on her transplanted gooseberry tree so she would not have to look at him. She needed to concentrate on the wide void of understanding between them instead of the heated longing.

"I dinna see it like that. As far as I am concerned, I have no direct quarrel with ye, Rosalind."

Speechless in the face of such logic, she hoped the look she bestowed upon him conveyed how absurd she considered his statement.

"I didna come to conquer Beaumont because I sought vengeance against ye. I took it for king and country. 'Tis sorry I am if it puts ye out, for I rather admire ye. I have no wish to bring ye sorrow."

Malcolm touched her cheek to encourage her glance, but she refused to meet his eyes, uncertain why he would pretend to be concerned for her. Stubbornly, she drew her slipper-clad foot across the soft earth, making designs in the dirt with the toe of her damp shoe.

"That is why I made sure we dinna trample one plant in yer fair garden whilst we build a proper wall about the southern side of the keep." He gestured toward the scaffold. "Ian has done well in this, has he nae?"

"I will be sure to thank him for it."

"Rosalind, look at me," Malcolm began again, determination in his voice.

When she turned toward him, she was shocked to see him so close to her on the bench. She started to scoot away, but his hands snatched her back before she could escape.

"Listen for a moment longer, and then ye may go. We need to understand one another on a few things."

She studied her enemy, so close she could see flecks of gold in his blue eyes, even in the pale moonlight. The black-as-sin hair was tied neatly at his nape, falling between his shoulder blades. Every inch of his form spoke of his strength, from the broad shoulders and chest that tapered to a lean waist, to the muscled thighs and taut calves.

Yet it had been her experience he was not quick to use his strength to gain what he wanted. Instead he chose to tread lightly through her garden and seat her at his side in the great hall.

Malcolm McNair *would* have taken Beaumont without bloodshed, she realized with sudden certainty. She'd scoffed at that promise when he'd sworn it from outside the ward, but she knew now he would have honored it. Truly, he'd honored it anyway, though Rosalind's resistance cost him several men.

The realization frightened her. Her whole foundation—her lifelong beliefs of the Scots—suddenly crumbled.

Any beef-witted idiot could tell Malcolm was not the conqueror here.

He'd been able to fight off this woman's flaming arrows, but he could not scavenge up a defense against the soft vulnerability in her eyes as she stared up at him. That gentleness, so unexpected in this fiery lass, caught him by the throat and squeezed. Somewhere between his first bite of capon and his last swig of ale at supper, he'd realized he couldn't simply hand her over to Ian. Not when Malcolm wanted her more than his next breath.

He longed to rail at her for distracting him from his task. His plan had been to barter with Robert the Bruce over Beaumont as a reward for his service, but Robert would never consider giving him a profitable holding *and* a valuable heiress. The Scots king was not so rich that he could heap many prizes upon one man.

And—damn it all—Malcolm wanted Rosalind. For what ultimate purpose, he didn't quite know. He could not despoil her. Did not wish to hurt her. But the want of her...

"A man canna think when ye look at him thus." He knew he should release her now that she'd grown still beside him. Yet she fit so soundly beneath his arm, her frame surprisingly small for a woman full of life. "Did yer mother nae teach ye of base men's thoughts?"

A smile tugged the corner of her soft lips. "Are you finally admitting you're a base man, heathen?"

"Sometimes ye make me wonder." With an effort, he pulled his hand from her shoulder, relinquishing his hold on her. His king would not thank him for ruining a woman who could be of political significance in the Bruce's wars.

Yet the thought of Rosalind's lush body and fiery nature being given to another man for the sake of furthering the Scots' cause made Malcolm's insides grow cold.

Casting about for any topic of conversation other than his sordid thoughts, he remembered the matter that required settling between them. One of the main reasons he'd called her out into the moonlight for a private discussion.

"I am concerned about yer brother." He'd been ruminating over the matter of the missing Beaumont, knowing Rosalind would never forgive him if he was forced to battle her sibling.

Rosalind blinked slowly, perhaps confused by the shift in conversation. Still, she straightened on the garden bench, drawing her skirts close to her body in the mild September night air.

"He is too young to know what he is about should he try to gather some men and retake the keep," Malcolm added. The longer he kept William Beaumont away, the better. Hell, the boy should hop a boat and sail to France before showing his face again, since Malcolm's king had been adamant about the need to acquire—and hold—Beaumont Keep. "He could easily meet his death if he shows up here. I want ye to contact him and warn him nae to come."

She did not look as troubled as he might have expected. Well, troubled perhaps, but not angry. She did not stiffen with indignation or fire back some dire prediction of Malcolm's imminent destination in hell.

"I cannot." She tucked a strand of flaxen hair behind one ear, her gaze flitting about the dark gardens like a nervous bird in search of a place to land.

"Ye canna or willna?" Did she not understand the consequences here?

"Both. I do not know how to reach him, and even if I did, I would not risk my chance of being rescued."

Malcolm went absolutely still, unwilling to think he'd heard her properly.

"Rescued?" If a voice could be lethal, he would probably have had the lass running for cover. "Ye think ye need to be *rescued?*" His pause was long and measured, but he did not for a moment expect an answer. "Ye are damn fortunate ye are an Englishwoman besieged by chivalrous Highlanders and nae a poor Scots lass taken by English knaves. If a Scotswoman raised a crossbow to yer countrymen, she would surely be tortured and hanged after being raped and beaten. Do ye honestly compare yerself to a woman in need of saving?"

Rosalind felt the anger radiating from Malcolm even though she now sat a few hands' lengths from his sprawling masculine form. Still, she turned to peer at him, to judge how angry he was already. The man she glimpsed now bore little resemblance to the controlled knight who'd taken her keep or the laughing laird who jested with his serfs as he toiled beside them in the fields.

Perhaps it would have been wise to keep her thoughts to herself, but Malcolm did not know her experience with the Scots. Although captivity in her own keep might be an easy sentence for now, who knew what might happen when Robert the Bruce came? He could order her killed with a mere nod of his royal head.

"Yes."

"Ye say *aye?*" Malcolm rose from his seat, casting a shadow over her like a mountain blocking sunlight. A low tremor threaded through his voice, hinting at genuine anguish. She wondered what the conquering Scots hero would know of defeat or the loss of friends and family.

"If ye would subject yer brother to me because ye are too stubborn to relent, then believe me, Rosalind, ye dinna know the grief of seeing people you care about suffer by the cruelty of another." His gaze, which had been so warm and inviting earlier, now became an accusatory lance.

The self-righteousness of his tone pushed her too far.

"The Hades I do not." She sprang from her seat to stand toe-to-toe with him, oblivious of his surcoat falling from her shoulders to the cold bench. Her blood rushed through her in a sudden flood of hot rage. "I've lost every member of my family to your—"

"What?" The word whispered through the night air,

a stark contrast to the raised voice Rosalind had resorted to.

"Which part did you not hear? Perhaps if you were not so consumed with running my keep and ruling over my every action you might hear more of what goes on about you." Her breath came shallow and fast. She had not been this angry since…ever. Not even when her family was killed had she allowed herself a time to rant and rave and be furious. She'd been called upon immediately after her kin's deaths to make sense of the chaos caused by the fire. And later, after order had been restored, who was there to be angry with? No perpetrator was ever brought to justice. A part of her felt almost relieved to be outraged now. The emotion was immensely freeing.

Malcolm's eyes narrowed in suspicion. "Ye lost *every* member of yer family?"

Dawning realization set in. Her anger, so long suppressed, had played havoc with her good sense. She thought to lie, but it was already too late. Malcolm scrutinized her face, and she had no doubt the quick-witted brute discerned the meaning of her slow response.

Collapsing against the trunk of a slender plum tree, upset with herself and her hasty words, she finally confessed the truth. "My brother is dead."

His eyes narrowed. "What trick is this?"

She shook her head, taking comfort from the familiar sights and smells of the garden as she inhaled a deep, cooling breath. "No trick now. I fooled you on the day of the siege when I dressed as a man to speak to you from the battlements. There has been no lord of Beaumont since my father and young brother died three years ago."

"William?"

She nodded, refusing to ruminate on Will's death. Three years later, it still hurt her deeply. He'd been a beautiful child—healthy, smart, full of promise. Rosalind concentrated on a rain-washed rose, willing the pain of her memories to recede. "He was but twelve years old."

"I'm sorry." Ducking beneath a low-hanging branch of the fruit tree, Malcolm reached for her. Perhaps he sought to provide comfort, but she could not accept it from him. Not when his countrymen had caused so many needless deaths. Furthermore, she did not wish to discuss the Beaumont fire for fear of displaying any more weakness in front of him. Bad enough that she'd lost control of her anger earlier. She would not show him any more unruly emotions this night.

Malcolm seemed to search her face for signs of deception. Apparently satisfied with her explanation, he finally nodded.

"'Twas you all along." He strolled about the shadowy garden, his dark brows furrowed in thought as he paused to finger a small yellow flower. "What is this little weed?"

"Hardly a weed." Wary at the shift in conversation, Rosalind kept her guard up. "'Tis the queen of the meadow."

"She doesna seem much of a queen among yer roses." Malcolm bent to sniff the blossom. "Although her scent is rather pleasing."

"Her looks are more impressive among the meadow flowers where she grows naturally, but she is a necessary herb and I like to have a fresh supply for healing purposes."

"Yer mother taught ye these arts?"

Rosalind nodded, still waiting for his reaction to the news of her deception. Was he angry? He must be, yet he walked about the flowers as if the garden were his only concern.

"And being raised a lady, ye know healing but ye dinna know much about defending a keep."

The criticism stung. "I managed well enough before you arrived."

"Only by the grace of God, Rosalind. Ye canna credit anything else."

"You think I have merely been entertaining myself, growing flowers?" She would not allow herself to become distraught all over again. She had already revealed enough of her secrets, thanks to her temper. "I learned to organize the harvest at the tender age of fifteen. A task even you were loath to take on. And I have worked hard to inspire the confidence of my people so they would not give away Beaumont's secret. News of a keep without a lord is not easily kept quiet, I assure you."

"Ye have been on yer own three years?"

"You cannot hide the suspicion in your eye, my lord. Do you think I lie?"

"It would nae be the first time, would it?" One brow lifted in skepticism. "In truth, I canna fathom how ye managed it. Yer former king was surely unaware of the fact. Longshanks would have had ye married within a fortnight."

"He did not learn of my father's death for some months." Rosalind lowered her eyes. She was not proud of her small deception on that note, though she knew the English king would sanction her marriage to Gregory Evandale once the younger man had proved himself. She'd known her actions were not fully admirable, but had convinced herself there was no need to disrupt her parents' wish that she wed her father's squire once he became a worthy knight.

"At which time, he would have insisted ye marry." Malcolm waited, so stubbornly practical. Honorable. She saw that now, even if she would rather not admit it aloud.

"Edward was also under the impression that my brother, the heir, lived." She sighed, realizing he would not let the matter drop without knowing the full story. "And since my father had mentioned a possible marriage contract for me to the king, Edward thought I was settled, as well. He saw no need to intervene even after he'd learned of my sire's passing."

"And why would yer king believe all of these lies?"

"I never put forth a mistruth to our king, but I also never saw a need to disclose the full extent of the trouble at Beaumont."

"Ye flirt with treason to play such games with yer sovereign. Who inspired ye to this madness? A greedy suitor, perhaps?"

Her discomfort grew as his guess came close to the mark. Of course Gregory was not greedy, but he had urged her to stay silent on the subject of Beaumont's woes. And she had been all too willing, for she did not want to wed some loathsome warrior with more might than brains.

"Beaumont is all I have in the world." She neatly sidestepped the question. "Without it I have no hope of marriage. I have no worth."

"Ye have plenty of worth either way. 'Tis fortunate the old king is dead and canna learn of yer lies. He wouldna have taken kindly to yer schemes, I can assure ye."

"No. You must know that if he'd discovered the truth about Beaumont, King Edward would have hied me off to a convent and given Beaumont to strangers."

"Mayhap," Malcolm admitted. "But more likely he would have wed ye to a strong knight to protect ye."

"One of *his* choosing."

"And ye would have one of yer own choosing then, ye fickle woman?"

"Is that so much to ask?" She wanted a chivalrous man. Someone who would appreciate her for something besides her ability to bear babes. Someone who would understand her dedication to Beaumont and its people. She did not want whatever knight her king deemed strongest and bravest.

"Ye wouldna be the first lass to wed with a man for duty's sake, Rosalind, and ye would have been safe these past few years."

"All went well until you arrived." She could not banish the bitterness from her voice.

"But I am here and I have no intention of leaving. Now ye must consider yer fate."

Chapter Seven

Malcolm watched Rosalind in the gentle wash of moonlight, wishing he could make her understand the need to be practical. What lofty expectations did she have for a husband that she would risk the wrath of her king to secure just the type of man she craved?

Couldn't she see that she needed protection? A woman alone in the disputed lands was unheard of. Even Isabel, for all her strength, had lacked a suitable protector. She suffered an English prison for her out-spokenness, and her husband gladly let her languish there. Malcolm hadn't been able to protect selfish Isabel, but he could safeguard Rosalind.

"Ye love Beaumont," he continued, wondering if he could be mad to entertain the notion flitting around in his head. "Ye love the people and ye take pride in their prosperity. 'Tis a good thing."

"Malcolm, I—"

He shushed her with a finger upon her lips. "Beaumont now belongs to the Scots crown. Ye canna stay here and continue to nurse the hope yer king will come to yer aid."

Instead, she could choose to protect herself and her lands. She could do the one thing that would reward her with a small stake in Beaumont.

She could marry him.

Malcolm thought even stubborn Rosalind had to see the practicality of a legal union between them. Once he acknowledged the notion that had been looming ever since the night he'd spied her among her roses, Malcolm realized it was a perfect solution. He could secure her lands for himself, and live among people he had grown fond of. Perhaps his king would be appeased if Malcolm handed over a bride price for her as part of the bargain in a gesture of sincerity.

He ran no risk of falling in love with ambitious Lady Rosalind, yet he could protect her. And for some reason, he possessed a curiously powerful need to keep her reckless self safe.

Rosalind shook her head, her expression distressed. "I will never swear loyalty to the Scots, even for Beaumont's sake."

"I dinna ask ye to." Relaxing into this new plan, he decided the notion pleased him immensely. Of course he was not marrying her just for the opportunity to share her bed, but he couldn't deny the prospect enticed him. "I ask instead that ye wed with me."

"What?" She looked a bit ashen for a would-be bride, but he did not let that discourage him.

He was a skilled battle tactician. He could win against seemingly impossible odds. All he had to do was argue the plan's logic. Certainly, Rosalind could be reasonable, especially when her beloved home was at stake.

"If we wed, there is no more question about yer status. The people of Beaumont would feel content that their mistress still reigns, yet gain the protection of a lord. I will hold this keep with or without ye, but I fancy ye would be happier if ye were to remain the lady of Beaumont."

"You mean to tell me you wish to wed to make your claim to Beaumont more legitimate?"

"Nay. I have staked my claim by power of the sword, and make no mistake, I can keep it that way. I care not whether yer king sees my claim as legitimate. But I do care about the people of Beaumont. They would be more content with their lot if their lady remained in her place."

"We do not love each other, and never could." She shook her head, her sculptured cheekbones lit by the pale offering of the moon. In the distance, he could hear the laughter of villeins finding their way home from the keep after the late meal.

"What of it?" He had not expected talk of love from her. He'd seen her as a worthy adversary. A tactician like him. He had not expected this kind of softhearted foolishness. "Marriage is a contract to benefit each party. Ye will gain the right to remain here. I will gain peace of mind that Beaumont will continue to be a place of calm and prosperity. It would give me somewhere to call home between campaigns with the king."

"Wars in which you are off killing my countrymen."

"Battles in which I am ensuring your safety from potential invaders. I will protect you, Rosalind." She didn't seem to be grasping the beauty of the idea. Malcolm picked up her hand and squeezed it between his own.

"How can you approach marriage so coldly?"

"It need not be a cold marriage at all." His voice dropped to a warm rasp just thinking about the possibilities. "I am certain 'twill not be hard for us to learn to enjoy one another."

For one moment, her jaw dropped, giving him an enticing glimpse of a mouth he longed to possess again. Then, she clamped her lips shut.

"Because of a kiss?" Indignation seemed to snap her spine straight, drawing her up as far as her delicate body would allow. "It was a mistake that will not be repeated. And as for the people of Beaumont, you are right, I do not wish to leave them, but I could not bind myself to a man who cares naught for me just so I might remain."

"Ye say that now, but ye might feel differently when ye are banished."

"You would not dare."

"Nay, but King Robert will give the order if ye dinna swear yer loyalty."

"I am a noblewoman."

"That makes no difference to yer king when he takes *our* women, Rosalind." Malcolm could not help the fierce note that crept into his voice. The English cruelties were too much to bear. "Why should it matter to Robert?"

"King Edward would do no such thing."

"Maybe nae the son, but the father would and did in his day. He did far worse than banish our women when he seized our keeps. He strung them up in hanging cages like animals."

She shook her head in denial. "You must be mistaken."

"Nay. I have seen a woman confined in this barbaric manner hanging outside the keep at Berwick." No matter how Isabel had treated Malcolm, his heart ached to think of the torment she suffered for loyalty to her country. He would not resign Rosalind to such a fate.

"How would you have seen this woman at Berwick after the keep was taken by English forces?" The skeptical tone in her voice told him she did not believe him.

Hellfire, he wished it was not true.

"King Edward loved to show her off." He growled the words through clenched teeth. "She is a proud and beautiful woman. And she is a *noblewoman*. Her rank didna matter to yer king, so dinna think yer rank will matter to mine." He gave her time to digest his words, knowing he fought unfairly to scare her, but wanting her to make the right choice. She needed him, damn it. "So, what say ye, Rosalind? Will ye wed with me?"

"To keep myself from being banished? I do not think so."

Damned stubborn woman.

Fresh out of alternatives, Malcolm did not allow himself to plot any more battle strategy. He simply followed the most obvious path to woo a woman. He closed the distance between them and pulled her to him, pressing the full length of his body against her.

Her response to his kiss earlier in the day had been gut-wrenchingly sweet. The memory of it had haunted him throughout the evening meal. This was his chance to take her lips again, to see if he had dreamed the impossible nectar of her mouth.

He held her for a long moment, feeling her tremors. He towered over her so that she had to arch her neck to see him.

"Malcolm." Her lips breathed his name. "I think…"

"Dinna think, lass." He raked his fingers through her tresses, treasuring the silken threads against his palm. "Nae right now."

Rosalind gazed up at him, lost in the stormy sea of his eyes. Following his command seemed so simple. The easiest course of action when her heart pounded with urgent force. She promised herself it would only be for a moment. Just long enough to find out if his last kiss had been an unusual accident. Rational thought drifting away, she allowed herself to enjoy the feel of being held. The sensation was heady and strange. Wonderful and wicked.

His gaze slipped from her eyes to her lips, and she knew what would follow. Perhaps she should make some protest. Say nay. But the only sound that escaped her mouth was a small sigh.

Her knees wilted beneath her. His mouth brushed hers, moving persuasively against her lips. A delicious languor spread through her limbs at his touch and she sank more fully against him. She delighted in the strength of him, so hard and muscular. The softness of her own body molded perfectly into his. Some sensual magic seemed to have sway over her, a thick trance of pure sensation and sizzling heat.

Malcolm's hands slid up her spine to wind themselves in her hair as his lips trailed down her neck. The warmth of his breath left her skin shivering with undefined longing.

"Rosalind…" The whispered word was a sigh and a plea.

Her senses reeled. She'd never felt anything so…elemental. The sudden need for Malcolm came from deep within, strengthened by all the years she had gone without physical intimacy of any kind.

His palm extracted itself from her hair to slip beneath the neckline of her surcoat. His fingers snagged her smooth skin as he caressed her exposed shoulder. The heat of his hand seeped through her chilled skin to warm her whole body. Awareness rippled over her flesh, making her wonder what it might be like to feel him touch her elsewhere. Everywhere.

A wave of longing washed through her, tugging her deeper into the haze of dark sensations. Her hands settled on his shoulders to draw him closer still, to steady herself against a world tilting quickly out of balance. The heat of him fairly scorched her, burning away all fears, all sense of propriety.

He filled her senses as if he'd been made to please her. His barley-scented skin made her want to taste him, yet she could not drag her mouth from the intoxicating wine of his lips. His tongue.

He stroked the inside of her mouth with persuasive swipes, the liquid heat of their mating calling to mind decadent visions of another kind of joining.

A keening cry echoed in the garden, and Rosalind was surprised to realize it was her own. She wanted this, wanted him, with a hunger that frightened her. She had no business touching him thus. Not when her kisses rightfully belonged to another man.

Heaven help her.

When Malcolm's lips followed the path of his hands beneath her collar, Rosalind knew she had indulged in his kisses for too long. Her control had slipped away until she felt barely able to think or speak. If she did not leave right now, she would be helpless.

"Malcolm, I cannot. You must—"

Her resolve faltered when his palm brushed over her breast. She gasped at the force of the pleasure that bolted through her.

If he noticed, he did not press his advantage, though his fingers trailed along her collarbone and neck. Her heart pounded as his touch moved lower, dancing around her breasts. Her flesh tightened and puckered in anticipation.

"I would protect ye always, I swear." He whispered the vow into her flesh, hovering just above the curve of her breasts. His tongue teased her, conquering and gaining new ground as it went until she moaned with the pure pleasure of it.

He lifted his head, one finger tilting her chin to meet his gaze. "Marry me, Rosalind."

His eyes held her in thrall, willing her to comply. She wanted, in that moment, nothing so much as to have him kiss her. To slide her bodice a bit farther off her shoulder.

She nearly said yes, so that she might explore the glorious sensation that spread through her like wildfire.

But then—finally—his words penetrated her brain. *Marry me.*

"I cannot." Panicking, she pushed away from him in a vain attempt to break the peculiar spell he seemed to have cast over her.

"Why nae?"

Time to be honest, if for no other reason than to remind herself why she must not touch him again. "I am promised to another."

His hands disappeared from her body as if by magic. Though she had sought freedom from his embrace, she felt bereft.

"Ye are truly betrothed?"

"Not quite." Her conscience pricked her, reminded her how much she owed to the man who had seen her through so much hardship.

"If there is no betrothal, then 'tis nae binding." Studying her thoughtfully, he added, "I dinna care if ye are no longer a virgin."

"How dare you?" Outrage filled her, an emotion she was grateful for since it helped burn away some of the raw need inside her.

"'Tis a natural assumption." He reached to straighten the collar of her surcoat, his fingers brushing lightly over her neck.

Rosalind swore that scant touch made her feel faint. Weak. She'd had no right to kiss him, let alone thrill to his every caress. "It is a wicked assumption."

"If ye are nae betrothed and ye remain a virgin, what is to stop ye from wedding with me?"

She cursed the heat that flooded her cheeks yet again but she held his gaze, determined to make him understand. "I swore an oath."

Guilt swamped her as she told him about the young squire who had helped her maintain Beaumont after her father's death, keeping the details of the fire set by the Scots to herself. She did not wish to argue with Malcolm about politics now, when the important factor here was her promise to another. She could not betray that vow.

Restlessly, she stalked the garden path in an effort to regain her composure.

"Who is this man?" A fierce note in Malcolm's voice unsettled her further.

"You do not know him." Would he seek Gregory out? Attempt to do him harm?

"I would have his name, else I know ye are lying."

"Gregory Evandale, my father's former squire." Shame crawled over her as she spoke his name, the heat in her face mingling with the gentle sting of her cheeks where Malcolm's bristly jaw had rubbed against her.

"Evandale? A real king's man, I'll warrant," he muttered. "And where is yer valiant squire-turned-knight now?"

"I do not know. One year ago he joined the old king. I have not seen him since."

"But he will show up here sooner or later to try his luck at winning back Beaumont. No doubt he looks forward to claiming this property with marriage to ye."

"As did you."

"I have already won it," he told her shortly. "Out of curiosity, what made ye swear an oath to Evandale?"

The fire.

But she would not speak of that. "Love."

"Ye fancied yerself in love? How convenient for yer young man." Malcolm glowered at her, evidently not pleased with the prospect of a rival for her hand.

Nay, a rival for Beaumont, she silently amended.

"I knew I could not make you understand." Incensed, she turned on her heel and started along the path to the keep. "But I do not intend to break a promise."

"Dinna count on yer faithful knight to take Beaumont back for ye," he called after her. "He willna get ye or the keep, make no mistake."

She managed to walk sedately through the hall, but once she reached the western wing, she ran up the stairs. Tears blinded her eyes in a hot flood as she flung open the door to her chamber.

"My lady?" Josephine's worried voice called after her as Rosalind tripped over the maid's pallet.

"A bath, please, Josephine. And a few moments alone."

The maid scurried into the corridor without commenting on the strange request at such a late hour.

Rosalind sank into her favorite chair and swiped at the tears she cried in silence. For Gregory. For her family. For herself. Malcolm had sounded so sure of himself when he said he would never give up Beaumont. He could kill Gregory.

Saints forgive her, she did not want Gregory's death on her hands. Her feelings toward him might be confused, but she knew she wished her childhood champion no harm. Her memories of Gregory became hazier with each passing month, but it seemed to her that Malcolm was twice his size. And he had many more years of battle experience.

"My lady?" Josephine looked questioningly from the doorway.

"I am fine now." An outright mistruth, but Rosalind knew she must brazen her way through this. "You may bring in the tub."

The maid hurried in with two young boys, who lay their burden before the fireplace. Rosalind gave each one a sugared fig from the sideboard, knowing they'd been awakened from their beds to do her bidding. Once her chamber had emptied, she undressed and eased into the warm water. A moment later the door burst open again to reveal Gerta, her cheeks pink with her haste.

"So what happened in the garden, my lady? The whole keep is whispering about your departure with the McNair laird." The elder woman rushed over to the tub, eyes wide with expectation. "Well?"

"I do not know why the Scot implied to the entire hall that I favored him, but nothing could be further from the truth." She hoped. Dear heaven, she could not favor her enemy over a gentle knight who had been beloved by her own father. Rosalind scrubbed her face vigorously, trying in vain to wash away the memory of Malcolm's kisses. "He remains the invader here, as unwelcome as before."

She knew the words to be a lie even as she uttered them. Yet how could she begin to explain the complex knot of feelings she had for Malcolm McNair?

Gerta sank heavily onto the footstool beside the tub. "Well, you cannot blame us for hoping."

"Hoping for what? That I would give my loyalty to a man who conquered my home? How could I hold faith with a Scot, whose people murdered my whole family?" She was hardly sure who she questioned—Gerta or herself.

"Begging your pardon to speak freely, my lady, but your father would have called it good politics, when all your people long for peace in their time." Gerta reached for a small urn full of scented oil and poured it into the bath, releasing a rose fragrance into the chamber. "And they rather like McNair."

"But Beaumont is English. If we bind ourselves to Malcolm, we become traitors. We would ally ourselves with the rebel King Robert."

"In the borderlands, what difference is there between Scots and English? Life goes on, and not too much differently for the villeins. All that the tenants care about is a good harvest and a fair lord."

"But I am nobly born." Was it not her duty to uphold her brother's birthright? "It goes against my heritage to turn traitor to my king."

"Your heart is with Beaumont, not with any royal

court. You must do what will be best for your home."
Gerta rose from the stool, her legs cracking softly with
age. "It is the men who make war, my lady. As they
always have. It is often up to the women to make what
peace they can."

Once Gerta had left, Rosalind settled deeper into
the tub in the quiet of her chamber, missing her family—her mother—with keen longing. She had battled
daily in that first year after the fire to move on with
her life, but she hadn't expected the ache of grieving
to still be so fierce. She missed her mother's gentle
counsel, her quiet way of making Rosalind see things
from her side. What advice would Shannon Beaumont
have if she were here now?

Wiping a wet cloth across her face, Rosalind told
herself the damp trails down her cheeks came from the
bath and not more tears. She'd wept too long and too
often to let herself be overrun by one willful Scotsman
now.

Perhaps she should follow her heart and her new,
confusing feelings for Malcolm McNair. Gregory had
not come to her aid in all this time. Surely news of the
plight of Beaumont Keep had spread to the king's
troops by now. And if Malcolm could bring peace to
her people, she would have all the more reason to align
herself with him.

Vowing to see her conqueror with new eyes on the
morrow, Rosalind decided to consider his proposition.
She would simply remind herself to make her choice
based on what was best for Beaumont rather than what
would best satisfy her newly awakened senses.

Chapter Eight

Two days later, the people of Beaumont attacked the golden wheat fields with scythes and muscle. The tall spikes fell in defeat and were dragged to threshing tables, where nimble fingers separated the chaff from the grain.

The scene in the southern fields might have filled Rosalind with contentment had she not been distracted by thoughts of Malcolm McNair's hypnotic kisses. She had not seen him after their argument in the garden, since he'd been consumed with final repairs to the south tower and other fortifications to the keep. While the rest of her people recovered from the barley harvest and observed the Sabbath, Malcolm and his kin had made a brief appearance at chapel and then continued to make battle preparations as if the English king would be at their gate any day.

In her new endeavor to see the positive side of marriage to Malcolm, Rosalind had to admit she admired his industrious efforts to protect the people of Beaumont. She kept an eye out for him now, curious to test the strength of his appeal and see if he held as much allure for her under the bright light of day. Breathing in the scents of fall and freshly harvested grain, she jumped when a masculine voice called to her from the edge of the field.

"Rosalind."

She swiveled about to answer, but saw only the forest. Thinking she must have been mistaken, she turned back toward the endless rows of golden grain.

"In here, Rosalind. Hurry." The voice sounded closer this time. And—heaven help her—more familiar.

Gregory.

Her heart stuttered to realize who called her. She looked about carefully to be sure no one else noticed. But none of the McNairs guarded the southern fields today. Only Balfour Dugan and Lachlan Gordon watched over this section of land, and their attention seemed to be lingering on the wheat for the moment. Scared but curious, Rosalind ducked into the concealing shelter of the trees.

"My sweet."

Before her eyes found Gregory, his arms slipped around her waist, pulling her to him.

Rosalind's first instinct was to push him away. What was wrong with her? Confused and annoyed with herself, she made a halfhearted attempt at hugging him back.

"It is not safe for you here. You must leave." She extricated herself quickly, wondering if Connor would note her disappearance.

She could scarcely believe Gregory Evandale at last stood before her. He was larger and more muscular now, though still of modest height. A richly appointed hauberk covered his broad shoulders. His hair was darker than the sunny blond she recalled, but it was clean and trimmed, along with a new, short beard.

He looked handsome enough, though he lacked the compelling quality that seemed to turn Rosalind's head whenever Malcolm came near her.

"I will not leave when I only just arrived. Have they harmed you?" His dark brown eyes narrowed as he studied her, his hands lingering at her waist. "John Steward told me the bastards threw you in the dungeon. Did they…harm you?"

"I'm fine." Although she noticed she could scarcely catch her breath. She should be happy to see him. She *was* happy to see him. She simply worried for his safety. If Malcolm saw him… The notion frightened her. Lowering her voice, she glanced over her shoulder to be sure no one had noticed her disappearance. "If you have seen John, you must know the Scots rule Beaumont."

"Now that Longshanks is dead, his son has made it clear the borders are on their own. We will have no aid from that quarter, I am afraid. Come on," Gregory added brusquely, pulling at her hand. "You can ride pillion."

She stood rooted to the spot, confused. Fearful.

"My horse is just over here." He attempted to pull her again, but she did not wish to be led.

"Where would you have us go?" After a year without Gregory by her side, she would not blindly follow him without the courtesy of an explanation.

"I would think you would go anywhere to get away from here." His clipped tones lacked the rolling sound of Malcolm's Highland notes. "But if you must know, I will take you to an English stronghold on the border. We can safely plot against the Scots from there."

Plot against Malcolm?

Two weeks ago she would have leaped at the chance. Yet now that she had kissed Malcolm, she couldn't help a niggling worry for his safety. She realized with sudden clarity she would not want Malcolm McNair to come to harm.

As if sensing her uncertainty, Gregory drew her into his arms. "My beautiful Rosalind. I will take care of you."

Before she could protest, his lips were upon hers. His hands moved swiftly, possessively, over her body. The physical aggression took her by surprise. His sweaty scent assailed her nose and she shoved at his shoulders, not ready for this kind of closeness when she had not seen him for a year.

When another man's kisses had tempted her sorely...

"What?" Releasing her, Gregory gazed at her, his brow furrowing. "You have no warmth to welcome me home?"

Guilt pinched her as her heart softened toward the man who had helped her through so much sorrow. He was the one she *should* want. She'd only considered Malcolm's proposal because she'd feared Gregory had forsaken her. But now that he was here, she owed him the loyalty she had long ago promised.

Much as it might unsettle her after she'd convinced herself to look at Malcolm with a more forgiving eye.

"I'm sorry." Hearing voices in the field behind her, she peered over her shoulder. "I must stay and help with the harvest. Since John is no longer here, I am the only one who can oversee it."

"You would help these bastards?" His lips curled in a sneer. "What has gotten into you?"

"I do not do it to help the Scots." What right did he have to judge her when she had made the best of so much hardship without him? "I do it so the tenants will not starve this winter."

"Let the damn people fend for themselves." He tugged her deeper into the forest, farther away from the fields. Farther away from Malcolm. "They look to their lady to free them from the Scots scourge, not to labor next to them in the fields."

"But would it not be more helpful to you when you retake the keep if I were on the inside? I could find ways to let you in."

"I need you with me." He whistled softly to his horse and then climbed atop his mount. "You must join me now."

She reached frantically for a way to reason with him. She could not name what strange fear possessed her, but she felt in her gut that it was madness to ride off with him without a word to anyone. And she did not want to leave her people.

Still, this might be her only chance to preserve her family's English loyalties. Perhaps if she left with Gregory now she could honor her vow to wed him, without conceding to Scotland's rule. Malcolm would keep her people safe at Beaumont, and according to Gerta, the villeins were content with him. But Rosalind had promised herself to this man long before she'd discovered the pleasures of Malcolm's kisses. She owed Gregory her loyalty for helping her through the darkest time of her life.

As the voices from the field came closer, she made up her mind and chose the only honorable path.

Reaching for Gregory's hand, she pulled herself up behind him just as Gerta and Connor began calling for her.

"Go," she urged, her heart racing with fear.

He needed no further encouragement, and within seconds they were galloping through the forest and over the meadow beyond. Beaumont was quickly out of sight among the hills.

"He will come after us," Rosalind shouted above the din of pounding hooves. "We must find shelter soon."

Gregory laughed. "You overestimate your worth to the Scot. Why should he bother?"

Why indeed? Perhaps Gregory was right. Malcolm might very well welcome Rosalind's escape. The result would be no different than had he banished her. She would be long gone from Beaumont and out of his way.

The thought stung her more than she would have expected. She did Malcolm a favor by leaving. He would be free to use Beaumont however he pleased.

"Do not worry, Rosalind." Gregory turned in the

saddle to offer her a smile. "You have escaped. Within the hour we will be safely ensconced in a secure English stronghold with our allies around us."

Wishing the thought would put her at ease, she clung to Gregory and prayed she'd done the right thing as they rode south away from the keep. Her body protested the rough ride and she checked over her shoulder frequently, still half expecting to see a force of Malcolm's clansmen come to take her back to Beaumont. But the trail behind them remained quiet.

She tried not to think of all she'd left behind. Gerta's friendship. Her extended family of all Beaumont's people.

And above all, she told herself not to think about Malcolm or the fact that she would never again experience the heaven of his kisses.

In Beaumont's northern fields that afternoon, Malcolm considered the scythe was a welcome change from the sword as he hacked his way through another row of golden grain. He enjoyed the simple satisfaction in watching his day's labor pile up before him in a tangible testament to his hard work. The tools of a knight's trade produced a far more grim result.

His muscles protested the unaccustomed swing, but he knew he could grow accustomed to this life. If Robert the Bruce would grant him Beaumont, he would devote his time to such simple pleasures—harvesting the fields, drinking ale with common folk, lying with Rosalind…

Thoughts of her invaded his dreams, robbing him

of sleep. He imagined the scent of roses at odd times throughout the day. Damned if he knew how he could be attracted to such a stubborn lass, but he could not deny the hunger he felt to possess her. He would make her forget her English squire just as soon as he finalized the fortifications on Beaumont.

"My laird!" An urgent shout rang over the gently rolling hills, tinged with the sound of the Highlands.

Tossing aside the scythe, he whistled for his horse, prepared to meet the rider who galloped into view as Malcolm mounted. Young Balfour Dugan? He'd been watching over the southern fields with Lachlan.

"It's the lady of Beaumont." Dugan's face was ruddy with the heat as he shouted. "She is missing and one villein swears she rode off with an English knight."

A knife twisted in Malcolm's gut. Betrayal, surely. But beneath that, fear for Rosalind sliced even deeper.

"Did ye ask if the knight carried a standard?" Knowing the identity of her captor—or worse, her conspirator—would help him find her.

"'Twas a kitchen maid who saw them leave, since she was swiving in the forest with one of the men-at-arms. The maid recognized the knight as Evandale, a former resident of Beaumont." Conner drew in a gasping breath. "But I am sorry to say Evandale must have had help to take Lady Rosalind because yer man-at-arms—Alexander Lawson—was apparently killed by an English sword."

Hellfire. A tide of fury rose up in Malcolm along with fear and the feeling of betrayal. A battle cry rose to his lips as he called his men around him. With terse words he instructed Ian and five men to follow him, leaving Jamie in charge of Beaumont, and taking those men with the best hunting and tracking skills.

He would find Rosalind and haul her back to Beaumont whether she wanted to join him or not. Had she been so appalled at the idea of wedding him that she would forsake her people and her keep to escape him? Or had Evandale used force to persuade her away? Malcolm was surprised to realize how much the answer mattered to him.

Either way, he would track her all across her godforsaken England, if necessary, to retrieve her. He had no great force of men to win her back, but he had his wits, and that had always been enough for a skilled strategist or a Scotsman determined to have the woman of his choosing.

Lucky for Malcolm, he happened to be both.

Rosalind had to admit she'd committed a colossal mistake in judgment when she spied Gregory tromping through an old rose garden outside of Baliwick Keep, where he'd hoped to find a priest who could marry them. She'd waited outside the gates in the long shadows of early evening with his horse and a handful of road-weary men-at-arms who apparently served him. She'd been surprised at the company Gregory was keeping when he introduced her to his rugged band of men a few leagues outside of Beaumont, but she remained silent on the matter because she knew he did not possess the means to attract more polished retainers.

But as she watched him trample one crimson bloom after another on his oblivious path back to her, she could no longer deceive herself that Gregory Evandale was the same man she thought she knew.

"Their priest is sitting vigil over a dying old woman," he called, shaking an uprooted vine off the toe of his boot. "He would not even hear my request."

The crew of dirty retainers grumbled about the disrespect to their leader, while Rosalind mentally gave thanks for the delay in her nuptials. She could not consign herself to marriage with a desperate knight who would haul her away from Beaumont without a care for her people or the friends she'd been forced to leave. *Their* friends. The only person at Beaumont he'd asked her about this afternoon had been the coarse kitchen maid, Moira. His interest struck Rosalind as highly inappropriate, especially since she remembered Gregory's penchant for seeking the maid out when he'd resided at Beaumont.

How strange that a year ago she'd not been able to see him for the kind of man he was, yet now she could almost see right through him. With new maturity to guide her, she was all the more certain they must not wed.

And it did not help that Malcolm McNair kept invading her thoughts as thoroughly as he'd conquered her keep.

"Perhaps we would be better off waiting." Rosalind did not mount to ride, holding her ground as she stood in the tall grasses in front of Baliwick Keep, the scent of impending rain filling the air. "You said you didn't ask King Edward for permission to marry me." Yet another reason her intuition told her she'd been foolish to run off with Gregory. "If we waited a few days, we would have time to send a missive."

That had been their plan long ago. They would send word of her brother's death and then ask permission to wed. A plan that had made perfect sense to her as a grief-stricken fifteen-year-old. But now she could see why Malcolm had scoffed at the notion of Edward allowing her to wed a young knight with no lands of his own and no experience at holding a keep.

Gregory went silent for a long moment before peering around at his men-at-arms. Searching for their approval? Rosalind could only think how Malcolm McNair needed no man's approval.

She had been such a fool to leave Beaumont.

"We will wait for the holy man to finish his vigil." Gregory nodded to his retainers, who seemed to understand his unspoken request, since they rode off toward the keep's gates. Once he was left alone with Rosalind, he stepped closer to pat her shoulder reassuringly. "The king cannot deny us permission once we are already wed. Besides, we have the blessing of your father. Isn't that all that matters?"

Guilt speared her as she remembered her parents mentioning Gregory as a possible match for her. She'd shared as much with him after their deaths, but she'd never told him they'd also discussed several other suitors. She'd been so sure Gregory would be the best man to marry because of their bond forged in the aftermath of the Beaumont blaze.

"I wish my father were here to give us his counsel now." Swallowing back her anxiety, she spoke her mind. "But in his absence, I would have the counsel of my father's overlord. Is it not too much to ask before our wedding day?"

She would find a way to extricate herself from Gregory's expectation of marriage later. Right now, she only craved time to think. Time to consider how she could return to Beaumont.

"There is no need." He stepped closer, smiling down at her with eyes that were not the rich blue of the sea. "My men will hasten the priest."

A vision of those weather-bitten louts dragging the holy man from a dying woman's bedside chilled her inside. Dear God, who had Gregory become?

"I do not wish to have a grieving family disrupted—"

Her words were cut off by Gregory's sudden seizure of her person, his hands clamping about her waist to draw her near. The scent of sweat and horses permeated his garments, assailing her nose once more.

"Mayhap you wish to greet your future lord with a bit more warmth than you managed earlier, Rosalind." He breathed the words over her lips, his gaze already fastened there, seemingly unaware of her discomfort.

Her utter distaste.

She would have cried out, tried to push him away, but his grip was strong. Harsh. His mouth crushed hers, bruising her lips painfully against her teeth. She squirmed, wriggled, knocked on his shoulders, but he remained focused on his task. Rosalind glanced around wildly for help, her gaze landing unexpectedly on a man bearing down on them from the direction of the woods.

A huge warrior with a long, dark cape swirling about immense shoulders rode through the twilight.

Malcolm.

She might have screamed had she been able to. Not that she was afraid for herself, but at that moment she knew Gregory was a dead man without her help.

Before she could think what to do, she was pulled from Gregory's grip by unseen hands, at the same moment Malcolm yanked Gregory clear off his feet.

Relief mingled with fear at the sight. Although Malcolm might save her from Gregory, now her childhood friend would have to face the vengeance of the warmongering Scot. And no matter that she did not love Gregory and had no wish to marry him, she also could not bear to see him killed.

"Please!" She lunged forward, almost breaking free of the man who held her. Ian, she realized.

Malcolm's knife hovered at Gregory's throat while other men appeared from the trees to circle their laird. No number of Gregory's men-at-arms could save him now, not when he had made an enemy of the most fearsome warrior she'd ever seen.

"Ye beg for yer lover's life?" Malcolm did not look pleased at the prospect, his wild eyes and fierce aspect communicating his fury.

"Nay. I beg you to spare a former friend who made a mistake in touching me." Willing Malcolm to understand, to free a man who was little more than a boy compared to the experienced Highland warrior, Rosalind forced herself to remain still. Calm. In control of her fears.

She'd made enough mistakes for one day. The time had come to grow up and take responsibility for herself. For Beaumont. Gregory would never be her savior, but she could save him in exchange for the friendship they'd once shared.

Slowly, Malcolm lowered Gregory to the ground. He stared the younger man in the face, towering over him. "Ye may tell yer king Beaumont is mine, as is the lady Rosalind. I release ye for her, boy, but dinna expect mercy twice in one lifetime, for I promise ye shall nae have it from Malcolm McNair."

Stumbling awkwardly, Gregory scrambled toward his horse, but one of Malcolm's men already held the reins. Looking confused for a moment too long, Gregory hesitated until Ian released a battle cry that must surely have been heard all the way to Edinburgh.

And Gregory ran into the forest as if demons were on his heels, heedless of his men-at-arms still within Baliwick's walls.

Rosalind did not realize she was shaking until Ian released her and she staggered forward.

"Thank God you're here." Rosalind clutched her chest, grateful and scared and overwhelmed by an onslaught of emotions she'd been holding back all day. She moved toward Malcolm as his men kicked their horses into motion, leaving them alone.

"Ye are pleased to see yer heathen laird?" He narrowed icy blue eyes at her as he lashed Gregory's abandoned horse to his. No doubt he was angry with her. Yet mad as Malcolm might be, Rosalind knew she was safer with the Scottish laird than her former fiancé.

She opened her mouth to reply, but he paused in his work to still her lips with rough fingers.

"Nay. I dinna want to hear more lies." He looped a rope about her wrists to bind her hands together. Imprisoning her.

He would never believe she had not left with Gregory of her own volition. And she had. But perhaps later, when he was no longer angry, he would understand that she did not want to wed the Englishman. Would never marry a man who treated her as callously as Gregory.

An irreverent laugh sneaked free as she considered the absurdity of her situation.

"Ye are amused to be bound and hauled back to Beaumont as my prisoner?" He gripped her waist in his strong hands, yet he did not hold her with the brute force Gregory had used.

"Nay." She breathed in the scent of him tinged by Gerta's soap. "I am merely surprised to discover I feel far safer with the man who would tie my wrists together than I ever felt with the man I once wished to wed."

Malcolm's dark brows cinched together in a forbidding scowl. Suspicion lit his blue eyes. "What trick is this, fleet-footed wench? Ye willna fool me twice."

She did not blame him for doubting her. And heaven

help her, she did not even mind riding back to Beaumont with her wrists bound, so long as she could return home. Another man might have run her through for her defection today.

"Thank you for freeing him." And many, many conquering Scots warriors might have gutted Gregory for spiriting her away. Malcolm's mercy had not settled well with him, yet he had granted it when she'd asked. But before she could say more about the kindness he'd shown her, she recalled a more pressing concern. "He rode with others who could yet come after us." She peered over Malcolm's shoulder to look for signs of the crude retainers in the growing darkness. "We cannot outpace them on only one horse."

Fear gripped her belly and gnawed. Had Malcolm truly sent away all his men who might have protected them from Gregory's errant followers?

"Ye are right, lass." He lifted her up on Gregory's mount. "Fortunately, we dinna have only one horse."

There would be no wedding today. She was going home.

As the rope on her mare's reins tugged even harder with Malcolm's increasing speed, however, she realized she was right back where she had started.

A prisoner yet again.

Chapter Nine

Alone with Rosalind, Malcolm turned to observe Beaumont's wayward lady at his leisure for the first time since he'd intercepted her this eve. Forlorn upon the dark Arabian Evandale had left behind, she looked exhausted even in the moonlight half-obscured by clouds. Her shoulders slumped a bit from her usual bearing. And before twilight had turned to full-blown night, he'd seen dark crescents shadowing the delicate skin beneath her gray eyes. Scratches marred both cheeks. A twinge of unwanted sympathy cut through his anger, reminding him she might have been through more hardship than he realized.

"We willna beat this rain, I fear." He called her mount closer so he did not have to shout.

"If you would but give me the reins to my horse, we could be home in no time."

"So ye can hightail yer way back to yer folly-fallen squire? Nay. Ye will have to get wet."

"We are not only in for a dousing. We will scarcely

be able to ride in such a downpour." Rosalind glanced up toward the threatening clouds shifting above them. The night sky rumbled ominously, the air heavy with the scent of rain. Still, she did not bother trying to defend Evandale despite Malcolm's purposeful provocation.

A wise decision.

"We will weather the storm." He would make sure of it.

"Yet you sent all of your men hurrying back to Beaumont. You must not have wanted *them* to catch their deaths out here."

"I dinna want them to suffer for yer sake. Ye, on the other hand, are a prisoner. Yer comfort matters not." Although he could not help thinking she looked too tired to ride. Too exhausted to remain straight in her saddle much longer. She'd been gone naught but six hours, maybe eight. Yet the day had stretched interminably for him. Had it been difficult for her, as well?

He found that hard to believe, since she'd run off of her own volition.

"What of your own comfort? You will have to suffer the consequences yourself."

"I consider it fitting atonement for ever letting ye out of the dungeon." He'd been responsible for keeping her safe. Yet he'd been swayed by the heady warmth of her kisses, the soft press of her curves. Hell's fury, but he could not believe he'd been taken in by a scheming lass.

A loud crack of thunder shook the very earth. The horses reared and whinnied in fright.

Wasting no more time, Malcolm urged his mount

next to Rosalind's and lifted her from the saddle. He'd barely settled her across his lap when the skies opened up. Rain soaked them with the force of a waterfall.

He rode hard for a hunting lodge he'd happened upon while tracking Rosalind to Baliwick. He'd made note of the shelter in case he had need of it, and now, after seeing her weary condition, knew he would not risk bringing her all the way back to Beaumont. Even Ian, for all his tracking abilities, would find it a challenge to find the way home in the deluge.

Although it was less than a half league distant, Malcolm still struggled to find it in the sudden blinding downpour. After circling the general area twice, he spotted the rough-hewn timber walls of the wooden lodging.

Rosalind studied the grim lines of Malcolm's mouth as they galloped through the rain. Although she recognized his anger with her, she couldn't help but feel safe and protected in the warmth of his arms.

He set her on the doorstep of the one-story lodge atop a small rise and went to secure the horses, leaving Rosalind to open the door with her hands still tied. It took her three tries to twist the knob before she succeeded. The cottage appeared abandoned. Its low rock walls giving way to wood at about hip height. Perhaps the structure had been a motte and bailey keep at one time, its foundations transformed for a nobleman's pleasure with a low, thatched roof that—thankfully— did not leak. Dust shrouded the sparse furnishings. But the room was dry, and for that she was thankful.

She still reeled from Gregory's brutal kiss and brazen assault of her person. He had kissed her chastely a time or two before he'd joined the king's forces, but never had his touch frightened her. Now it seemed the old insensitivity that she'd blamed on his youth had escalated into outright selfishness. Aggression. Had he ever cared for her? Or had he only wanted Beaumont all along?

Her nerves thin and her daring squelched in the echoing emptiness of the darkened cabin, she desired nothing so much as to be home in her chamber, to sleep and to gather her strength.

With a sudden whoosh of cold wind and rain, the door opened and Malcolm stepped inside, his hauberk clinging to his skin as water poured off him to pool at his feet. Slick and wet, his dark hair clung to his head. His features stood out in sharp relief, the bold angle of his jaw mirrored by the downward slash of his brows. Unease slid over her at the sight of him and the sudden awareness of their absolute solitude. Together. Alone.

His arms full of wood, he stepped forward and deposited the timber by the single grate in the one-room shelter. There were a few dry logs already in place on the hearth to start a blaze, and once a flame burned brightly, he threw a wet log onto the pile. It smoked briefly, but the chimney drew well and soon the fire crackled.

His task complete, he appraised Rosalind with a cool blue gaze, then strode closer to untie her bound arms. "Ye will catch yer death in that garb." Tossing the rope to the floor, he retrieved a sack that had been among his saddlebags. "Gerta packed ye a gown with amazing speed for an old woman. I think yer busybody nurse must have known of yer disappearance before me."

Rosalind shook her head, denying his accusation as she ignored the hostility in his eyes.

The warmongering Scot had been resurrected, but this time, she would not be intimidated by him. "Where should I...?"

He jerked a thumb toward what was probably the sleeping area, since a low wall divided the room. It would not afford her much privacy, but she knew arguing would hardly help her cause. She longed to tell him of her revelations about Gregory today, along with her new certainty that she could never wed her childhood friend, but she did not expect Malcolm would believe her until he'd calmed down.

Plucking up the bag he'd indicated, she trusted her instincts, which assured her he was too angry to look in her direction, anyhow.

She shivered on the way to the sleeping area, bag in hand. It held one clean surcoat and a kirtle. Longing for a linen to dry with, she peeled off the wet clothes as she crouched behind the partition, donning the dry ones at once. She peeked over her shoulder often, but Malcolm paid her no heed as he unpacked ale and cheese from their linen wrappings.

"I am starving," she ventured, determined to get through the evening with as much grace as possible. If only the rain would cease, they could depart for Beaumont and she could still sleep for a few hours in her own bed before dawn.

Malcolm stared hard at her new garments and frowned forbiddingly. He'd removed his own hauberk, revealing a tunic that appeared only slightly damp.

"What?"

"Yer hair will soak yer gown. Why did ye nae dry it?" He snatched the sack from her hands and dug through its scant contents until he found a comb. "Sit." He motioned to a small fur he had laid before the fire.

The intimate setting of the hunting lodge in the middle of nowhere was already playing havoc with her senses. Rosalind didn't want to risk even more proximity, inherent in what he suggested. "It is fine, really. I—"

"Sit."

Had he raised his voice, she would have stubbornly stood her ground. But he spoke softly. Nay, almost kindly. And that she could not resist.

Willing her legs to carry her closer to him, she swallowed back her nervous awareness of his strength. Of his allure, more potent than ever. She recalled all too clearly the way she'd nearly forsworn her family loyalties the last time she got too close to Malcolm Mc-Nair. What might she agree to now that she no longer felt any allegiance to Gregory?

Even her duty to the English had been called into question since Malcolm had shown Beaumont mercy. Protection. She'd vowed to look upon him with new eyes the night before, but she'd never expected her perspective to be so thoroughly altered in the course of one day. Gregory's arrival had made her question her own judgment, but it had also assured her that Malcolm was a man of infinitely stronger character.

Seating herself on the fur, she reached to unfasten her dripping tresses from the intricately twined braids and pearls woven about her head.

"Nay." He halted her hand in midair, gripping it in his own. "Ye didna get it right the first time." His touch was not gentle, but neither was it painful as he replaced her hand in her lap.

"You will only succeed in knotting it." Shivers broke over her skin at his nearness. Nay, from the rain and cold. She could not allow herself to be so affected by his mere presence now that she recognized her marked lack of reason when it came to men. "It is more difficult to unwind than it looks."

"I have solved more challenging problems than taking down a lass's hair, ye can be sure." He grumbled as he worked, now and then muttering in his thick Scots tones about hasty-witted women and idle-headed maidens.

Still, some of the anger seemed to have faded from his diatribe now that they'd left Gregory far behind for the remote haven of the hunting lodge. Surprisingly, Malcolm's hands were adept at seeking out pins and uncoiling the wet locks. As he freed each section, he dried it on a coarse length of linen he must have had among his own belongings. Soon all of her hair was undone, covering her arms and a portion of his muscular thigh as they sat before the cedar-scented fire.

The sight of those pale waves curling along the dark wool of his braies sent a warm swirl of pleasure through her. She should not want this closeness with Malcolm, should not crave the heated touches he'd used before to enflame her senses. But all the warnings in the world seemed inadequate when she was faced with the temptation of the McNair laird.

What was it this man that called to her despite her long resentment of his people, despite his blatant disruption of her domain, her rule, her whole life? He'd turned her world on its ear in the last month, making her question old notions and forcing her to see her situation from a new perspective.

And yet there was more to it than that. The breathlessness she experienced around him had naught to do with anything besides pure feminine attraction to a virile, powerful male. Everything within her seemed to respond to him, from her heartbeat jumping erratically to her inability to catch her breath.

When he reached for the comb, she forced herself to protest. "You needn't—"

"Sit still." His former growl subsided to a gentle admonishment as he eased the comb through the strands.

She started when his hands slid under the hair at her neck.

"Are ye cold?"

Her pulse quickened as his breath whispered over her ear. His body loomed incredibly close to hers on the thick pelt of fur, certainly much closer than when he'd begun. But as much as she wished to simply lie back into the warm strength of his arms, she feared making another mistake.

She understood that Malcolm was a better man than

Gregory. More noble. Kindhearted. And yet if she had so thoroughly misconstrued Gregory's character, how could she be certain she did not misinterpret Malcolm's actions now?

"I'm not cold." Straightening, she swept her hair over one shoulder, away from its warm resting place along his thigh. "Just a bit hungry, perhaps." She hoped this announcement would bring an end to his ministrations before she could add even more mistakes to her list of blunders today.

Bad enough that she'd left Beaumont with an errant knight. No sense falling into the arms of her Scots captor, no matter how enticing.

"There is ale and cheese that Ian managed to snatch on short notice." Remaining half-sprawled on the fur, Malcolm nodded toward the flagon he'd left sitting on a bench.

"Here?" Sharing libations with him upon their decadent seat before the hearth seemed unwise when her fingers already itched to touch him, her arms ached to wrap around him. More than anything, she wished to forget the brutal force of Gregory's touch.

"There isna anywhere else." He gestured toward the nearly empty room. "Unless ye wish to take yer meal seated upon the bed."

The narrow pallet stripped free of any linens caught her eye. "Certainly not."

She rose to fetch the flagon and cheese, her ears straining to hear any slowing of the rain pounding the roof. Wishful thinking since, if anything, the storm dumped water more heavily now than when they'd first arrived. A fact that did not bode well for her sleeping in her own chamber this night.

Swiping her tongue along lips gone dry at the thought, Rosalind stumbled over her own feet as she made her way back to the fireside. Quickly righting herself, she eased down to the fur again, careful to put the food between them.

"Have ye nae eaten?"

"No." She drank straight from the flagon, since there were no cups to be found. "I did not plan to leave the keep today, and had made no preparation."

She could not tell if he believed her, his expression inscrutable as he cut a bit of cheese with his knife.

"From the trees, it sounded as if Evandale was most eager to exchange vows." Malcolm did not say how much he had overheard, but his words gave Rosalind hope that he'd at least seen enough to know she had not welcomed Gregory's kiss.

"Aye." Regret stole through her, more for her own foolishness than for a betrayal a wiser woman would have seen coming. "Even at the expense of dragging a holy man from a dying woman's bedside."

"Yer friend's haste speaks well of yer charm." Tugging the ale from her grasp, he took a long swallow before his blue gaze glittered back at her in the firelight. "He risked much to have ye."

"His risk was no more imprudent than my own." She longed to make amends somehow for the trouble she'd caused Malcolm, but the words to make him understand she at last recognized her mistakes eluded her. "I never should have left Beaumont."

"Ye think to avoid the dungeon with pretty speeches and fluttering long lashes?" Lying back on an elbow, he studied her from the lazy sprawl of his masculine frame. "I'll spare ye the trouble and assure ye I dinna care to hear it."

The cold wall of his anger seemed as resolute as ever, and yet Rosalind could feel heat pulsing from him even more strongly than it flowed from the blaze in the grate. What madness was this to feel such warmth—nay, such fire—for her Scots captor when he made a point of showering her with his disapproval?

Fie on him.

Curses take him.

Or perhaps his kisses could simply take them *both*. Steal their breath. Abscond with her good intentions. Leave her reclining breathlessly in the heathen's arms for a few stolen moments.

Reaching for the ale, she hoped to find her wits with the help of the brew. Perhaps the strong drink would chase away her wicked thoughts and resurrect cool reason.

She closed her eyes for a long moment, concentrating on the sound of raindrops on the roof instead of the slow rhythm of Malcolm's breath beside her on the fur.

"Mayhap the rain will stop soon so that we may be on our way." She congratulated herself for redirecting her thoughts.

"We will not proceed to Beaumont until tomorrow."

Her eyes flew open at the pronouncement.

"It will surely cease in a few hours." It had to, because she could not spend the night alone here with a man who tempted her sorely.

"Even if it does, it will be dark and wet. We willna leave until morning, at the earliest."

"We cannot stay here." Her cheeks heated at their awkward situation. "What would the people of Beaumont say?"

"Ye didna give much thought to what they would say when you ran away from them to join yerself to another man. Ye were nae too concerned with what anyone thought then."

"There was hardly any joining involved." Embarrassment blazed through her, but she would make sure he understood.

"Nay? Dinna forget I watched him devour yer mouth like a starving man his last meal. Ye appeared well joined at the time." Although he kept his voice light, she did not miss the raw anger—perhaps a bit of jealousy?—threaded through his words.

"I did nothing to invite such an unwanted…" she paused, scarcely able to find words to describe Gregory's behavior "…invasion."

"Perhaps he took yer willing assent to run off with him as invitation enough." Reaching for the flagon, Malcolm removed it from her fingers and set it aside on the hearth before his hand settled along her jaw, grazing her cheek. "Ye would consider taking a bloodthirsty parasite to yer bed because he is English, but ye would nae listen to an honorable proposal from me because I am a Scot."

Her gaze locked with his as his palm held her still with little more than the promise of touches to come. He skimmed gentle fingers into the soft warmth of her hair, now dried by the fire. Pleasing chills tripped along her skin in anticipation.

After the onslaught of every conceivable emotion today, she did not trust herself to make a rational decision where he was concerned. Especially not when he wielded the compelling weapon of her own desire as deftly as he brandished a sword. Her whole body quivered, ready to ignite if his hands remained upon her.

"I cannot consider anything now when I am…" Overwrought. Undone. *Dangerously hungry for you.* "I think you'd better release me."

"I dinna think so, Rosalind." He brushed his hand down her neck to the vulnerable curve of her throat. Lingering but a moment, he skimmed lightly over her collarbone to nudge her linen kirtle to the very edge of her shoulder, where it teetered precariously on her hot skin. "Something tells me ye'll be swearing yer loyalty to me long before sunrise."

Chapter Ten

Had there ever been a man so bold as the one reclining beside her?

Spellbound by his gaze and the rhythmic drum of rain against the lodge walls, Rosalind stared up at Malcolm for long moments, gauging his words carefully. She'd learned that he was a man of infinite strategy, a tactician far more skilled than she in wresting what he wanted from life. Answering him now required caution.

"Swear loyalty to the man who makes me his prisoner?" She had not forgotten her bound hands on their ride from Baliwick tonight. She'd understood his reasoning, but in light of his distrust, she could not imagine him ever granting her any real authority at Beaumont again. "Remember, it is no true oath if I do not give it of my own free will."

She could not fathom how he could wrest such a pledge from her.

But then his finger pushed the neckline of her kirtle off the curve of her shoulder, exposing her warm skin to his gaze. In a flash, she recalled the most forceful weapon in his arsenal.

"Who says ye will not give it of yer own free will?" A slow smile spread across his lips, the first she'd seen since he'd saved her from Gregory's marauding hands.

She could have protested, but her thoughts skittered to a standstill as he molded his hands to her hips and pulled her to him. Her body pressed against his and a thrill shot through her when his breath warmed her cheek and rasped in her ear. She did not want to meet his gaze, though she could feel it boring into her with the intensity of a peregrine eyeing its prey. Pride forced her to look at him.

"Have ye ever considered that maybe allegiance to me willna be as loathsome as ye think?"

"I do not expect it would be loathsome." Because— heaven help her—she was definitely seeing Malcolm with new eyes tonight. She also happened to be feeling him more intimately than she should, and she could never call his touch anything but pleasurable. "But I am not sure I could ever swear loyalty to a Scot."

His hands fell away from her too quickly. "Because of Evandale? Are ye so blind ye canna see the man for what he is?"

"What do you know of Gregory?"

"Evidently more than ye do, lady, if ye would rather bind yerself to him than me. He has earned a reputation as a knight gone awry, since it is said he canna keep his killing to the battlefield any longer, but seeks out other chances to spill a man's blood."

"You are mistaken," she protested, yet feared he was not.

"Nay." Malcolm caught a lock of her hair and rubbed it absently between his fingers. "I knew of his reputation before I came to Beaumont. But even if I didna, it would have been proved to me this afternoon when he allowed one of the knaves who follow him to slit the throat of one of my men."

Cold revulsion filled her belly.

"Who?" She realized in that moment she would genuinely grieve if Ian or Jamie or old Lachlan Gordon were dead.

"Alexander, who has a fair wife back home. It pains me to lose him, and even more so because…" Malcolm lay back on the fur to stare up at the ceiling, muttering a cold curse. "'Tis no way for a good man to die."

"It is my fault." She should have listened to her instincts, which had told her something was amiss with Gregory the moment he'd kissed her in the forest at the edge of the wheat field. She'd ignored her instincts, blindly following old loyalties that were apparently sorely misplaced. "That young man might still be alive if I had not left today."

"We agree in this at least." Malcolm reached for her hand and traced a slow pattern over it, as if offering her a way to find peace. Healing. "Yer place is at Beaumont, where ye can be safe. Ye shouldna have left in the first place, but what is important to me is that I gain yer word ye willna try to leave again."

"How can I promise so much when I do not know what the future holds?" Gazing into the hearth flames, she longed for the clear vision of her youth, the convictions that had seemed so unshakable. Now she did not know who to trust. "While I swear I would never leave willingly with Gregory again, how can I vow to stay at Beaumont if your king decides to turn me out? And for your part, you will have other wars to win, other keeps to capture. What will it matter to you if I stay at Beaumont when you are long gone and I am under the rule of whatever Scots lord your king invites into my household?"

Malcolm allowed her words to drift over him, wishing he could settle her fears as easily as he could conduct field maneuvers. He half feared what action his king would take in regard to Beaumont himself. Indeed, his concerns only increased the more he became attached to Rosalind. He could find another keep to possess if Robert the Bruce did not wish to grant him Beaumont, but what would happen to Rosalind in his absence?

The thought of leaving the headstrong lass to her own devices scared him far more than any enemy blade. Her youth and passion made her a force to be reckoned with, but hellfire, she did not have the life experience to teach her caution. Or patience.

"Ye say ye would not leave with this milk-livered lout Evandale again." Devil curse him. "Did he hurt ye?"

If the knave had harmed her, Malcolm would personally kill him when Rosalind's gentle gaze was no longer watching.

"Nay." Her gray eyes clouded. "He did not beat me, but I saw a different side of him that grieved me tremendously."

"I'm sorry." He knew the words were hopelessly inadequate for whatever had transpired between them. Malcolm had never considered himself a man of any great human insight, but he'd come to know Rosalind well enough that he could see the anguish in her gaze. "He isna a good man."

And while Malcolm wished he could tell himself *he* was different from Evandale because he could let go of Rosalind long enough to let her make up her own mind about what she wanted, he feared he would not get through this night without touching her again.

The light scratches on her cheeks called to his fingers as if requiring his aid to soothe their sting. Reaching toward her, he hesitated, halted. Knew he had no choice but to skim a thumb across the angry red slashes.

"How did ye get these?" Tension thrummed through him, the desire to rage at the man who'd subjected her to harm.

"We rode away from Beaumont in a hurry through the woods." She closed her eyes as Malcolm's fingers strayed from her cheek into the soft silk of her hair. "I fear we tangled with a few tree branches."

"He is a careless idiot." Drawing himself up to sit beside her, he tugged her near.

She came to him easily, but he did not attempt to kiss her. He merely provided comfort. Or so he told himself. He could not confess to any comfort of his own, since the rose scent of her hair and the gentle sigh that drifted from her lips drove him to think of all the other ways he'd rather be holding her. Touching her. Making her his own.

To kiss the lady of Beaumont again would be madness now that they did not have the protection of her people surrounding them, a constant reminder they were not wed. The privacy of the abandoned lodge provided too much insulation from the rest of the world. As if whatever happened between them tonight could be kept secret. Silent.

His hands stroked the length of her hair over and over again. He hoped in vain that he could concentrate on the silken feel of the fair locks against his hand rather than the delicate curve of her spine or the arch of her neck beneath the tresses. If he held her long enough, she might fall asleep against him, and then he could extricate himself from the lush temptation of all that femininity curved alongside him.

Finally, her eyes closed as the fire burned slowly to embers. She shifted deeper into him, her surcoat sliding wantonly over her legs, exposing pale, supple skin. Ach, but what he would give to curve his hand around her slender calf, drag his palm up her thigh and cup the swell of her hip.

His whole body tensed painfully at the thought, his gaze fastened inextricably to that bare skin. And although he cursed himself mightily for his inability to release her, he thought his stillness a damn sight better than kissing her soft mouth the way he wanted to or plunging his hands deep beneath her skirts to explore her womanly warmth. Or plunge himself inside her, claiming her as his own for now and always....

When her knee grazed his, he knew he could no longer trust himself. The desire for her surged through him until his teeth ground painfully together. A man could bear only so much temptation. Easing away from her stiffly, he thought perhaps a few hours standing in the pouring rain outside might cool the fire within.

Nay, a few days, perhaps.

"What?" She sat bolt upright, blinking groggily.

"'Tis time to sleep, lass."

"I am cold." Wrapping her arms about herself, she unwittingly drew his gaze to the generous fullness of her breasts.

Devil's teeth. He'd trade his sword arm to feel cold for a few moments.

"'Tis because I left yer side." He padded over to the door long enough to crank open the wooden barrier and feel the night wind and rain on his face. She would surely rather be cold than have him overheating beside her, of that he was damn certain.

Although he'd sooner trade places with a peasant than speak of his discomfort to her.

Ignoring her grumbled complaints of the chill, Malcolm finally closed the door and retrieved the ale.

"Drink," he commanded, passing the flagon to her. "'Twill help you rest."

Dutifully, Rosalind drank the libation he offered.

"Ye feel better?"

"Much." Rosalind settled the flagon back on the

floor. "But I think we need a better fire to see us through the night if you still do not think we may leave."

More heat?

Ach, but he was ten kinds of an idiot to have brought her here with him tonight. She'd been through enough of an ordeal that she did not need his advances.

He moved toward the hearth to stir the embers, hoping she would go back to sleep and leave him to suffer in peace. But as she sighed contentedly behind him, her delicate limbs stirring as she repositioned herself on the fur, Malcolm knew the dawn could not arrive soon enough.

This promised to be the longest night of his life.

Easing back into the warmth of the fur, Rosalind watched Malcolm lean over the grate, a huge shadow in the dark. Gradually, as the fire leaped beneath his ministrations, she could discern his features.

The severe whiteness of his tunic shimmered in the half-light. The play of shadows on his arms only enhanced the deep furrows carved by muscles as he moved logs in the hearth. Inky black hair strayed from its queue to fall against his back.

His profile was stark and strong, the cheekbones high and sharply cut, the jaw squared and rigid. She remembered more than saw the fullness of his lips. The generous shape of his mouth softened the more severe lines of his face.

Being awakened from her slumber with a man sharing her chamber had toyed with her overwrought senses. Her blood flowed thickly through her veins as she watched him, as if she had been robbed of her daylight defenses in this isolated shelter, leaving her armed with naught but feminine curiosity where Malcolm was concerned.

She had not forgotten the sweet fire his kiss aroused in her, a blaze more dangerous than any his hands might call forth from the grate. She closed her eyes against the wayward thoughts and hoped she could find her way back to sleep to escape the wicked slant of her imaginings. But her body conspired against her, granting her keen awareness as he finished his task and moved about the cabin. His footsteps echoed, magnifying the yawning emptiness within her.

Forcing her eyes open, she peered about to see him testing the construction of the pallet far from the fire.

"It is surely rodent infested." She could not allow him to sleep on such a bed while she reclined in luxurious warmth. "I promise I will not disturb your rest should you wish to share a bit of the fur."

Perhaps she could remain awake while he slept, and somehow convince herself they had not slept together.

He grew still for an unnaturally long time.

"Don't tell me I've offended you somehow?" She could not envision Malcolm caring much for the overly pretty laws of chivalry that would demand they not rest too near one another.

Finally he stalked forward, his expression only coming into view once he'd gotten very near.

"Nay." His words were clipped and harsh. "But I

dinna know if I can lie so close to ye and not commit some offense of my own."

Tension poured from him, so thick she would have to be quite insensible not to feel it. Confused, she could not imagine this man who had treated her so nobly ever proving anything but honorable.

"I insist." She would not displace him to the cold, mice-infested pallet. Reaching for his hand, she thought to draw him down beside her to rest as comfortably as they had earlier.

Only when his hand gripped hers with surprising strength did she understand the tension emanating from him. Heat flowed from his grasp to every pore of her skin, washing through her like a fiery wave.

His utter stillness allowed her to choose what to do with all that heat. Aye, his grip held her hand, but she knew he would let go immediately if she protested.

If she could scavenge up the will to object.

Instead of pushing him away, she wound up drawing him nearer, unable to resist the heated promise in his eyes. And then he was beside her, dropping to the floor to pull her against him, wrapping her in the strength of his arms.

His hand landed lightly on her cheek. He stroked it for a moment, as if testing its softness. His touch was gentle; her reaction was anything but. The mere brush of his fingertips roused a longing she could not name. His lips settled on hers as she opened her mouth to ask about it.

Heat coursed through her like liquid fire. In some recesses of her rational mind she knew it might be wrong to stay this close to him, but could no longer find it within herself to care about propriety. She'd had little enough comfort the last three years of her life. If she found some small measure of it when he held her, so be it. Tonight she would take what peace Malcolm could offer her.

Arching her neck to get closer, she angled her mouth beneath his to better accommodate the questing slide of his lips. His tongue dipped possessively into her mouth and she sighed her pleasure. The thrill she had struggled to forget reverberated through her. She had tried to convince herself that her reaction to Malcolm's kisses was some accident of her memory. Now she realized the futility of her denial.

His mouth upon hers was sheer bliss.

Lost in the heady swell of sensations, she tasted the ale lingering on his tongue, grazed her teeth along his lower lip. She scarcely noticed that he leaned her back slowly, until she reclined fully upon the fur. Only when he stretched out beside her did the impact of their intimate position occur to her.

"Malcolm?"

"Aye?" His hand ran down her shoulder and eased over her hip, leaving her skin tingling beneath her surcoat.

"We must take care." She could not think when he touched her thus, his hands now slipping beneath her outer garment to the sheer kirtle, so fine it hardly counted as a barrier. Soft tremors shook her, made her unable to catch her breath.

"I will take such care of ye as ye never knew." His eyes, glittering with heat, scanned the bodice of her kirtle. With one hand, he covered the expanse of white skin from throat to neckline. Her heart slammed beneath his fingers, craving still more of his touch.

Her body yielded to his every caress as she pressed against him more fully.

"Such promises," she whispered, winding her arms about his neck to draw his mouth back to hers. Kissing, she decided, bordered on the divine.

But his lips found distraction along the way, nuzzling her exposed neck. He ran his tongue over the jumping blue vein that throbbed in time with her heart.

She gasped as he pulled at the lacings of her kirtle and continued his kisses below the garment's neckline. The warm stroke of his tongue had her wriggling beneath him, her hips edging closer to his, her thigh brushing his leg and the hard male length of him. She would have rocked closer, but he kept himself at a safe distance, fastening his mouth around the taut tip of her breast.

Fire radiated to every nerve in her body. The exquisite sweetness inspired a melting ache deep in her belly. She shifted beneath him in a silent, hungry plea.

He had promised to take care of her, and she believed he would, whatever that promise entailed. Right now, she could not find it in herself to care what might happen tomorrow, so long as tonight she did not have to give up the delicious feel of Malcolm against her. She wanted to lose herself in this, in him. Burn away the old fears she'd nursed alone for so long.

Malcolm growled, low and fierce. His hand roamed over her shoulder to slide beneath the kirtle and expose her other breast. He squeezed the mound gently, eliciting a cry of wanton delight.

Sliding her kirtle over long, lean curves, he followed the path of the garment with his mouth. He kissed the hollow between her breasts, his tongue exploring the valley of her belly, pausing to discover the tiny depression of her navel.

The sultry warmth of his lips and the stiff scratch of whiskers on his chin thrilled her in their contrast. This pleasure must surely be forbidden, for all its lush sweetness. Nothing this decadent could be hers for the taking.

"Rosalind." He sighed her name between kisses. "Ye must be still."

"I cannot. It feels so exquisite, Malcolm, I—" Her words ended in a gasp of astonishment as he raised her hips in his hands and greeted the juncture between her thighs with a flick of his tongue.

Ooh.

The torment grew unspeakably wonderful. She would surely perish in her pleasure. He held her tightly to him, ignoring her soft cries of distress and—heaven help her—ecstasy. He teased her womanhood, drawing upon her until she teetered on the point of blissful agony. Even as she feared the overwhelming sensations that grew within her, she could scarcely wait for their culmination. She burned with sudden fierceness, crying his name in weak abandon as the crest of passion's wave shattered her.

Her muscles clenched within, tightening in lush contractions she could not control. Sultry heat flushed her skin until her limbs grew weak from the tide of sensations. Body still pulsing its satisfaction, she was startled when Malcolm lowered her to the warm softness of their shared pelt and pushed her thighs apart with his knees.

The dark look in his eye did strange things to her insides. Robbed of speech, she could only gaze in wonder at him, male and magnificent above her as he discarded his tunic and untied his braies. Even after the incredible fulfillment he'd given her, she longed to be wrapped in his muscular arms, to explore the light rasp of hair on his chest with her fingertips. She could not be close enough to him.

Thick fingers stroked the inner side of her thighs as he lowered himself over her, covering her body with his own. She reached tentatively to touch his cheek, the bristle of his whiskers prickling her fingers. Slipping her hand into his hair, which was now undone, she found it to be nigh as long as a Viking's, though dark as a moonless night.

Their eyes met in the flickering light of the fire, and Rosalind felt her heart turn over. Though inscrutable, his eyes hinted at the depths of the man. The capacity for passion, for honor. She wished, not for the first time, that he were an English knight. What might her life have been like if Malcolm had been the man she'd promised herself to three years ago?

He would not have forsaken her. Would never have left her alone for a year to make a name for himself. And the heat of her marriage bed would have surely kept her warm—nay, burning—on many a drafty night.

"I have no choice but to claim ye for my own, lass."

His hands smoothed over her belly, cupping her hips and, at last, lifting her closer to the rigid length of his shaft.

His words echoed her thoughts somehow. For tonight, for this once, she wanted nothing more than to be claimed by Malcolm McNair. If his king banished her tomorrow or next week or next month, she would rather have the memory of this one night to nourish her soul. And if she ended up in some brutal man's bed, wed to a harsh lout like Gregory, she would need every tender remembrance, every stored impression of Malcolm's touches, to carry with her.

"Maybe I have no choice but to claim you, as well, my laird." She drew out the word in the fashion of his Scottish speech, savoring the way the words lingered on her lips. Perhaps his lilting accent accounted for the talents of a tongue well versed in slow deliberation.

His arms flexed as he held himself above her, his skin bronzed by the firelight. She arched higher, needing the final completion he yet withheld. Any maidenly fears she might have experienced had melted away in the conflagration of the sweet fulfillment he'd already brought her.

Holding her hips steady, he aligned their bodies and slid himself inside her. Slowly. Achingly. The hard press of him against her most delicate flesh stole her breath. Made her see tiny points of light behind her closed eyes. All of her opened to him, her whole body unraveling for his. She reached to guide him closer, to urge his flank nearer. Her fingers grazed the scarred flesh on his side where she had stabbed him. Wounded him.

She regretted that rash act now as she settled her palm over the taut skin.

"I wouldna hurt ye." He held himself utterly still, unmoving, until sweat beaded across his brow.

A soft swell of emotion burned inside her, mingling with so many other feelings for her Highland warrior. She quelled those softer sentiments, wishing only to lose herself in the heat of him. Lifting herself up to him, she nipped his ear, flicking her tongue along the ridge of his jaw.

"I think it will hurt far more if you don't offer what I seek, heathen."

He drove fully into her then, breaching her maidenhead and possessing her completely. She cried out with more pleasure than pain, the sting fading already into a flow of desire. Her whole body sang with the feel of being beneath him, at his mercy. At the same time, his ragged breath told her this huge, hulking Scot was just as much at her mercy. The knowledge overwhelmed her, providing her with a secret thrill as heady as any carnal delight he might bestow.

Winding her fingers possessively through his hair, she held him closer, dizzy with the thought of having him inside her. She arched up to take all of him, wanting more. His skin burned against hers, as if the same dark flames consumed him from within as now took hold of her.

But then he rotated his hips, taking her higher. Higher still. Thought became impossible as he withdrew and then entered her again and again, finding a rhythm that pleased her so much she clung to him, crying out for that nameless fulfillment he'd brought her to before.

His shout mingled with her cry at last, his body going rigid as he pulsed his seed deep within her. Bathing her womb. The realization startled her, but she was too breathless and spent to consider what that joining meant. She only knew she could not have denied this chance to know Malcolm's kisses tonight had her life depended upon it.

And come what may in the harsh light of morning, she could not regret one moment spent in his strong arms.

Chapter Eleven

Malcolm pulled Rosalind closer to him in sleep, covering her bare limbs with his tunic and much of the rest of her with himself. She'd fallen asleep beside him too soon after their coupling to discuss what needed saying between them, but he'd known she was exhausted from the moment he'd found her in Evandale's arms.

Never again would the worthless knave get his hands on her. Not when Malcolm planned to wed her with all due haste. He wanted his king's blessing to ensure Rosalind could remain mistress of Beaumont, but if the Bruce did not swiftly give him the permission he sought, Malcolm would celebrate their nuptials anyhow. He would protect any issue from their union with the McNair name.

Vowing as much while he watched over her in sleep, he found it less simple to discuss the matter with her in the morning. At sunrise she slipped from their makeshift bed in the few moments he was gone from the cabin, dressing quickly as if to arm herself anew for battle with him. Having learned the value of patience, he decided to wait her out on the matter. Perhaps he would learn more of her thoughts if he let her broach the topic. But as they rode back to Beaumont in silence, he began to wonder how long he would have to wait.

The borderlands were soaked with newly fallen rain and the day already grew warm, causing a thick white mist to rise from the ground and surround them in an eerie, damp cloud.

And still she did not speak.

"Ye're confounding me with yer infernal quiet." To Hades with strategy and patience. What transpired between them had been too important to languish unacknowledged, unaddressed. "What happened to the lass who made bold with my person well into the night?"

"I am attempting to learn prudence." Her cheeks flushed lightly as she stared fixedly at the road ahead. "I would think you of all people would applaud my new commitment to greater caution."

"When it comes to running off with whey-faced varlets, aye." What was all this talk of prudence when at last they'd found passion instead? A damn poor time to consider caution. "But where I am concerned, I think I prefer the more reckless lass."

"I made a grave error in judgment when I trusted Gregory to honor me above all others." She guided her horse around a wide puddle in a low-lying trench. "I must ask myself how I have grown any more shrewd in the last year, or if I can trust my opinions now, when I was so thoroughly fooled in the past."

"Ye've aged. Grown. Matured." The answer seemed obvious to him. "I expect defending yer own keep and taking care of yer people by yerself have given ye a new wisdom a lass can trust."

She could trust *him,* damn it.

She shook her head, her forehead furrowed with worry. "But when you stormed the gates a mere month ago, you pointed out several flaws in my reasoning with how I defended the keep. How wise can I be when I have risked so much to the detriment of so many?" Turning toward him with genuine anguish in her eyes, she shook her head slowly. "Nay. I have not grown wiser. Just yesterday I ran off with Gregory. Then I sought something I shouldn't have with you. That is…"

Giving up the cause, she simply shrugged.

Foreboding descended over him, as thick as the white fog that covered the landscape. Hell, he could see through the mist better than he could see his way to converse reasonably with Rosalind.

"Ye canna make such broad comparisons, lass. How can ye be expected to know aught about defending a keep?"

"Why? Because I am a woman?" She straightened in her saddle, looking offended when she had no right to be. "I've run Beaumont, with very little help from a man who found more cause to flirt with kitchen maids than to draw up plans for defense. If I could not preserve the keep, I had no business attempting to hold it in the first place, did I?"

"Ach." Reaching for her reins, he tugged her horse to a stop beside his. They could not move ahead until she understood him. "Ye must nae condemn yerself for mistakes. Everyone muddles things. 'Tis unavoidable."

"Is that so? And what mistakes have you made, Malcolm McNair?" She met his gaze evenly, sitting still in the saddle while the Arabian stomped restlessly beneath her.

"I, too, have trusted unwisely." Not that he planned to trot out all his missteps for her entertainment. "But I dinna allow that to keep me from taking new risks. Seeking new challenges."

"I fear you say as much only to soothe me, my lord. May I inquire who has betrayed you?" Her query was softly spoken. Gentle even. Did she think to pity him for his long-ago foolishness?

"'Tis hardly of any importance now." He reached for her cheek, sliding the back of his knuckles over the soft skin there, where her scratches from the day before were still raw. "What is important is that ye understand we will wed as soon as possible."

"What?" Her cheeks lost their color.

"Did ye think I would forget my vow to take care of ye?" She would see he was not the same sort of man as her father's worthless squire. "I would make sure we legitimize my heir if ye are to bear my child."

Her hand moved to her belly. Protectively, perhaps, since her gray eyes gazed back at him full of cold accusation. "Is this how you ensure you will maintain control of Beaumont? Insist upon a marriage I have not even agreed to?"

Her whispered words cut him deeper than he would have expected, her assumption that he would maneuver her thus stinging more than the cool reception she'd been giving him since waking. His hand fell away from her cheek.

"Ye came to me willingly, Rosalind." He would never have seduced her into a marriage she did not want. "Most men would take such passion as a sign ye wish to be wed."

"Well, fie upon you and your assumptions. I have never expressed a desire to wed." Spurring her horse, she ended their conversation abruptly, although she was not so rash as to ride away. The cheeky wench simply rode with her back straight as an arrow all the way to Beaumont.

Hellfire.

One way or another, she would be his wife. She would see reason. Had to see reason. Their night together had been beyond anything he'd ever experienced with any woman. Her soft vulnerability combined with unexpected strength…there was something irresistible about the she-demon who had started all this with one well-aimed shot of her crossbow.

She was smart. Yet she could be tender, too, as witnessed by her remorse at the death of his man-at-arms. In short, she was altogether pleasing.

And she tasted like honeyed mead.

Feeling his body respond to the thought of her, he squelched the memory of her sweet form beneath him. Instead, he concentrated on his plans to woo and win her once they were back in the quiet routine of Beaumont.

Marriage to the heathen? The passionate, maddening, delicious heathen who had made her throw all caution to the wind the night before for just a taste of his kisses?

Steering her horse through the woods beyond Beaumont's southern fields, Rosalind told herself she had no right to be angry. Or even surprised, for that matter. He tendered the offer an honorable man should. He would wed her for her recklessness. And in doing so, he would be rewarded with the keep he wanted for his own.

Surely he had not planned to use her desire against her in some sort of seductive ploy. She knew him better. Trusted him too much for those games.

If not for the fear she could not make a sound decision to save her life, perhaps Rosalind would have simply smiled gratefully at the notion of being the laird's bride. But merciful heaven, she could not find it in her heart to trust anything she felt after she'd refused to see what was in front of her eyes all along with Gregory. She'd been too desperate for him to be the true love who could save her. Save her people.

Who was to say she wasn't equally desperate now?

Still, only a madwoman would deny Malcolm for a husband after giving herself to him the night before. She had bestowed upon him the only favor within her power to grant and—once given—it could never be taken back.

Confused and bone weary, she welcomed the sight of Beaumont's outer ward as they broke through the last barrier of trees outside the keep. But any hope she might have nursed about sneaking unnoticed to her chamber was quickly dashed by the presence of a band of richly decorated horses in the courtyard. Twelve warhorses stamped and snorted in the cool air, their hooves clanking against the cobblestones.

"The Bruce," Malcolm announced from behind her, breaking the silence that hung between them more heavily than the fog rolling off the hills.

Fear niggled at her. "Your king?" The same king he'd once suggested might banish her?

"Aye." Although Malcolm looked unconcerned, he straightened his tunic as they approached the entrance to the keep.

Sliding from her horse, she hastened her step to keep up with him as they entered the main doors.

Robert the Bruce, King of Scotland, sat leisurely before the fire in the great hall, his boots propped on a trestle table nearby. Engrossed in a book and devouring a pear, he seemed oblivious to the juice that ran down his bearded chin. He could have been any young English nobleman with his relaxed posture and informal manner. Although his long legs appeared strong and powerful, he lacked Malcolm's height. Sandy brown hair framed a broad forehead and long nose, while his mouth disappeared beneath a full mustache.

His head shot up as they approached.

"My good man!" He shoved aside book and pear alike. "Ye must excuse my lack of manners."

"'Tis pleased I am to see ye, Yer Highness." Malcolm bowed to the king, but Robert halted his effort and greeted him with a hearty embrace.

"No need to stand on ceremony, McNair. I havena

let this crown go to my head, as ye can see." He gestured merrily to his bare pate. "But dinna waste another moment, Malcolm. I would know the identity of this fair creature at yer side."

His eyes were full of roguish good humor as he smiled at her. Were he not the enemy king who possessed the power to banish her, she might have found him charming.

"This is Rosalind, the former lady of Beaumont, my lord."

The king took up the hand she did not offer and kissed its palm, his dancing eyes never leaving hers.

"'Tis truly a pleasure to meet ye, Lady Rosalind, though I would it were under different circumstances. I have heard much about ye from Malcolm's brothers." He continued to imprison her fingers as he spoke. "I promise ye I was unaware that ye were a lady on yer own here, else I wouldna have thought to take Beaumont. I had it on good authority that yer keep was held by a young male heir, whom I thought to easily overrun. 'Twas never my intent to deprive ye of yer household." He bowed gallantly over her hand and then released it.

She did not believe his pretty speech for a moment, though she supposed it was true enough that no Scot had suspected she alone held the keep. Had the rebel king known that fact, he probably would have deprived her of her home all the sooner.

"I hope I will have the pleasure of being yer dining companion this eve, my lady?" The king lifted her hand once more, kissing the back of it with greater restraint than he had the palm. He continued when Rosalind nodded. "If ye will excuse us then?"

Rosalind curtsied politely and took her leave. She prayed the Scots king was not dismissing her so that he might discuss her banishment with Malcolm, although she knew she should not expect any better from the sovereign of a rebel nation. Would Malcolm speak in her defense? she wondered. Would he ask his overlord for permission to wed her?

She supposed two such powerful men could order her to wed on the morrow and she would have no say in the matter. Or would she?

As a woman possessed of so little power, all she had left, really, was her choice. Her narrow escape from Gregory had taught that she could not be cavalier with making this decision in the future.

Of course, ideally, she would have seized upon such wisdom before she unraveled like a wanton beneath Malcolm McNair's tempting lips.

Finding her own chamber, she called for a bath and started to undress. Her hair, her clothes, her skin—everything about her carried the scent of Malcolm. Thoughts of their night together tantalized her as she remembered every touch, every moment of their joining, which had culminated in a pleasure so fierce she feared she would never forget it.

She stroked her belly absently. Could a babe grow inside her even now? A surge of protectiveness coursed through her at the thought. She would have no choice but to wed then—and quickly. But until she knew for certain, she planned to take her time thinking through her options.

Slipping into the rose-scented bathwater, she allowed the steam to clear her mind and cleanse her spirit. Gently, she scrubbed the bloodstains from her thighs, her skin still sensitive from Malcolm's hands upon her. All over her. Her muscles ached from the night before, but she could not find it in her heart to regret a moment.

Only when the water grew tepid did she arise and dress to sup. She donned her best kirtle of soft green linen and a heavy surcoat in a shade darker. Her silken hose were dyed a pale shade of spring mint and tied with matching embroidered garters. She called in Josephine to help with her hair. They wove a yellow ribbon into a small braid, which they wound around her head like a circlet, leaving the remaining strands loose. This Rosalind covered with a gossamer veil that shimmered subtly in the candlelight, and topped it with a simple gold fillet.

She debated wearing her father's amethyst dagger to dinner, finally deciding to—not out of disrespect to her Scottish guests, but because the amethyst complemented her kirtle so nicely. Two intricately shaped golden bracelets, molded by ancient Viking craftsmen, adorned her wrists—pieces she loved because they had belonged to her mother, and had somehow managed to survive the Beaumont fire, along with her mother's silver pomander.

So garbed, Rosalind descended to the hall and out of doors to greet the villeins as they arrived from their day's work in the fields. A few traveling minstrels were already present, discussing their planned entertainment animatedly. The sun still warmed the evening, but it would set before the meal was complete. Candelabram graced several of the tables to help ward off the dark.

The tables overflowed by the time Malcolm and the rebel king appeared. Rosalind hastened to greet them in an effort to put her people at ease, since Beaumont had not hosted royalty—rebel or otherwise—in her lifetime. Swallowing back a bout of nerves at the sight of Malcolm, she smiled and curtsied before his king.

"My lords, let us be seated and I shall give the order for the meal to commence."

Bowing over her hand, Robert the Bruce winked.

"Ye have but to lead the way, my lady, and I, for my part, will be well pleased." He held her gaze longer than was polite. "Yer beauty is welcome to the eye, yer good cheer heartening to my weary soul."

She seated the king at the small dais table with Malcolm and the McNair brothers, along with a few of the king's more highly placed retainers. Unsure where to seat herself, Rosalind hesitated, but the king solved the dilemma by gesturing for her to sit beside him.

When she nodded, the feast began. Trenchers were soon served to all the company, followed by trays heaped with the first course of lamprey or eel, according to each guest's preference. Rosalind noted her household did a credible job of serving the large crowd promptly.

"Yer kitchen does ye proud, my lady," the king remarked halfway through his first course. "'Tis rather uncommon to find such service in a country keep such as yers. But then, I sense there is nothing common about ye, Rosalind Beaumont."

"The credit belongs to a loyal household, my lord. I like to think I have endeavored to make their lot in life a pleasant one."

"Another way in which ye are an unusual creature, yet very wise. I commend ye on yer gentle tactics." He chose a large portion of stuffed piglet from the tray that now came around. "'Tis no wonder one of my most formidable warriors is taken with ye."

Surprised, she shook her head. "I fear you are mistaken."

"Nay. 'Tis obvious." He held out a morsel of cheese for Rosalind, which she accepted from his fingers. "He has asked me for permission to wed with ye."

The cheese lodged uncomfortably in her throat. Eyes burning, she reached for her wine, requiring something to soothe the new fears and frustrations heaped upon her with Malcolm's pressure to solidify a union between them.

"A natural request if he is a man in search of lands, my lord. Perhaps he only wishes to gain control of Beaumont on your behalf." She prayed she did not speak too boldly, but it seemed the rebel king was determined to catch her off guard tonight with his affable manner and pointed remarks.

How could Malcolm have approached Robert about a marriage when they had hardly discussed the matter? Aye, two days ago he had made an offhand suggestion that they wed, but he had not made a formal proposition this morning after their night together. He'd simply announced the need to wed as a fact. Like a skilled battle tactician assuming control of his quarry.

Her, in this case.

"Ye know McNair well, it seems." The king toasted her with his wine.

Surely her cheeks flamed bright red at his implication. "My lord, I'm sure I don't know what you mean."

"I only wished to suggest ye have seen McNair's shrewdness in a way that others do not." The king turned his gaze to where Malcolm sat between his brothers. "Ian is the eldest and therefore has been entrusted with his father's lands, but the younger McNairs are every bit as impressive on the battlefield. I hate to lose Malcolm to a life of leisure as lord of his own keep, but I might be seen as rather stingy with my followers if I dinna offer up occasional rewards for services rendered."

Rosalind followed the king's gaze to where the McNair men sat farther down the bench. They made an imposing trio, but her eyes lingered over Malcolm. As he laughed at one of Jamie's jests, his face lost its fierceness. She remembered how she had gazed into his eyes the previous night, longing for him to be a different man, one she could pledge herself to without forsaking her family's English loyalties.

The Scots king had done nothing to ease her fears that Malcolm wished to wed her only so that he might rule Beaumont as his own. If anything, Robert the

Bruce seemed even more convinced of cunning maneuvering at work than she had been.

"So you think to offer my hand as a reward?" She knew marriages were made for such base purposes all the time. But she had always hoped for more for herself. Was it so much to yearn for a bit of affection between husband and wife?

"I have not yet made up my mind if I can afford to lose both Beaumont and ye, Lady Rosalind. I thought to seek yer opinion on the matter."

"You wish to know what I think?" The very notion dazzled her, even while she reminded herself he might not take her feelings into account in the end.

"Aye. What's yer pleasure, lass?" He leaned closer as he spoke, his words carefully spoken for her ears alone.

What game was this? His proximity put her on guard, warning her that his amenable conversation this eve might be a way to soften her, to convince her to part with her secrets or—saints protect her—entice her favor.

"I am not of a mind to marry yet." Straightening, she hoped she was not too abrupt, but she could not afford to give Malcolm's king the wrong impression.

At that moment, a flushed Gerta approached the table, oblivious to the seriousness of their conversation.

Gerta's old face was wreathed in smiles. "Is it not time for you to call the entertainment? We are eager to begin the merrymaking."

Rosalind glanced about the lawns to see that the villeins had finished with their meals, drinking and laughing while they waited for the fun to commence. With the descent of the sun, the evening had cooled to a comfortable temperature.

"Of course." She eased back from the table before seeking Robert's permission. "If you do not mind, my lord?"

"Nay. I look forward to partnering ye in a dance this eve, Lady Rosalind, if ye would do me the honor?"

"I look forward to it." She curtsied deeply, already considering ways to excuse herself early from the festivities. She signaled for the entertainment to begin and slipped away from the king to make further preparations for the eve. Tables were removed to make room for the minstrels and the dancing that would follow as part of their harvest celebration.

"Ye are nae wasting any time charming the king, I see."

She turned to see Malcolm lounging in the shadows against a stout pine.

Her heart stalled at the sight of him. Had it been just the previous night that she had lain in his arms, eagerly succumbing to his caresses? A shiver of awareness skated over her skin at the memory.

"It is the king who is doing the charming, I assure you." Continuing on her way to the keep, she refused to be trapped in a web of intrigue between Malcolm, his king and her own treacherous desires.

Malcolm had no choice but to reach for her. She thought to leave him here to wrestle with his conscience and play whatever games his king had in mind?

Bad enough that he had not been able to think about anything but her all day, even when Robert had been discussing his favorite of all topics—the strategy of his war. Malcolm had been able to think only of winning the battle for Rosalind Beaumont's bed.

"The Scots king is already married, Rosalind." He tipped a small flask to his lips, unable to forget the vision of her smiling engagingly at Robert over the meal. "Ye waste yer time to trot out yer womanly wiles."

"You know perfectly well I do not seek to marry a Scot." She yanked her arm from his grip, her stiff posture a good indication she did not appreciate his words. "It just so happens that your king was an entertaining dining partner."

"Ye might be careful he doesna attempt to partner ye in another way. I hear he isna the most faithful of husbands." Malcolm did not wish to offend her, but he could not bear the thought of Robert winning her affection when Malcolm had not yet developed his own strategy, devil take the king and his penchant for dalliances.

"How dare you insinuate such a thing? And about your own king."

"I insinuate nothing, Rosalind. He is just a man, subject to yer charm like any other. 'Tis more than obvious he finds ye pleasing. If ye would not end up in his bed tonight, ye would do well to be on guard." Malcolm paused to swill from the skin, praying mightily that she had no wish to end up as the king's newest liaison.

"You insufferable lout." She glared at him as if she

could make him quake in his boots at the sight, but her vicious frown only made him want to kiss her senseless. "As if I would run off to bed with any man who cast his eye upon me. You may not trust your own king, my lord, but rest assured, I am no lust-ridden creature given to dallying at whim."

"I did not suggest… I know ye are no wanton." He capped the wineskin and slung the strap over his shoulder, wondering if Rosalind would shout down the keep if *he* chose to haul her off to bed right now. Truth be told, he felt a bit like a lust-ridden animal. "But I dinna want ye to be deceived into thinking the king would care more for ye than I would."

"You suggest you care for me, and yet you can hardly trust me to conduct a conversation with another man." Hurt glowed in her eyes, apparent even in the shadows. "Perhaps your king is more of a gentleman than you suspect, heathen, for his manners have been far kinder than yours this eve."

"Mayhap ye wouldna feel the same way were it Robert who seized yer castle and was forced to throw ye in the dungeon." Could she not appreciate the awkwardness of his position? "Ye might find me a gentleman were I the one to ride in and offer ye my protection the way Robert has today. Just remember, 'twas the well-mannered king who called for Beaumont to be taken from ye, not me."

She might have argued, but over her shoulder, Malcolm spied Robert's approach as the music for a stately round drifted on the night breeze. Hellfire. It seemed

Malcolm had no choice but to play the courtier if he wanted a chance to win her hand.

"Dance with me, Rosalind." He grasped her fingers, not wishing to give her a chance to say no. But she stood still. Unmoving. Calling forth the more civilized words that she seemed fond of hearing, he murmured, "Please?"

She nodded. A barely perceptible sign of agreement, but he spied it nevertheless. Slipping his hand around her waist, he guided her toward the small clearing where the dirt was packed and pine needles carpeted the earth. The minstrels plucked their lutes with grave expressions, the mournful tune quieting the crowd while dancers bowed and circled one another. Candlelit torches surrounded the space, casting golden light and shadows over all the participants and reminding Malcolm of the way Rosalind's skin had looked in the firelight the night before.

At last, the round dissolved into a more gentle tune that gave him an excuse to draw her near, his hand pressing lightly on her back, just above the enticing curve of her rump. Her flushed cheeks told him her thoughts traveled the same path as his as he drew a light circle on her hip with his fingertips.

"Ye are thinking of last night, are ye nae?"

Although he felt a shiver run through her, the lass shook her head, avoiding his gaze. He took some satisfaction in knowing she could not find a voice to deny it aloud.

"Ye dinna tell the truth." He gave his gaze free rein over her body, sweeping leisurely from her shimmering veil to her velvet slippers and lingering in between. "'Tis in yer thoughts as much as mine."

"Nay." Her hand that lay lightly on his shoulder fisted. Relaxed. Fisted again. Then, meeting his gaze, she sighed. "Perhaps a time or two I have thought of it. But only because the events of the night were rather…irreversible. I realize I must give some consideration to my future now."

"Aye." Thank the saints she was beginning to see reason. "The wise course of action—nay, the only course of action—is to wed. I have already spoken to—"

"Has it ever occurred to you that I may not choose the course you find most rational?" Abruptly her hands fell away from him. And although Malcolm discerned the music was at an end, it seemed Rosalind had stepped back rather hastily. "Perhaps I have other options open to me that you know nothing about."

She stalked away from the dancing arena with a flounce of green skirts and pale tresses. Away from him.

So much for brilliant strategy where she was concerned. It seemed his king had outmaneuvered him when it came to wooing a fickle lass like this one. Frustration gnawed Malcolm's patience ragged, and he drained the rest of the wineskin he'd set aside earlier. He would speak to Rosalind and settle this matter for good, whether she wished to provide him with an audience or not.

Fortunately, he knew one sure way to make her listen. One tactic that Robert the Bruce had better not even consider, should the king know what was good for him.

And lucky for Malcolm, the most effective method of communication would be every bit as rewarding for him as it would soon be for Rosalind.

Chapter Twelve

Rosalind smiled at her guests as she moved toward the keep, sharing jests with Lachlan Gordon, who looked as if he was trying his best to woo Gerta into a shadowy corner of the yard. Not that Gerta seemed all that unwilling.

It seemed everyone at Beaumont was too busy celebrating the good harvest to care about their lady's traitorous union with her Scots conqueror. Guilt nipped her from every corner of her brain as she slipped into the north tower to find her solar and a little quiet.

The whole keep would be empty, with everyone celebrating on the lawns below. Although disappearing from her own festivity ranked as highly discourteous, perhaps the hour was so late that no one would take offense. She simply could not face Malcolm again tonight, not with his touch still singeing her waist, her hip…

Her sole regret about leaving the gathering was losing the chance to speak with Robert the Bruce. Perhaps she had misread him earlier, after the meal. And if the man wanted to know her preferences for her future, why not share them on the small chance he did not deceive her? She had nothing to lose by making her hopes known. She just wished she knew exactly what they were.

Tie herself to an unyielding Scot who could set her whole body aflame but might never touch her heart? Seek an English lord with whom she could rest easy, knowing she did not betray her family's loyalties? Or gamble on whatever else Robert the Bruce might offer her?

None of it promised her gentle companionship or the possibility of true accord or—most importantly— real love.

Inside the keep, her chamber remained cold and utterly dark. Josephine must have thought her lady would not retire for many hours yet. Rosalind moved with tentative steps about her solar in the dimness, seeking a candle to bring to the torch in the hall so she might have some light.

As her hand closed around the heavy silver holder, a low masculine voice rumbled from the shadows. "'Tis a bit early to leave yer own party, is it nae?"

Malcolm.

She almost dropped the heavy candelabrum in her surprise, barely managing to keep it from falling to the floor.

"Allow me, lass. I will gladly light yer fire for ye."

She felt more than saw his approach, her eyes still unused to the darkness of the chamber. Anticipation curled through her, reminding her of all the heated feelings his touch had inspired last night.

"You do not belong in here." She cursed the breathlessness in her voice as he neared. "You have no right to enter my chamber, McNair."

"Ah, but ye mistake me, lass, for I only came to apologize for offending ye during our dance. Surely there can be no harm in that?" He pried the candelabrum loose from her shaking fingers. "Give me the tapers and I will bring ye enough light to see."

Hoping to lock him out, she tripped after him as he went to light her candle. She stole quietly toward the entranceway, the one part of the room she could see clearly, since the torches in the corridor still burned. Yet she did not see Malcolm shadowed in its light. Had he already stepped through the portal?

Finding no other explanation for his disappearance, she hastened to the heavy door and threw it shut. The key dangled at her waist beside her pomander and she promptly turned it in the lock.

"Ye'll nae be wanting any candlelight this eve, Rosalind?"

She jumped at the sound of his voice, unbelievably close in the pitch blackness.

"'Tis just as well. Yer eyes will adjust and ye'll have no need of it, anyway. I must admit I am rather surprised ye wanted to lock me in here with ye, though." He paused, as if considering. "Perhaps I made a more favorable impression on ye last night than I dared to hope?"

Truly, the man was too much to bear. Sighing in her

frustration, she resigned herself to his presence until he'd spoken his piece. As much as she did not want him in her chamber, she knew he would not harm her. She did not need to fear him, curse his eyes. She only needed to fear her twitchy fingers, which even now longed to reach out to touch his broad warrior shoulders. His deliciously muscled arms.

"What are you doing in here?" She willed her thoughts quiet, urged her breathing back to normal.

She could be normal, couldn't she? Except that it wasn't normal to have a man in her chamber. A man who gave her heart palpitations when he wasn't bringing her to the brink of sensual release.

"I might ask ye the same question, darlin'. 'Tis rather early to retire. Why do ye seek yer bed so soon?" As he talked, her eyes began to acclimate to the darkness in the room. She could discern his large shadow, sprawled across a wooden bench a few feet away.

"I sought my chamber to escape your attentions, yet magically, here you are. I am quite annoyed with you."

"When ye left during our dance, I knew ye would retreat to one of two places. And my old friend Lachlan looked to be cutting off yer escape route to the garden, so I thought to seek ye here."

The more Rosalind became used to the dimness, the better she could observe him. It was a strange feeling to watch him when he did not realize she could see him. His body, usually so alert and ready for action, reclined lazily before her. She could not recall ever seeing him so much at ease. Well, perhaps one other time. A swell of warm memories swamped her at the thought. Right now, he propped his weight on one elbow, his leg draped over the arm of the bench. His foot swung idly from its careless perch.

He did not look in her direction, but fixed his attention on a small object in his hands, which she could not discern.

"Now that you have found me, it would be best to speak your mind and then go. It is unseemly that you be here with me, locked in my chamber."

He glanced up at her, meeting her eyes in the dark. "So ye can see where ye're going at last." He winked at her before turning his attention back to what was in his hands. "Does this belong to ye?"

He tossed a dully shining object to her, which Rosalind deftly caught. Turning, she examined it in a shaft of moonlight shining through the room's only arrow slit.

"'Tis my mother's pomander. I always wear it. I do not know how—"

"It fell from yer waist when ye were searching for yer key to lock the door. I felt the engravings but couldna make out the images."

"My mother was Celtic." Rosalind fingered the pomander's familiar markings as she had many times before. "I do not know what all the symbols mean. She did not explain them all to me before she died, but I do know they are symbols of pagan worship. The serpent, for instance, was a powerful link to their ancient goddess, I believe. The serpent whispered wisdom into the ears of Celtic priestesses."

"I am surprised yer priest has not demanded ye discard it. The Church does not look favorably upon the old religions."

Rosalind sighed, squeezing the pomander tightly before attaching it to the chain on her girdle. "I do not make a habit of showing it off. I keep it purely for sentimental value and not to align myself with old gods."

"And how did the good lord of Beaumont end up with a Celt?" His voice curled comfortably about her in the darkness. It seemed easier to talk to him under cover of the gloom.

"Apparently he kidnapped her." She leaned against the wooden table bearing her small vases and dried flower arrangements.

"Ye canna be serious?"

"'Tis true. My father visited several Celtic kingdoms as a young man and fell in love with my mother on sight. Her family would not give permission for them to wed, so he stole her away."

"Was yer mother angry?"

"To hear her side of it, yes. My father held that she loved him in return, she just did not realize it at first. Either way, they fell deeply in love and were very happy."

"What of her father?" Malcolm prodded. "Did he nae come after his daughter or seek justice?"

"My father sent him a large shipment of wool and spices as payment as soon as he returned to Beaumont, and that satisfied the man. I guess my grandfather had feared that William Beaumont was not rich enough for my mother."

"It must have been difficult for yer mam, accepting a foreign culture as her own, moving to a strange land."

"Yes, I have heard she hated the climate and the strange ways of the English people when she first came here and—" She broke off, her words striking a sudden chord.

Malcolm grinned, his white teeth visible in the shaft of moonlight. "And she came to like her enemy, anyway?"

She nodded absently, considering how her mother rose to the challenge.

"Yer mother was a noble woman to overcome her misgivings. She must have learned to look into the hearts of men instead of at their place of birth."

Rosalind considered Malcolm. Reclining no longer, he sat forward on the bench, his alert body full of the tension she had grown accustomed to. As his eyes followed her, Rosalind sensed he could guess her very thoughts.

"You'd better go, Malcolm. I—"

"My real mother died when I was but a lad."

His stark admission touched Rosalind. Before she could offer her condolences, Malcolm continued. "Jamie's mother raised all three of us. Ian and I are honored to call Lorna McNair 'Mother.' She accepted us as her own, when she could have easily preferred her natural-born son over another woman's children."

Rosalind struggled to envision the woman who had raised the McNair men. "She must be a strong person."

Malcolm furrowed his brows as if he had not considered the notion before. "Aye," he admitted slowly. "Mostly, she is as tender as the Highland winter is long. She made my father's keep a real home. She oversaw every meal herself, cared for all the tenants and brought a sort of magic to holy days for all of us." Malcolm paused to glance at Rosalind, his love for his stepmother apparent in his dimpled grin. "Lorna is a gentle spirit."

And no doubt had the stamina of a warrior and the strength of a northern wind, Rosalind thought. She found it interesting that Malcolm preferred not to see those obvious qualities in the woman who had raised him. He seemed to prefer a more delicate female over the crossbow-wielding kind.

Not that she cared. Much.

"You are fortunate she is still around," Rosalind mused. "My own mother would no doubt have lived at least long enough to see me wed if death had not robbed me of her."

Malcolm must have sensed the bitterness in her words, for he leaned over and encased her hand in his. "Rosalind, listen to me. Ye canna continue to revile all the Scots, no matter how atrocious their crimes."

"It is not a mere matter of like and dislike any longer." She allowed her fingers to remain nestled within his for a moment longer, relishing their strength. "But I find it difficult to align myself with your people and be a traitor to my own family."

"Ye dinna have any family left to be traitor to. I am sorry for yer loss, but think of what ye have left. Why risk any more over a cause that no longer matters?"

Could she share with him her fears? Her parents' deaths, long unavenged, remained a burden to her heart. It might help to speak of it, to ask Malcolm his opinion. He was an experienced warrior, and an honorable one at that. Maybe he would have some insights.

But what if he did not? Or worse, what if he chose not to help her avenge her family, out of loyalties of his own? She could not force him to make those decisions when she already feared he had captured an irretrievable piece of her heart last night. She could not put him in an impossible position and then be disappointed if he did not make the decisions she preferred.

"I do not wish to burden you with my past."

"What other choice do ye have?" He scowled, all traces of gentleness gone. "Ye canna wish to turn to young Gregory anymore. Ye have no brother to rescue ye. Yer king doesna care what happens in the borderlands." He rose to close the space between them, and waited, allowing the full impact of his words to settle upon her.

But it was not easy to consider her future rationally when he stood so close to her. He brushed his fingers over her cheek, lingering near her mouth the same way his lips had the night before. She fought an overwhelming urge to nip his finger, to draw the digit into her mouth for a small taste of him. His scent surrounded her, warm and male and vaguely tinged with the cedar fragrance of the hearth smoke.

She blinked up at him, her heart slamming so wildly in her chest he must surely feel it as he touched her. More than anything at this moment she longed to sink into his arms, to know the heat and passion they'd shared the night before. His hand curved warmly about her waist and she all but fell against him, her skin burning with tiny flames of desire that leapt to life at his nearness. She skimmed her palm up his shoulder, pausing only when she realized he did not touch her to draw her closer.

Nay, his hand upon her waist was only reaching for the key that hung from her belt. No sooner had he freed it than he was striding toward the door.

"Ye canna withhold all yer secrets forever, Rosalind." He turned back after unlocking the door and depositing the key on a small chest. "Ye must consider where ye will place yer trust."

The door slammed behind him, leaving Rosalind in total darkness again.

He wished to leave her wanting? To distract her with honeyed touches and confuse her so much she knew naught but that she craved his touch? She would have submitted to him in a heartbeat just now, risking everything to be with him again. Yet he'd left her desires unfulfilled, her need still aching heavily within.

The depth of her disappointment terrified her. She hadn't felt so much since her parents died.

Cracking open her door to retrieve a taper and bring some warmth to her chamber, Rosalind vowed she would explore all her options before giving in to Malcolm McNair again. She could not risk any more of her heart on a man who would leave her.

Surely there had to be a more logical answer to her dilemma than to cling wantonly to a Scots laird who would never love her.

Chapter Thirteen

"Ye canna up and leave after only two days, Robert. Ye havena even told me yer plans for Beaumont." Malcolm tried to keep his anger in check, but the king's news did not sit well with him.

Robert mounted his horse at the edge of the fields, seemingly unaffected by Malcolm's foul mood. He'd planned his departure shortly before twilight as the wily King was well aware the borderlands were rife with enemies. He often traveled by night, his stealth keeping him safe.

Malcolm had hoped he would grant him possession of Beaumont before he departed, but Robert was wily as ever about such a grant—hinting he might, but never actually committing to it. "Can ye at least tell me what plans ye have for the deposed heiress? What would ye have me do with her?"

"As if I had any real choice." Robert grinned. "Any lack-wit can see ye want her so badly yer eyes are fairly crossing in their sockets." His smile fading, he leveled a finger at Malcolm's chest. "I give her to ye as part of yer spoils, but bear in mind I rather like the lass. I wouldna have ye mistreat her."

He was off in a swirl of dust before Malcolm could reply.

Rosalind was his. Malcolm could scarce believe his good fortune. He did not have to worry about Robert trying to seduce her. She belonged to Malcolm now in all ways but in the eyes of God.

As would Beaumont, once he wed her.

Perhaps this was the king's way of granting him the keep without riling the prickly lass who would be his wife. Malcolm picked up his scythe and called an end to the workday. The sun was nearly set. The villeins would find their own dinners tonight, but there would be another feast at the keep two nights hence for Michaelmas.

Tonight, he would find Rosalind and talk sense into her stubborn ears. How many women in her position could wed for love, anyhow? She was being awfully choosy for a conquered orphan with no options left. Marriage would give her a way to maintain her pride and her keep—at least to some extent.

For his part, he would gain peace for the people of Beaumont, and his longtime dream of a home. Certainly a man could do worse than claiming the fey Rosalind for a wife. Their night together had hinted at a depth of passion he could not wait to experience again.

As he approached the gates of the keep, a shadow stirred in a nearby clump of trees.

Evandale?

Malcolm had already begun implementing new defense measures to ensure Rosalind's thwarted groom kept his distance from Beaumont, but no defense could take the place of alertness. Readiness. He kept moving with the others, not wanting to arouse the suspicion of the shadowy figure. He did not have long to wait. Whoever it was darted among the trees, moving agilely through the low brush and undergrowth.

Malcolm detached himself from the group to pursue the figure. He gained ground easily, his quarry obviously unaware he was being followed.

Malcolm felt a little foolish when he realized the lurking figure was a mere boy—Brady Millerson, an impish child taken in by the Beaumont household. Malcolm was about to tackle the lad and give him a good scare for wandering out past dark, but the youth's determined step and watchful eyes made him hold his attack for a moment longer.

Brady soon stepped into a clearing where an older boy waited for him.

"Here is your coin and your message. My mistress says it is most important, too," Brady stated.

"'Northfield,'" the boy read aloud as he looked at the letter. "This will get there in a sennight, without fail." He moved to tuck the letter into a grimy bag on his shoulder when Malcolm stepped into the clearing, his sudden presence scaring both boys speechless.

"Brady, ye know I dinna allow any messages to leave Beaumont unless I give permission." He withdrew the letter with the odd green seal from the other boy's fingers. "Who gave this to ye to deliver?"

Brady's face crumpled, all trace of boyish bravado gone as tears threatened.

Hellfire.

"Ye will not get in trouble, lad, as long as ye dinna do such a thing again. Who gave the letter to ye?"

"Gerta. But I do not think she is the one sending it."

Malcolm examined the green floral seal on the envelope. "I dinna think so, either." He stuffed the envelope into his tunic and turned to the messenger. "Ye may keep yer coin this time, lad, but there will be no more missives coming from Beaumont. We deliver our letters from the keep, not from the forest. Ye ken?"

After sending off the elder boy, Malcolm collared Brady and marched him back to the keep.

Rosalind had not arrived in the hall yet, so Malcolm hastened to his chambers, moving quickly in the hope that he would still have a moment to read the missive. But as anxious as he was to know what it said, his curiosity mixed with another feeling that rendered him distinctly uncomfortable.

Fear of betrayal.

A damn idiotic fear, he knew. Rosalind made it clear she would never be loyal to him, but in his arrogance he continued to think she would see reason eventually. The letter he held in his hand, addressed to Lord Gareth of Northfield, could very well put an end to that hope.

When Malcolm reached the hall, Rosalind was still not at her seat. Now he would have time.

"Good evening, my lord."

Her musical voice stilled him. He tucked the missive back into his tunic before she could spy it, then turned to greet her.

"Good evening, Rosalind." He gestured toward the hall. "Shall we enter together?"

Nodding, she took his arm. They were greeted on all sides by castlefolk, who made no effort to hide their pleasure in seeing the former lady and the new lord of the keep together. Why couldn't Rosalind see that the whole damn keep wanted them to wed?

"'Tis lovely ye're looking this eve." Jamie made a courtly bow, no doubt going out of his way to pay attention to Rosalind because he knew it would rile Malcolm.

"Yer way with a scythe puts us all to shame, my lord," called one of Rosalind's men-at-arms, who had worked in the fields beside Malcolm.

"We need to talk." He turned on his heel abruptly, unwilling to sit through another cursed meal beside Rosalind while wondering all the time what mischief she concocted behind his back.

"Now?" She peered back over her shoulder toward the hallful of murmuring onlookers.

Withdrawing the missive from his tunic, he brandished it under her nose. "Aye. Now."

Any hope that her letter contained nothing damning vanished at the sight of her tight nod. If his feisty she-demon would quietly agree to skip the meal she normally enjoyed presiding over, her missive must surely bear news he would not appreciate.

Bloody hell. Tearing open the seal as they moved down the corridor, he braced himself for the worst.

* * *

Marching up the stairs to her chamber with a stonily silent Scot at her heels, Rosalind cursed the man with every oath she could think of, many of which were newly learned phrases she'd overheard his warrior brothers use.

Slipping into her solar, she seated herself on the same bench he'd taken refuge on the previous night. At least here they could discuss in private the matter of her last-ditch effort to escape him. And her solar was located far from the keep's dungeon, where he'd put her once before.

Yet there were distinct disadvantages to being alone with him now. She studied him as he locked the door behind them, his tense movements making him look ready to pounce at any moment. His dark jaw, shadowed from a day's growth of whiskers, clenched and flexed as he gritted his teeth.

His right hand still clutched the piece of parchment she'd labored over half the day.

"What the hell is this?" he growled, waving under her nose the missive to an old friend of her father's.

She had thought to be logical by writing to the kindly English widower and confessing her awkward situation at Beaumont. She'd hinted that she would be willing to consider marriage, although she hadn't found a delicate way to express her need to wait long enough to ensure she was not carrying Malcolm's babe. If she was already breeding, she would somehow find a way to resign herself to a loveless marriage to the child's father.

"That letter is my failed last chance at a practical resolution to my predicament, it seems." She ignored his obvious anger. He could rant and rave all he wanted, but he'd intercepted it before it could work any harm against him. Why should *he* be upset? Her life lay in utter shambles, not his.

"What do ye mean, last chance, woman? Ye'll only come up with some new scheme to escape tomorrow. It seems yer a never-ending source of trouble." Malcolm glared at her, standing mere inches from her, but she did not feel intimidated so much as she felt…

Bloody hell.

The new expression she'd learned seemed quite fitting for the confusing deluge of feelings coursing through her whenever Malcolm came near.

"If only I could think of something else, I *would* try it out tomorrow. But you have effectively vanquished my last hope of settling myself to my satisfaction." Her logical plan would not work, apparently.

"Ye really want this marriage?" His blue eyes narrowed as he ceased his pacing. "Ye would consider it a favor if I marry ye off to a doddering old man with nary a tooth in his head just so ye can say ye wed a man born on the proper side of the border? Ye have lost yer mind." He tossed her missive into the fire. "And what makes ye think this Lord Gareth would take ye, when ye yerself say ye have *nothing at all* to bring to the marriage?"

Her cheeks heated at his crude reference to the letter and her subtle way of telling Northfield she was no longer a virgin. "He is an old friend of the family."

"With the emphasis on 'old,' I dinna doubt. Well,

lass, ye have taken me by surprise once again. Heaven knows I shouldna underestimate ye after yer escapade with yer wee lordling Evandale, but I'll be a hedge-born malt worm if I saw this coming."

"I told you I would have difficulty swearing loyalty to a Scot." She watched the parchment curl up at the edges before it took flame, the ink glowing bright for an instant before the sheet blackened completely. She shivered at the sight, trying not to allow old ghosts to haunt her.

"What is this noble notion ye have about needing to stay loyal to yer country? No one will blame ye for giving in to the inevitable."

"Because I am a woman?" She whirled on him, hoping her anger would help her keep more distance from him tonight than she'd managed in the past. "What would you do if you were in my position? Would you ever switch sides just because someone told you that you must?"

"'Tis the way of the world that men make the wars, while women tend the hearths. Women are peacemakers and healers. Ye shouldna be ashamed of yer role, Rosalind. 'Tis as noble as any man's, and as honorable." He tilted her chin up to encourage her gaze. "But different."

"It is not fair for men to rob us of our choices." Rosalind took a deep breath to steady her nerves. "I do not wish to be a peacemaker in this instance."

"Then ye are too stubborn for yer own good, lass. And too stubborn to care about the people of yer precious Beaumont."

"What do you mean by that?" she asked, trying to hide the little tremor of fear that gripped her.

"I mean that by being too proud to swear loyalty to me, ye give up yer place as lady here and forsake the people who have counted on ye and yer family all of their lives. 'Twill hurt them to have their lady leave them."

"Are you threatening my people with harm?" She had not expected such crass means from Malcolm.

"Nay. Ye should know me better than that." He settled on the bench beside her. "But ye know very well ye are an integral part of their lives. Everyone in the village seeks yer aid for their illnesses and yer advice on any number of things, from bringing in the crops to growing a rosebush. Thomas Cole loves ye like his own daughter. Young Brady forbade me to punish ye over this Northfield incident and bravely offered to take yer punishment in yer place."

"He did?" She attempted to swallow the growing lump in her throat.

"Aye. My own men look out for ye. Ian has been smitten with ye since ye pecked him on the cheek for saving yer garden. Lachlan Gordon worried himself right into his sickbed when ye ran off with yer Evandale. Even old Lachlan knows that one's reputation."

"I had no idea." It was the first time Rosalind had heard a reference to that particular incident, although she recalled Lachlan had been ill when she returned home.

"Well, perhaps ye should consider all of the people who care about ye and depend on ye before ye try any more of yer schemes to leave Beaumont forever. Ye may scoff at yer woman's position, but ye hold life together for yer people. 'Twas obvious to me the first day I saw ye here, surrounded by folk who would willingly lay down their lives for ye."

Knowing in her heart he was right, she fingered her mother's pomander, gazing at it through tear-misted eyes.

Dimly, she felt him stroke her hair. She never felt so safe and protected as when Malcolm was at her side. How could she call him her enemy?

As he fingered a strand of her hair, Rosalind studied the strange carvings that covered the silver ball she always wore at her waist in memory of her mother. Beside the serpent, there were figures of a mother with her child, and a woman and man seated side by side on a throne of sorts. But there was a puzzling figure between these two images that Rosalind was never able to decipher.

Until this very moment.

She'd always recognized the symbol as some kind of bird due to its outstretched wings. Only now did she comprehend the rest of it. Jagged lines bracketed the strange bird's feet, which Rosalind realized depicted fire. The bird was a phoenix rising from the flames. Even more interesting, it had the voluptuously curved body of a human female. The winged creature that rose from the ashes of destruction was also the figure of a woman.

"It is a phoenix." For a moment, Rosalind had the overwhelming impression that the image was her own.

"What is?" His fingers halted in her hair.

She passed him the silver ball, pointing out the figure.

"Ye will rise from the ashes." He pointed to the final image on the ball—man and women seated next to each other. "And then this will be ye and I."

Rosalind wondered if he could still mean it, even after her missive to Lord Gareth.

"I would make ye my rightful lady."

"But you do not love me. Why wed me when you already have everything you wanted of me?"

His warm palm covered her cheek and stroked the length of her throat. "But I dinna have everything I want from ye, Rosalind Beaumont, not even close. We have both been betrayed before, so now that our eyes have been opened, we can give one another something more lasting and intense than foolish notions of love." His hand slipped around the back of her neck to draw her lips to his. His eyes held hers in thrall until he closed them at the very last moment. "Something far more pleasurable."

His mouth was on hers, gently prodding her lips apart with the insistent stroking of his tongue. When at last she gave in and parted them, she was rewarded with unspeakable sweetness that flooded every fiber of being. His mouth drank hungrily from hers until she thought she would swoon. As if sensing her reaction, Malcolm slid his other arm around her limp body and secured her against him.

"Malcolm." Rosalind was surprised to hear his name on her lips, and even more surprised to hear the breathless plea in her voice.

"Rosalind," he whispered reverently as his mouth left hers to caress the long column of her throat. The warmth of his palm covered her belly. "Let me have all of ye."

The heat he'd inspired in her two nights ago flamed faster, hotter this time, her body instantly recalling every decadent caress, every lush kiss. She twined her arms around him, heedless of logic and utterly unconcerned with love.

Aye, she was a wanton for this man. This good, honorable man. Mayhap their union would not be about love or logic, but about fire and passion. Surely there were marriages based on much less.

His fingers already unlacing her bodice, he placed kisses along her shoulder and in the hollow between her breasts. The warmth of his breath on her skin incited her to spear her fingers into his hair, to draw him closer. If the heathen smiled knowingly against her skin at her greedy movements, she did not care. Could not care. He had shown her too much pleasure, introduced her to delights she had never anticipated.

Her nipples tightened and thrust upward at his touch. Anticipating her need, he cupped one plump breast in his palm, his teeth nipping the taut peak gently before his tongue soothed the ache. A cry sighed forth from her lips as his hand crept below her hemline to find her calf and massage the muscle there. Working slowly, he took his time untying her garter and rolling down her stocking.

Her leg bared, he continued his journey up to her knee and over her thigh, pausing before reaching the juncture of her womanhood and caressing the curve of her bare hip.

Rosalind shuddered, needy for more. Had it only been two nights ago she'd lain in his arms for her first taste of passion? It seemed aeons since he'd touched her.

"Please." She did not know what she asked for, precisely, but she would gamble all of Beaumont that *he* knew.

"I will give ye everything ye ever wanted, lass." Plucking her off the bench, he seated her sideways on his lap, where she could feel the length of his hard arousal against her hip. "But first ye must promise to wed with me."

"You have resorted to seduction to win a bride?" She ran her hands over his chest, seeking a way to circumvent his tunic to feel his skin.

"I think I will resort to seduction frequently in this marriage." He traced his fingertips up her inner thigh, teasing her. Tempting her.

"You are a scoundrel and a knave." Finding the ties of his tunic in the middle of his muscular chest, she quickly undid them and slipped her fingers into the mat of dark hair she exposed.

"Ah, but I will be a married, well-satisfied knave."

Suppressing a smile, she leaned forward to brush her uncovered breasts against him, and a guttural groan escaped his lips. He lifted her up and carried her to the bed, depositing her on the soft feather mattress before she even realized they were moving.

He stood above her for a long moment, his blue eyes darkened to the color of midnight as he removed his tunic and raked her form with his unflinching gaze.

He was the most magnificent man she had ever seen. Tall and imposing, the muscular form that had once terrified her now filled her with aching need. His dark hair escaped its queue to fall against his shoulder.

Leaning over her, he peeled her surcoat and kirtle away. He stroked her all over with his hands—over her hips, down her thighs, back up her belly and breasts. His hands skimmed her so lightly that soon Rosalind trembled with hunger for more. She squirmed, waiting for the fulfillment his touch could bring.

"Ye like that, lass?" he asked, his husky whisper conveying that he already knew the answer.

She moaned, unable to think, let alone voice her thoughts.

"Would ye like more of my touch?"

"Far more. Much more." Desire snaked through her belly until she thought she would perish if he did not continue the exquisite torture.

He increased the pressure of his strokes, one hand moving to cradle her womanhood in his palm.

"Yes," she gasped with a ragged breath, his touch almost her undoing. The sweet fulfillment of his hands upon her sent fire through her veins.

Stretching out on the bed beside her, he steadied her chin so he could kiss her lips. Rosalind closed her eyes, losing herself in the wine-tinged flavor of his mouth, the velvety stroke of his tongue over hers. He nipped her lower lip, tugging it into his mouth before kissing his way lower. And lower still.

Her hands could not remain motionless against the

rippled strength of his muscles. She twitched beneath the play of his mouth over her hungry skin, the rising tension in her belly urging her on.

His mouth fastened on her nipple and drew on it gently before rolling it delicately between his teeth. The more he teased her breasts, the heavier they seemed. She arched her back in pleasure.

"Malcolm." She cried his name brokenly, the need for him so strong that all else faded away.

"Ye have but to ask." He lifted his head lazily, his eyes glittering.

She twisted and sighed beneath him, hardly knowing what she wanted, but unable to remain still. "I do not know, but I am so—"

He trailed his hand slowly over her body to settle on her belly. Her hip.

"Ye mean this?" He raised a questioning brow, his fingers already grazing the silken hair that shielded her most secret places.

Her hips rose off the bed of their own volition.

He slipped his finger into her cleft and stroked the length of her, imitating the motion with his tongue along the valley between her breasts. A deep heat took hold of her. She wriggled beneath him, remembering the incredible pleasure he could give her.

The fiery sensation spread all over her, but burned most hotly deep in her belly. Then his tongue flicked over her most sensitive flesh and she lost herself to the feelings that rocked her body. Coiling. Tightening.

The pleasure burst into full bloom, expanding in her womb until it seemed to flow through her whole being.

Sultry fulfillment pulsed within her until she almost sang with the joy of it.

When she had recovered in some small measure, she became aware of Malcolm's hands stroking her hips absently.

"Ye are the most passionate woman I have ever known." His wicked smile made heat rise in her cheeks to the roots of her hair.

But she could not stay embarrassed for long, when he rubbed his roughened cheek slowly against the smooth skin of her belly, causing a ripple of pleasure to trip down her spine. His eyes darkened again as he looked at her, his hands reaching up to trail lightly over her breasts.

To her surprise, the heat came rushing back, the hunger building all over again. What magic was this? She had found release but moments ago, and now…

Once again she wanted, she yearned, raking her fingers down his back to draw him closer.

When his arousal pressed against her thigh, she reached tentative fingers to touch him. A wondrous implement, this shaft of his. So very pleasing.

Stroking her fingers lightly around him, she gasped when he gripped her hand in a fierce hold.

"Nay. Ye are killing me, lass." He moved over top of her, his manhood pressing at the soft center of her.

"Do tell, my laird." She smiled to think she could incite the same pleasures in him that he could wield within her. "You have only to ask."

He pinned her arms above her head, imprisoning her. "Ye may regret such a hasty promise."

Somehow, she didn't think so.

She stilled beneath him, wanting him so much she could hardly catch her breath. Her fingers clenched around his, imprisoning him as much as he restrained her.

And then he drove into her completely.

The pressure grew, thick and hot and incredible. She eased her thighs apart, taking all of him, wanting more. He withdrew almost all the way from her body before plunging forward once again.

She could not help the little shout that escaped her. "It is wonderful," she gasped, reveling in the delicious sensation of his body within hers.

Malcolm gathered her close and held her to him. "Ye are mine, Rosalind."

In that moment she believed him.

"Aye." She wrapped her legs about his hips to bring him more fully into her, locking her ankles tight.

"Rosalind." He cried out her name as he crushed her to him, filling her with his seed in a rush of heat.

Immense satisfaction filled her, too. She knew she would second-guess this moment later, but right now she wanted nothing so much as to belong to Malcolm, to be protected and cared for by him. She covered his damp shoulder with kisses, wishing she could hold him all night long.

"Ye are a minx to unman me with yer words," he accused when he'd collected himself enough to speak. He rolled away from her and pulled her into the crook of his arm to rest her head upon his chest.

"I?" Rosalind asked, oblivious to his meaning.

"Aye. Ye brought me to a finish far too quickly with yer exclamation that 'twas wonderful. If ye had behaved yerself I could have given ye a longer bout of enjoyment and mayhap fulfilled ye all over again." He kissed the top of her head.

"Oh, I feel very fulfilled." She snuggled more deeply into his arms.

And indeed she did.

She'd never felt more wonderful in her entire life. For a brief moment she considered that this man was Malcolm McNair, the Scotsman who was taking everything she had, but then she recalled the feminine phoenix on her mother's pomander and was filled with an immense sense of power and well-being. She felt certain that the bird was a message for her, and that she, too, would rise from the ashes in triumph.

Unfortunately, she had no idea how she would wrangle such an achievement when she could not even find a way to wed for love *or* logic. She had only Malcolm's promise of pleasure, which, while it might be tempting in the present, did not address her fears for the future.

Praying she would find a way to seal a more secure fate, she drifted off to sleep, Malcolm's name a final sigh from her lips.

Chapter Fourteen

A haze of sunlight filtered through the bed curtains the next morning, soft and diffused. Dawn, Rosalind realized, as she stretched languidly next to the warrior knight who still shared her bed.

Malcolm looked peaceful in sleep, the fierce set of his features banished from his face. Even now, his arm curled possessively around her body. The night had passed in a delicious swirl of touches and kisses that sometimes led to gentle unions and other times hasty, hungry joinings that left her breathless. All night long they'd drawn each other close if they strayed too far apart.

Had she been foolish to allow Malcolm McNair into her bed? She feared the real danger had more to do with letting him into her heart. He'd claimed to want a marriage between them for pleasure's sake and not for love. Was that enough to bind them when she knew he intended to gain her keep?

The questions tormented her. She could not bear another disillusionment. And she had other fears to contend with. In the soft light of dawn a thought niggled at the edges of her mind, preventing her from returning to sleep.

The Beaumont fire.

There was something inherently wrong with feeling so content and happy this morn when her parents, her brother and the many tenants and servants who'd perished in the fire were not avenged. How could she be entitled to happiness until the score had been settled on their account?

She peered longingly at Malcolm's sleeping figure and ran her hand over his jaw. He would never have ordered such wanton destruction of life and property. He was not heartless enough, for one thing, and he was far too practical to allow a perfectly good keep to go up in flames.

Robert the Bruce, she was certain, had a ruthless side to his character, but he could not have ordered the torching, either, else he would not have chosen Beaumont for his border stronghold. It was taking Robert a great deal of time and money to fortify the devastated south tower. Time and money he probably would not have wasted on a worthless keep in poor condition.

But then who could have committed such an act?

Unwilling to lie there and be haunted by the past, Rosalind threw off the covers and left the bed, wincing at the soreness in her limbs.

The time for taking another chance with the Scots had arrived. If she ever hoped to avenge her family, she needed to know who had set the fire. And if anyone was in a position to take on the seemingly impossible task, it was the man who shared her bed.

She dressed in a fresh kirtle and surcoat, rinsing her teeth quickly and swiping a clean cloth over her face. Malcolm stirred as she finished.

"Ye are risen early, considering all the merry ye were making last night." He peered about the chamber, his gaze lingering on the bed curtains she'd already shoved aside. "Dinna tell me ye ride to Northfield today, lass. I dinna think ye've left me with enough strength to do battle for yer fair form again so soon."

Her cheeks heating at his teasing words, she settled herself at the foot of the bed, determined not to be distracted with all the myriad ways the knave had of diverting a woman.

"I've something to discuss with you." Now that she'd made up her mind to enlist his aid, she found she could scarcely wait another moment. "Something of grave import to me."

Nodding, he pulled himself from the bed, his fine masculine frame a sight from which she could not look away. He tugged on his braies and rinsed his own face and teeth before pouring a bit of wine from the decanter on the chest at the foot of her bed.

When at last he declared himself ready, Rosalind launched into her tale, dredging up the past and all her old hurts in the hope he could make some sense of the Beaumont fire that had claimed so much. Nearly an hour later, after making her relate the story twice in full-blown detail and then quizzing her on the incident, Malcolm shook his head as if to refute her words.

"Ye say there was no attack that night. No looting before the fire, no raiding afterward?" He lifted a heavy dark brow as if to confirm those facts.

Rosalind nodded.

"Nae even any sheep driven off?"

"No."

He paced the chamber, absently stroking his jaw, and Rosalind envisioned what he must look like before battle, plotting his strategy. His blue eyes were alight with his thoughts as he paced and muttered.

"Ye must figure out who yer father's enemies were, Rosalind. I can assure ye, the fire at Beaumont was no random attack by a rogue band of Scots, but a deliberate strike against yer family."

"I know you feel protective of your people, my lord, but I have lived in the borderlands long enough to know our people can commit violence against one another for seemingly no reason."

"Aye, but this is different. Robert the Bruce never sanctioned such a raid or else he wouldna have bid me to take Beaumont on his behalf, for he would have already held it. A crime like this doesna happen without a lot of tussle at the gates. Knights murdered at the perimeter. A cry going up from the gatehouse. A warning sounded." He ceased his restless stalking to pin her with a fixed gaze. "From what ye know of the usual border raids, what happens when the Scots come down here?"

"The sheep are stolen. Sometimes crops are burned, along with tenants' cottages."

"Aye. The Scots come down to steal yer sheep. That

way they ruin yer livelihood and further their own. They burn the crops to set ye back all the more. But how often do ye hear of a keep being set afire, with nothing stolen? Why would any self-respecting border Scot bother to commit such a cowardly act and have nothing to show for it?"

Rosalind shrugged her shoulders.

"He would nae," Malcolm boomed, his voice bouncing off the walls of the chambers. "There is no sense in it, lass. And we Scots are a practical folk. I tell ye, the crime doesna sound like something a Scotsman would do in the name of war, anyway, but when ye tell me that nothing was stolen, that seals it. There is no way a Scot would bother to bring down the wrath of England and the mighty sword of Edward Longshanks when there was nothing to be gained from the act."

"Mayhap the attackers thought that with the keep burned down, there would be no one left to tell the king of the crime."

"As if Edward wouldna notice one of his best border keeps missing. And who do ye think he would pin the blame on, without any question? The Scots. Ye see why that makes it a good crime for an enemy seeking vengeance? The attacker thought the Scots would be blamed, so he doesna have to worry about anyone pointing a finger in his direction."

She had to admit his reasoning made sense. "But I do not think my father had any enemies. Everyone respected him."

"What about within the keep's walls? He didna

have an envious younger brother? Any knights who resented his success on the battlefield?"

Rosalind shook her head. "You don't really think the blaze could have started from within the keep?"

"Ye said the men on the keep's walls that night made it out safely. Only those sleeping within the south tower were trapped." He settled on the foot of the bed beside her. "I am afraid ye must think who would have wanted yer father dead, lass. 'Tis the only reason I can see for such a horrible crime."

"I never thought…" Her words dried up, her mind muddled with the new light Malcolm had shed on the problem. The scenario made sense and yet she wanted nothing more than to reject it outright. "I find it impossible to believe anyone at Beaumont would do this."

Silence hung in the chamber, laden with unspoken thoughts.

"What?" She peered at Malcolm, who seemed to be waiting for her to draw some conclusion she could not fathom on her own. "You think you know who could have done something so heinous?"

"What of yer former love?"

"Gregory?" The notion didn't fit with her memory of him. Even knowing she'd been wrong about him before didn't make the pieces come together. "I realize he's a man rather lacking in honor, but that is because he has changed since our youth. He was not always such a reprobate."

"I thought ye said he was fond of cornering the kitchen maids when he thought ye were not around?"

"I thought that was because he was young." She could not credit Gregory with such wickedness. "Besides, winking at village girls does not make a man a ruthless killer. He may be a thoughtless knave, but I know he would never be so cruel as to take the life of the man who had fostered him."

"Even if that man stood between him and ye? Marriage to ye was his one sure path to lands of his own. Are ye so certain yer father planned to give yer hand to him?"

A cold chill whispered through her at the thought. "My parents had mentioned several possible unions for me." Fear gripped her, with anger following fast upon its heels. "Gregory was but one."

"What if yer father threatened to take ye away from Evandale?" Malcolm reached to refill his wine cup, his practical mind already ticking through all the reasons his theory could be true. "Evandale might have moved quickly to ensure yer father couldna act upon the threat. He thought to win ye over as his bride and ye would never be the wiser to yer father's disapproval. 'Twould explain how the fire was set from within and why no cry went up from the watch. By the time anyone noticed the blaze, it was already too late."

Horror pierced her heart as she considered this version. Somehow the cold cunning required by such an act chilled her even more deeply than her long-held belief that the Scots had set the flame.

"But how would I ever gather proof?" Much as she wanted vengeance for her parents' deaths, she would not risk accusing the wrong man. "I would not be satisfied that Gregory had committed such a terrible deed unless we could somehow prove it. If anyone had known of his involvement, they would have come forward by now."

"Maybe not, if they thought ye planned to wed the lout. Yer people could still be holding their tongues for fear of retribution by the man they thought would one day be their lord." Malcolm reached for her, turning her to face him. "But either way, 'tis nae yer worry. I can find the answers ye seek, Rosalind. I wield a mean blade, but my king would be quick to tell ye he values me more for my battle vision than my might. Thinking through impossible obstacles is what I do best."

Rosalind had never thrilled to his touch so much as she did at that moment. Much as she'd relished every sensual caress during the night they'd shared, none of them compared to the warm strength of his hand upon her cheek now, his persuasive assurance that he would stand by her side.

"I would be grateful for your help. I am sure you understand how heavily it has weighed on my heart."

"I canna imagine what a trial these last few years have been for you." He threaded his hands through her hair, cupping the back of her head so she peered up at him. "And then yer life was complicated further by a band of warmongering Scots. I can almost see why ye might have been tempted to raise yer blade against me that first day."

"I am sorry for that." She reached to touch his jaw, to smooth her fingers along the rough bristle there. "Truly, I am."

"If ye keep touching me like that, lass, I fear I may have to forgive ye." He pressed a kiss into her palm. "But I have much to do, now that ye've trusted me with this task. I will be busy much of the time until Michaelmas, but I promise to have news for ye then."

"So quickly?" She wondered how he would be able to find the answers that had eluded her for so long.

"Aye. If nae news of one kind, then I will have news of another." He rose to his feet, but did not elaborate. "Ye will have yer own hands full with the preparations for the feast day, I assume?"

"I will show you the way an English keep celebrates the saint." Smiling, she hoped she had at least gone a little way toward healing the rift between them. If there could be no love, there could at least be some measure of accord beyond pleasure. "You will not be disappointed."

"As long as I have ye to warm my bed that night, lass, I'm sure I willna." Leaving her chamber with a roguish wink, he abandoned her to her thoughts of a future that suddenly seemed full of more possibilities. Without the weight of her parents' deaths preying upon her, perhaps she could find some happiness for herself.

Even with Malcolm McNair.

She would consider marriage to him, or at least bide her time as his plans for the future revealed themselves. For now, she was content that he would assist her with the biggest responsibility she'd ever borne in all her days as lady of Beaumont. Ready to seize the new day with both hands, she prepared to leave the chamber and find Gerta to discuss the Michaelmas menu. But before she reached the door, the weight of her father's dagger reminded her of the need to make a new beginning. Removing the jeweled weapon from its sheath, she lay the blade upon the chest in her chamber.

There would be no need for arms in the peaceful days ahead.

Malcolm had failed miserably already in his duty to Rosalind.

Damning the attraction between them, he stormed through Beaumont's corridors, eager to leave behind the temptation its fair lady represented. How could he have neglected to discuss with her Robert's bestowing Beaumont upon him the previous day? Malcolm had been so angry with her thwarted letter writing that he'd forgotten the good news of his installation as the new lord. For that matter, he'd solidified no real plans for a marriage to Rosalind, which only proved to him what a poor excuse for a husband he would make.

Hellfire. He could plot battles and create strategies for luring fair Rosalind to his bed, but when it came to conversation, he admitted he was hardly a silver-tongued courtier. He usually left that to Jamie.

But in this case, discussing his marriage to Rosalind was not something he would permit his younger brother to do. Malcolm would settle the matter of his nuptials with her as soon as possible. As soon as he could wrest his mind away from thoughts of tasting her again.

Spotting Ian on the way to the stables, he outlined

his need to speak with the villeins whose domains rested closest to the keep. Ian and Jamie were in need of the extra work, both itching to be off to more challenging tasks than harvesting grain and training Beaumont's ill-equipped men-at-arms.

Perhaps, if Malcolm's study proved what he thought it might, his brothers could accompany him on a task of vengeance. If Evandale had aught to do with the blaze that night, Malcolm would discover anyone who'd aided the cause, and make sure they never brought such wicked harm to anyone else. But until then, he needed to focus on maintaining order at Beaumont and preparing for nuptials that must be celebrated as soon as possible after Michaelmas.

Assuming—curse his eyes—he found an opportunity to ask Rosalind to wed him. Mentioning it during their discussion of the Beaumont fire had not seemed like an appropriate time. And the night before…distractions had abounded as he'd slept beside her lush body, her sighs warming his skin, her curious fingers straying over him when she thought he slept.

No man could have found the wits to speak of priests and marriage ceremonies while a woman's thigh twitched invitingly against his own.

Now, saddling his horse to ride the perimeter of the keep and speak at length with the men who'd armed the gatehouse and the walls the night of the fire, Malcolm told himself that the Michaelmas feast would be as good a place as any to inform Rosalind of the happy news. She would be his forever, along with Beaumont.

* * *

Although the garden ranked as Rosalind's favorite place in summer, when the fresh blooms faded every autumn that distinction went to the herb-drying room. While the garden in bloom emanated fresh scents of new life and growth, the herbal room smelled of the fully ripened harvest, carefully preserved for various healthful concoctions to be used throughout the winter.

Of course, the small work chamber was not strictly for herbs. Rosalind took great pleasure in drying mountains of roses every year, too. The petals were beautiful even in their withered state. Their scent became more distinctive as they dried. She liked to fill small urns around the keep with the petals to freshen the stale air of winter indoors.

"A few more of the yellow blooms," Rosalind requested as she peered critically at a bunch of flowers she was preparing to string.

Deftly, the women wound lengths of string about the stems to ready bunches for hanging. The flowers would hang upside down for a few weeks or more, depending on the weather, to dry fully.

"So what did he say, Rosalind?" Gerta wheedled, her gnarled old fingers moving rapidly in defiance of their age.

"He is adamant that it could not have been a Scots raiding party."

"Och. He would say that. Who, pray tell, does he think did it then?"

"Someone seeking revenge. He pointed out how strange it was that there was no looting, no raiding, no driving off the sheep, and that no self-respecting Scotsman would commit such an act without some gain to show for his efforts."

"He has a point there. It is true that they usually come down here for reaving and thieving."

"What if he is right?" Rosalind turned to her friend, craving for answers that had long eluded her. "What does that mean for us?"

"It means you must let go your old fears and embrace that big ox of a Scot. You should let my lord Malcolm demonstrate the wrath of Beaumont."

Rosalind laughed in spite of herself. "I bet McNair knows how to serve that kind of justice. But he is not mine."

"So you would like me to think."

"He is not. Malcolm and I have found a certain understanding, but not the kind that is most important for a lasting union." She recalled that he had made no more mention of a marriage between them, even though they now had a much higher risk of breeding after all the times they'd been together the night before. "I am not sure we are even fond of each other."

"The greatest romances never start out with *fondness*." Gerta winked knowingly.

"Gerta!" Rosalind's cheeks heated, though she wondered if passion could ever turn to love.

"I am only trying to tell you not to be so hasty in your judgment. He is a good man if you care to look beyond that fact that he took Beaumont from you."

"It is much to overlook, I am afraid. And just how do you come by your great knowledge of our heathen lord?"

"By using my eyes and my ears, my lady, and not letting my good sense be clouded by old notions as, begging your pardon, yours sometimes has been."

Rosalind was about to defend herself, but Gerta thrust a new batch of fresh flowers at her and held up her hand.

"Every man who follows Malcolm McNair has a tale to share about him. He has personally saved the lives of more than half of them, has rescued various mamas and sisters from ruffian bandits, has fed and sheltered several who came to him when forced out of their homes by the English…. And these are not all noblemen, whom he would have been honor bound to take into his home. Many who knocked on his door half-starved were farmers, and still he took them in, even training the young sons to be warriors so they might raise themselves up in the world."

"You make him sound like a saint." Rosalind was surprised Gerta had made such an effort to learn about the new lord. Did she show more sense than her mistress by asking Malcolm's followers about him? Nay, as lady of the keep, Rosalind was in no position to make such inquiries.

"Hardly. You know all too well he is a hard man, but he seems to have a noble heart." Gerta paused thoughtfully. "You have no idea what it was like here when you took off with Gregory that day. Did you know Gregory killed one of Malcolm's watchmen? I feared McNair's vengeance when he found ye."

Rosalind continued tying the herbs in silence, imagining Malcolm's fury when she'd left. And yet he had granted Gregory mercy when she'd asked. Mercy that might have been sorely misplaced if he'd had anything to do with the fire.

"I hope you have no plan to run off to Lord Evandale again. I do not think he is the man you believe him to be."

"I learned exactly the type of man Gregory is when I escaped last time, and I have no intention of ever getting near him again."

"Thank goodness. We always thought he was a snake."

"We?"

"The servants, the tenants…you know. Evandale might have been gentle with you, my lady, but he could be short of temper with the rest of us."

"Do you think he could have had anything to do with the fire?" She dropped her flowers on the drying table, half fearing the answer.

But Gerta looked genuinely taken aback. "I never suspected him. But perhaps if he had any reason to think he would not be able to wed you…"

The older woman's voice trailed off and Rosalind wasn't sure she wished to ask any more questions. She'd learned more than enough to turn her world on its ear today.

Chapter Fifteen

The next evening, Malcolm made his way to Rosalind's chamber. He had missed the meal, had missed *her,* in his effort to discover the answers she sought. All day he had asked questions of the villeins. All evening he had spent closeted with members of the household staff and the men-at-arms who'd watched the gates that fateful night. He'd unraveled her past, discovered more secrets about the people of Beaumont than he cared to know, but at last he'd reconstructed a plausible theory for what had happened and who'd been responsible.

No real surprises there, devil take Evandale. But Malcolm had been surprised to learn some of Evandale's other secrets, including his humble birth, which he'd hidden from Rosalind's father, and his dalliance with the cheeky serving maid who had spoken coarsely to Rosalind.

Devil take them *all* for hurting her.

Slowing his steps outside her chamber door as the

midnight hour was tolled by the chapel bell, Malcolm hesitated. Should he wake her for the selfish pleasure of touching her? Tasting her? Assuring himself she was still safely within the walls? Still safely his?

Or should he give her a few more hours of peace before he confronted her with more news that could damn well devastate her? She deserved to know the truth. Needed to know the truth. And yet the facts of Evandale's long deceptions would hurt her. How much, Malcolm was almost afraid to discover. She'd begged for him to show the man mercy, proving she must have some strength of feeling for the knave yet. Would this latest news stamp out that idealistic yearning for love she embraced with the fanciful longing of a girl? Truth be told, that openness about her, the desire for marriage with a happy ending, appealed to something in him, the part of him that remembered his parents' marriage. Even if he could not give her the trust she longed for, he vowed to make it up to her with peace and pleasure, two commodities he would shower her with for the rest of her days.

Unwilling to wait to see her, he opened her door. Her maid gave a start on the small pallet on the floor, but Rosalind slept on in her bed. He excused the maid, passing her a coin for being inconvenienced.

Once they were alone, Malcolm tugged aside the privacy curtains and stoked the hearth fire enough that he might see Rosalind more clearly. She clenched her pillow with both hands as she slept, hugging the silk to her breast.

Satisfied with the leaping blaze in the grate, he

struggled to keep a lid on the heat building within him. No easy task when just looking at her enflamed him. Edging closer to her bower, he peered down at her as she slept, her night rail a thin veil of well-worn linen cupping her shoulders loosely. If he could but pry the pillow away from her, he might be able to untie the laces and indulge his view.

Madness. Selfishness.

And yet he could think of nothing else but burying himself inside her. Holding her. Damn it, he wanted to be holding her when he told her the truth about the fire.

Or was he simply justifying what he wanted for himself?

Stalking away from the woman wrapped in rose-scented linens, he cursed this growing fascination with her that hadn't been eased one bit by taking her to his bed. If anything, he'd only become more enthralled, the need for her so great she seemed to be a powerful drug in his bloodstream, always present and frighteningly potent.

Arriving at one of the chests that she kept by the fireplace, he discovered a gown folded neatly atop her other garments. Silken hose and garters. A white kirtle. A heavy velvet surcoat. Unable to resist, he lifted the kirtle to his nose, indulging himself in the scent of her. Roses and other flowers, a sweet testament to her fondness for all green and growing things. He slid his finger over one of the silken hose, envisioning exactly what it would feel like if her leg were inside the fabric.

A loud snap and hiss from the fire called him from

his thoughts, made him remember that both Rosalind and her flawless legs were tucked neatly between the sheets an arm's length away.

He only had to claim the lass to touch her.

"Malcolm." Her whisper in the darkness surprised him.

"Aye?" He replaced her garments on the chest to return to her side. "I am here, lass."

But as he stood at the bedside, he realized she'd spoken his name in her sleep. She still hugged her pillow, her eyes closed as she slumbered on, each breath smooth and even.

"Ach." Removing his hauberk, he knelt beside the mattress, speaking softly to her. "If ye are thinking of me in yer sleep, surely it doesna do any harm for me to join ye there in yer dream."

She did not move as he pried the pillow from her grip, her arms slumping onto the coverlet. Her hair spilled all around her like a sunny halo, the pale tresses covering the pillow and sheets. Brushing aside the locks, Malcolm exposed one shoulder to his gaze. Her skin awaited his touch, creamy and soft, yet he would not rush this slow awakening.

Finding the laces of her night rail, he tugged on first one end and then the other until the ribbon slid wide, opening her garment. One breast spilled into view, the rosy peak already taut. But he had to nudge the remaining fabric aside to see her other breast, the plump mound rising and falling with each soft breath she took.

So fair.

He bent closer, overcome by the need to brush a kiss across first one and then the other. She tasted warm and fragrant, the heat from his mouth releasing more of the floral scent her clothes had held. He cupped the weight of her breasts in his palms, his thumbs lightly skimming the tight crests.

She moaned in her sleep, and Malcolm had all he could do not to slide between the covers and awaken her with her thighs splayed, himself deeply buried within.

Patience. He was no lad with his first woman. He could wait. Draw out the pleasure. Prove to Rosalind they had something substantial upon which to build a marriage.

Stripping away his tunic, he bent over her, nipping at her breasts, rolling the peaks between his thumbs and forefingers. He applied only the lightest of pressure, but it was enough to make her lids flutter open. Her gray eyes went wide at the sight of him there.

"I couldna stay away, lass." He skimmed his hand down her belly, easing her night rail farther down her body as he found the curve of her hip, the lean strength of her thigh.

"I was just dreaming of this," she whispered back, her body covered in a light sheen of warmth. "Wanting you has been plaguing me most fiercely."

Malcolm marveled that she would admit as much. But she seemed warm and receptive, her hips shifting as he slid his hand between her thighs.

"Tell me of this plague upon ye." He cupped her mound, rotating the heel of his hand against the soft down of her womanhood. "I wouldna wish ye to suffer."

She cried out, her arms looping around his neck to drag him closer.

"There is an ache," she confessed in his ear, her teeth nipping his lobe between words. "A keen pang of emptiness that you alone can fill."

Desire blasted through him, her words spiking the fire inside him. He rubbed her cleft, his finger sliding easily in the damp warmth he found there.

"I would know the place of this ache, lass, if ye want my help." He stretched out alongside her beneath the covers, his hard strength finding naught but feminine softness. She seemed to melt all around him, over him. "This pain you speak of, is it here?"

He eased a finger deep inside her, calling forth a squeal of pleasure from her, and her nails raked his shoulders as she clung to him. Her hips rolled with the movement of his hand, prolonging the sensation.

"Please, Malcolm." She kissed his jaw and his neck, her lips fastening on his to swirl her tongue sweetly about his mouth. "I am in great need."

He didn't think her hunger could be any greater than his at the moment. His blood pounded through his head like a hammer, his whole body stiff and unyielding with wanting her.

He rolled her on top of him, so that she might show him exactly what she desired. If he was to bring her pleasure for a lifetime, he would know her every secret longing and uncover her most sensual of wishes.

But right now, he could not trust himself to do either unless she was on top and in some control. Positioning her above his rigid length, he entered her with a sharp thrust of his hips. She threw her head back with a cry, while the rest of her remained perfectly still.

He half feared he had hurt her, and lifted his hands to her chin so that he might better gauge her expression. But then she began to move—slowly, achingly. She lifted herself off of him and then took her sweet time to ease back down his staff.

He might have swallowed his own tongue at her brazen assault if she had not chosen that moment to kiss him, then draw his tongue into her mouth.

And he'd started this torment? Sweet heaven, the lass would drive him over the edge in moments if he did not put an end to this.

"I think I am developing an ache of my own," he muttered, flipping her to her back, where he could keep her still for a few moments. "Ye want me to show ye where?"

He withdrew from her partway, just enough to catch his breath. But she thrust her hips upward, taking all of him and scrambling his thoughts to gibberish.

"I think I know where, my lord." She stretched beneath him, extending her arms over her head to lift her breasts close to his mouth. "I am happy to help, if you'll let me."

Catching one pink nipple in his mouth, he drew on her, savoring the taste as he pinned her beneath him. Finding a rhythm that pleased them both, he listened to each soft whimper, noted every flex of her fingers on his skin as he took her higher. Soon he knew exactly which caresses pleased her most, which spot on her neck made her squeal with delight and which one made her constrict her legs about his hips.

He went to that hollow now and stroked his tongue along that stretch of sensitive skin, his hips picking up their pace as she squeezed him. Locked him against her. Ignoring the pressure from her thighs, he listened only to her ragged breaths, caught up in the sound of her passion.

When at last she moaned in release, he allowed himself to find his own. His blood surged powerfully, the force of it making him dizzy. He clung to her, holding her to him, needing the reassurance of her steady heartbeat while he recovered. As his own heart finally slowed, he twined his fingers through her hair, stroking the silken strands.

He knew he needed to talk to her, to discuss so much that he had not been able to share. Robert's gift of Beaumont into Malcolm's care. Malcolm's desire to plan their wedding. His findings about the fire.

No question, he should have found a way to discuss at least the former topics with her before now. But he had grown overly cautious the last few years, unwilling to share any part of himself with a woman who might use it against him. Rosalind was not that woman, he knew.

"You are deep in thought?" she asked from her place beside him, breathing warmly on his chest.

Every fiber of his being urged him to set their wedding date, to solidify their union and claim Beaumont together. But before he could speak the right words, he found himself asking her something else entirely.

"Ye never mentioned where ye learned to wield a crossbow." So much for good intentions. What woman wished to discuss her skill with a bow while lying naked against her lover?

If he'd offended her, however, she did nothing to show it. She traced idle patterns on his chest. "The topic never came up."

"'Tis very heavy for a woman to lift, let alone aim and fire." He'd been too surprised by her arrival on the parapets that day to consider how she'd managed such a feat.

"I have great strength when the need arises."

"Ye didna have all that much strength when ye stabbed me that day, however. Ye barely nicked the skin."

"You were bleeding all over the hall." She lifted her head to peer up at him in the firelight. "I do not think the stains have come out of the floor to this day."

"Ach. Dinna tell my brothers lest I never live down the dishonor of being bested by a lass."

Rosalind propped herself on her elbow, the linens barely skimming the tops of her breasts. "Your warrior brothers seem eager for more adventures than Beaumont has to offer. Do you think you will stay through the winter, or will you all be off on another campaign before then?"

Guilt chewed his conscience for not having told her of his king's dictate that Beaumont would belong to him. The time had come to share his plans.

"Jamie and Ian will leave shortly." After Malcolm's marriage. "For my part, I plan to remain here, since my king has seen fit to give Beaumont to me."

He wondered if the news settled as awkwardly upon her ears as he feared. He hadn't really considered how to deliver the tidings in a way that wouldn't upset her, since he'd never needed to factor a woman's wishes into his own plans before.

"Your king left two days ago." Rosalind drew the covers more tightly to her chest, her gaze narrowing. "Yet you have only just *now* decided to disclose your ownership of my keep?"

"I only discovered his plans just before he left, and then, if ye recall, I was distracted with the news ye were arranging a marriage to a withered old man." Malcolm sensed a cold draft circulating through the chamber that hadn't been there a few moments ago.

She levered herself up to her knees, keeping the coverlet firmly tucked around her. "But wouldn't you agree that we have had plenty of moments of accord between us since then when you might have mentioned your new position as my overlord?" Massaging her temple, she closed her eyes, shaking her head impatiently. "For that matter, did you learn anything else of my position here that you have not shared? Am I to be banished? Married off to one of his knights as a battle prize?"

It hardly struck him as an auspicious way to propose marriage, but there could be no helping the timing.

"The Bruce gave his blessing for us to wed."

"He has ordered you to marry me?" Her words sounded a bit strangled. She blinked slowly, the rest of her body going absolutely still.

"Nay. I sought his permission for all the reasons I have told you before." Hellfire. Hadn't he already suggested a union between them not once, but twice? "I canna fathom why ye would be surprised."

"The reasons you gave me before were…let me see if I can remember." She tilted her gaze heavenward as if struggling to capture her thoughts. "Pleasure and…I do not think you ever gave me another reason."

"I told ye yer people would appreciate having their lady in their midst." He reached for his garments, his skin chilled from the frost growing thicker by the moment. The fire in the grate had faded to little more than embers, the taper by her bed casting the only remaining light in her chamber. "And more importantly, I told ye we would wed to legitimize any issue from the nights we've lain together. I would think that would be more than enough reason."

Lacing his braies haphazardly, he fumed at the need to argue over something that should be so simple. Clear-cut. He knew Rosalind was a more honorable woman than his Isabel had been, but he had not forgotten the pain that noble lady had caused him at her defection. And seeing the hurt Ian had gone through at the loss of his wife only reinforced Malcolm's decision to base his marriage on passion and respect instead of something as fickle and potentially painful as love.

Plucking up her pillow, she hugged it to herself once again, the way she had when he'd first gazed upon her that night. Only now, instead of engaging in sensual dreams, she looked ready to strangle the very life out of the feathers.

"How foolish of me to forget the need to legitimize our *issue*." She lingered over the word as if it were distasteful to her tongue. "Forgive me for wanting…"

He shrugged his tunic over his shoulders, waiting for her to finish. The anguished expression on her face gave him pause. "For wanting what?"

She tipped her head to the pillow she clutched, hiding her face from him for a long moment. What did she want? To his way of thinking she had won far more by his arrival than she'd lost. Discovering Gregory Evandale was a treacherous lout had saved her from a lifetime of heartache.

Although, now that he considered it, he was certain this would not be the right time to discuss his conviction that Evandale had set the fire. Malcolm would not wish any more upheaval for Rosalind than he'd already brought her this night.

"Nothing." Lifting her head from the pillow, she tilted her chin, met his gaze. "I do not expect anything more from you, Malcolm. Instead, I'm sure I should be grateful you have not dismissed me from my lands altogether."

"I would never turn ye away." He reached for her hand, to cover it with his own, but she tucked it deeper under the linens before he had the chance.

"Do you have a date in mind to celebrate the nuptials?" She stared up at him politely but coolly, as if she were determined to hear the details even though she didn't give a damn about marrying him.

But in this matter, he would not waver.

"After Michaelmas." He adjusted the blade at his hip and wondered idly where the dagger that she used to be so fond of carrying had gone.

"Two weeks after? Two months after? I would prefer to know so that I might ready myself." Her gray eyes grew all the more steely.

"I thought two days after might be more appropriate. My brothers can witness the marriage and then be on their way home before the cold weather sets in."

"Two days?"

"Aye." The sooner they spoke their vows, the easier he would rest. If Evandale reappeared to make any claim against Beaumont, Malcolm wanted the sanctity of the Church's blessing already binding him to Rosalind.

"Very well then." She straightened in her seat on the bed, her bearing as regal as a queen's despite the wanton garb of a linen sheet. "If you will excuse me, a wedding will require a fair amount of preparation."

"I appreciate ye being so practical about this." Seeing no way to soothe her angry pride, Malcolm gave a quick bow and pivoted on his heel.

He would not cater to her temper. But perhaps once they were wed, they would find more grounds for mutual understanding.

Still, he hoped the nagging sense of regret in his gut went away by the time they wed, since some small part of him acknowledged she'd deserved to know her fate sooner. Perhaps tomorrow, at the Michaelmas feast, he would find a way to make peace with her. Speaking to her about the fire and making plans for their future together would be a practical use of time, a way to assure her she would still be a vital part of life at Beaumont.

The plan soothed him, helping him ignore his real fear that she had already become a vital part of *him*.

So it had not been the marriage proposition of her dreams. Rosalind had developed a practical side, as Malcolm so helpfully pointed out. That sensible facet of her more mature self could surely understand the benefits of wedding Beaumont's new lord.

The new laird.

She would be a Scotsman's bride, no real hardship if she could convince herself Malcolm was right in his suggestion that his people had naught to do with the Beaumont fire. Still, even if her practical self calmly overlooked her traitorous allegiance to a Scot, she could not help but remember she had not made the choice to wed Malcolm McNair.

A foolish concern. A trivial matter.

Yet it nagged her relentlessly as she lay in her bed, cold and alone now that Malcolm had left her side. Would it always be thus? Would they meet for occasional heated trysts that left her breathless, only to part company afterward for separate chambers? The practice was common enough, but it would slowly eat away at the tender regard she already felt for him. With gentle nurturing, that caring might have turned into something more. Something like love.

But with Malcolm's commanding ways and assurance that his choices alone were the right ones... Rosalind feared that fondness would wither into resentment. Even the physical pleasure he touted as so important to their union would not escape that kind of slow deterioration.

Settling deeper into the feather ticking of her mattress, Rosalind prayed she might find some sort of peace with Malcolm. Ever since her family had perished in the fire, she'd known her only chance to experience affection again would be through her marriage. Her heart stung sorely at the thought of relinquishing that dream now.

After longing for the safe haven of wedded union these past three years, she would finally be granted her wish, it seemed. And while she would be grateful to align herself with an honorable man, she could not help but mourn the loss of any chance for love.

Chapter Sixteen

By late afternoon, preparations for the feast of the archangel Michael were in full swing. Extra cook fires and spits had been set up beyond the kitchens to handle the overload of food preparation. The scent of ginger permeated the keep and wafted over the lawns. The meal would be taken outside in the courtyard, as the weather was still fine for late September, though crisp and cold.

Rosalind tended to all of her regular duties, failing to find the usual pleasure in them. She was bedeviled still by Malcolm's abrupt announcement of their nuptials and her own foolishness in thinking she could ever sway a man who had been very forthright with her about his expectations in a marriage.

She positioned small urns of Michaelmas daisies on each trestle table in the courtyard and told herself it didn't matter. What difference did it make that her feelings had begun to change? Clearly, Malcolm's had not.

"Oh." Rosalind stepped back as water splashed on her surcoat from an urn she set too roughly upon the table. In her frustration, she was slamming things about with as much delicacy as a drunken serving maid.

It was time to bathe and dress for the feast regardless, though she worried about the upcoming meal and the time she would spend seated next to her future husband. But, mindful of her duty and her people's expectations of her, she trudged up the hill to the keep and made her way to her chamber for a long, hot soak.

Only when she stepped from the tub and began to dry herself did she spy the new gown draped over her bed. She had ordered it in the spring for this very occasion, but had somehow forgotten about it.

The kirtle was a delicate shade of rose, and fashioned of the softest linen. The neck was round and low, exposing the tops of her breasts. The surcoat was a deeper shade of berry, with a neckline that matched the kirtle, rising within an inch of the other bodice so that the soft pink showed through at the neckline, down the sides and at the sleeves. Heavily embroidered with tiny pearls and small garnets, the velvet surcoat seemed ideal for a cool fall night.

Acknowledging her sin of vanity, Rosalind had to admit the dress revived her a bit. With her toilette complete and the exquisite new garb in place, she approached the looking glass secured safely above one of her chests. She saw the features of her mother for a moment in the mirror before her own became clear. As she gazed at her reflection, it occurred to her that the girl who'd ordered the rose gown four months ago had vanished. She was a different person now. A woman who had weathered much upheaval.

Still thinking of her mother, Rosalind hung the small pomander from its chain at her hips, along with her eating knife and two important keys to the keep.

The image was complete. As full of sorrow as the day had been, she felt powerful, strong, ready for battle. Surely she would not let Malcolm McNair and his staunch practicality get the best of her. He might not wed her for love, but who was to say he might not find those more tender emotions once they had more time to know one another? She turned from the glass and descended the stairs to join her tenants for her favorite feast, already contemplating ways to reach the more gentle side of the mighty McNair.

"Holy Queen of Heaven." As she made her way down the steps, a masculine voice drifted up from the great hall, pulling her from her reverie. Ian McNair stood at the base of the stairway, clutching his heart in mock astonishment.

"Are you surprised I invited all my Scots invaders to celebrate the saint's day with us?" She smiled in spite of herself, having long ago decided the rowdy McNair men would not make such bad brothers.

At least, Ian and Jamie would be passable siblings by marriage. She'd already come to think of Malcolm in a far different way.

"'Tis nae more than I would expect of yer gracious self, lass. It is just ye quite stole my breath. Ye are such a fey creature, Lady Rosalind, and not o' this world for certain."

"You will charm the women of Beaumont with your

gallant words." She had not seen Ian so amiable before and she wondered if he would soon be ready to think about finding another wife after the heartache of his first marriage.

"Aye, but not ye, I'll warrant." He offered her his arm and she allowed herself to be swept through the hall and out the front entryway. The sight that greeted their eyes lifted her spirits more.

All the candelabram were lit on the tables below them, the tiny points of light seeming to ward off the chill, even though it had cooled enough now that she could almost see her breath in the crisp air. In a few more weeks the snows would fall and bring quiet months of solitude to the keep, but for tonight, they would feast heartily and celebrate the turn of the year.

"Rosalind." Malcolm's deep voice rumbled in the shadows, tripping over her senses like the Scotch mead he had once shared with her. Garbed in shades of night, he cut an imposing figure as he stepped from the shadows. "My God, ye look beautiful."

He raked her from head to toe with his eyes and she felt her insides soften with the pull of desire.

Hope curled through her anew at the idea of a future together. Surely she could touch his heart the way he had already touched hers. She knew in that moment that she truly loved Malcolm. Perhaps had known it ever since he'd plucked her from Gregory's oppressive grip that day she'd run off with him like the reckless soul she'd once been.

"Thank you." She could not seem to take her eyes from him now that she'd acknowledged the truth.

"Ye come with me." He extracted her from Ian, giving his brother a black look. Then Malcolm wrapped his arm firmly around her and guided her to their table.

Their guests scurried to find places at the tables while Malcolm seated Rosalind. He lifted his drinking horn to address the company.

"Our king has departed, my friends, and ye have made a wonderful impression on him. He canna wait to return to Beaumont to visit its gracious folk, and truth be told, to enjoy the bountiful hunting.

"Whilst he was here," he continued, "I asked for his permission to wed yer lady." There was a collective intake of breath. "And now I ask ye for yers. Will ye grant me yer blessing to wed with yer lovely lady of Beaumont?" He drew Rosalind up to stand by his side, and her body followed the command of his hands as it had so many times before.

She had not expected him to do this now. Here. And in such a public forum. But it made sense. If some small facet of her mourned that he did not consult her first, or at least apprise her of his plans, she squelched the thought in the interest of compromise.

She could make this marriage work.

Rosalind smiled at Malcolm and then all the people of Beaumont, while the crowd roared in approval. She glimpsed Lachlan Gordon twirling Gerta round and round like a doll, then kissing her soundly. Others clapped and called out their good wishes.

Malcolm gestured for silence and raised his cup once again. "Then I toast ye, good people of Beaumont. Thank ye for yer goodwill, for my bride and for yer hard work. To yer health, yer good fortune, and to a merry night for us all."

His drink disappeared in one gulp, and Malcolm commanded the start of the meal.

"I think the news of our nuptials was well received." Determined to simply enjoy the feast and the time together, Rosalind sampled the goose that was a Michaelmas tradition. The scents of ginger and other spices in the air had brought an unexpected wave of nostalgia for feast days she'd once celebrated with her family. She seemed to miss them most keenly at times like this, when their presence loomed so near.

"Everyone looks well pleased." Malcolm lowered his voice for her ears alone. "Except perhaps for ye."

"I am only thinking how much I wish my parents could have been here to see me wed."

His hand closed over hers. "I expect they will be here in spirit. No father misses his daughter's day to speak her vows."

Touched by the simple comfort, Rosalind peered up at him gratefully just as Deirdre, the dairymaid, stumbled across the dais, a heavy serving pitcher in her hand.

"Careful." Rosalind hastened from her bench to aid the gangly girl, helping her set the pitcher on the table. Confused as to why Deirdre would be struggling with a server's tools, anyway, Rosalind peered about the trestles in search of her usual server. "Serving the high table is not your chore, Deirdre. Where is Moira?"

She hoped the two women had not been arguing again.

Deirdre's gaze skittered to Malcolm and he rose to his feet.

"Moira has left Beaumont and she willna return." He waved Deirdre away and reached for Rosalind's arm. "Perhaps we can speak privately?"

Confused, she wanted to protest Deirdre's defection to ask the girl more questions, but Malcolm's strong arm guided Rosalind to the shadowed fringes of the feast.

"I don't understand." Nervous tension caused her heart to pick up speed, the hairs at the back of her neck tingling eerily. "Where would she go? No one simply departs from their family and the lands they were born to unless…" she peered warily up at Malcolm's face "…she had no choice?"

"I've been meaning to speak to ye—"

"*You* did this?" Frustration burned away all Rosalind's good intentions. She'd wanted so desperately to give their marriage a fair chance, but how could she when Malcolm refused to discuss even the most basic of concerns with her? "She is a member of *my* household. She is not a knight, nor a man-at-arms, nor any strong-armed vassal who will plow your fields for you. Am I to have no say over my own kitchen maids now?"

He tugged her even deeper into the shadows, although her raised voice would surely not be heard in the general mayhem of feasting and conversation in the courtyard.

"She knew who set fire to Beaumont, Rosalind."

His words called an abrupt end to her outrage. Fear took its place, as she contemplated the weight of his statement.

"You've uncovered the mystery behind the blaze? You've been about the task for naught but a couple of days, and you know this already?" She should have searched for answers long ago, but she'd been so certain she knew the truth.

God, she'd been so naive.

"I didna wish to spoil yer feast day, but Moira admitted to a...a liaison with Evandale." Malcolm gripped Rosalind's shoulders, his warm touch permeating the heavy velvet of her new gown. "Between what she told me of his activities before the fire and the stories of other folk about the keep, it became apparent yer father's squire was behind the foul deed."

Even having prepared herself for news of Gregory's ultimate betrayal had not readied her for the devastating grief—nay, anger—that roiled in her belly. The lies Gregory had heaped upon her while he pretended to lament her family's deaths came back to her with stinging clarity.

"You're certain of this?" She could not fathom how Malcolm had possibly had enough time to be sure.

"Aye." He rubbed his hands lightly down her arms. "I spent all yesterday speaking with every member of yer household and all the villeins who reside close enough to the keep to take note of unusual goings-on. Evandale had...a meeting of sorts with Moira outside the south tower earlier that night. By all accounts, he remained out of doors even after she sought her bed."

"That places him near where the blaze started, but it hardly proves he set the fire." Something else niggled at her about Malcolm's explanation, too, but she couldn't quite put her finger on it.

"But it seems Moira had long told her peers that she would be running the keep one day—nae as the lady, but as the most important member of the household." Malcolm shooed away a stray cat that rubbed up against their ankles, his boot gently edging the creature aside. "She boasted of this long before the fire, before ye made any promise to wed Evandale, and some of yer father's older knights told me yer sire had some doubts about Evandale's trustworthiness."

"But then why did they not confide in me when they saw me begin to trust Gregory?" She would have welcomed insights from her father's men. She may have been young, but she had not been so foolish that she would have ignored their words. "Why allow me to throw myself into the arms of a..." she gulped, the words drying up in her throat "...a killer?"

The sentiment whispered from her lips as she scooped up the mangy kitten to offer the scraggly beast some small comfort. And perhaps to receive a bit for herself, as well. The night breeze seemed far colder since they'd walked away from the festivities.

"'Tis a dangerous thing to go against a nobleman, lass, and once yer father had died, they considered themselves bound to bide their time and follow young Evandale if he secured permission to wed ye from the king." Malcolm stroked a knuckle across the dark animal's head. "And they had no proof that Evandale had set the fire. Everyone seemed willing to believe it was more handiwork of the Scots, even though there wasna any proof and yer gates had never been breached."

"They have never been strategists, as you are, my lord." She recognized that Malcolm's battlefield wisdom had probably given him a different insight on the incident than anyone at Beaumont could have offered. The people who'd lived through the horror of that night had not brought cold reason to the matter, but a wide range of passions and their own personal losses. "We recovered as best we could."

"I am only sorry ye have to grapple with the matter again after it has already hurt ye so much in the past."

"But I deserved to know the truth." Setting the kitten back on its feet, she relinquished its comfort. She understood now what had bothered her about Malcolm's explanation earlier. She'd been too busy absorbing the facts of the fire to fully appreciate the other bit of news he'd imparted. "I wish you would have shared your findings with me as soon as you had learned of all this."

"I weighed the idea, Rosalind, but I couldna stand the thought of this miserable bastard Evandale hurting ye again."

She might have softened if he'd seemed the least bit sorry for shutting her out, but if anything, he only looked more resolute as his jaw flexed, his mouth set in a grim line.

"But you knew I craved answers after being in the dark for so long." She'd asked for his help, curse his arrogant hide, not his autocratic control over the whole matter. "And since you obviously knew much of the truth by the time you visited my chamber last night, I can't help but wonder if you were more concerned with taking your own pleasure than sparing my feelings."

"That's damn well not fair, and ye know it." He glared down at her in the moonlight, his blue eyes taking on a frosty glint.

"Nor was it fair to withhold information from me that you knew I desperately sought. But perhaps you thought I couldn't handle the truth." Straightening, she knew she would find no comfort from Malcolm this night. "I have agreed to marry you even though you have assured me there is no hope of love between us. But I cannot go through with a marriage where there is also no trust."

Pivoting on her feet, she left him to his logic and reason, her emotions swelling too high and dangerous within her to be shared with a heathen Scot, who would only hold them against her later. Thankfully, she still had her retreat. One place where she could be herself without fear of censure.

Leaving the feasting to her people, she sought the sanctuary of her garden. Hurrying through the darkness to the back of the keep, she stumbled onto the grassy area where cobblestones faded into lush lawns. Perhaps a few moments alone would help her collect herself. She'd been so certain she could suppress her needs and give her marriage a chance, but what if she'd overestimated herself? It might not be so difficult to swallow her pride and stifle the cries of her heart if she did not already love the resolute Scot who seemed to think he knew what was best for her.

And truly, maybe he had known better than her about many things when he'd first arrived and she'd still been blindly hoping for Gregory's return. But hadn't she proven a willingness to make sensible decisions since then? He'd known how much her family's deaths had devastated her.

Voices from the Michaelmas feast faded as she arrived at the entrance to the walled plot. Welcoming the quiet, she tugged at the gate, which squeaked in protest.

Before she could take refuge, a blow struck the back of her head with a force that sent her staggering to her knees. Rosalind tried to cry out, but before she could make a sound, a damp palm covered her mouth. She sank senselessly into a man's waiting arms as the dark night turned blacker still.

Chapter Seventeen

Malcolm refused to follow in an angry woman's footsteps. Rosalind could have been born a Highland lass with that temper of hers.

Or so he told himself for the first hour after she'd departed. But as time stretched interminably without her, he brooded at the fringes of the Michaelmas feast, wondering if perhaps she had fair reason to be frustrated. Now, scowling at a dismal jongleur, who sang of lost loves for the entertainment of a bunch of dreamy-eyed females, Malcolm acknowledged that had his position been reversed with Rosalind's, he would have been livid at being kept in the dark.

Perhaps he had underestimated her commitment and loyalty to her people. She had supervised the estate to great triumph. The people were happy and thriving. They loved her well. They trusted her. While he, devil take him, had not.

Cursing an oath at his own thickheadedness, Malcolm unwittingly roused the ire of several swooning lasses engaged in rapturous admiration of their warbling troubadour. Pivoting on his heel, he left the women to their entertainment to search for Rosalind and admit he'd been selfish. Nay, ignorant.

Perhaps a bit of both.

Picking up his pace, he realized that Ian would have never been so stubborn with his wife. And their sire had taught them well to respect women. But Malcolm had allowed his experience with Isabel to taint his perceptions, and he'd taken it out on a lady who did not deserve his lack of trust. She'd given up her body to his passions. Had promised to wed him even though he'd promised naught but his protection in return.

Damn.

Unable to find her in the courtyard, he retreated indoors, certain he'd locate her in her chamber, as he had another time she'd tried to escape one of her outdoor revels. But shoving his way into her solar, he discovered nothing. Darkness greeted his eyes instead of a warm woman and the chance to make things right.

Where the devil could she be? Had she executed the latest in a long line of schemes to rid herself of him? But even as the thought formed in his mind, he dismissed it. Knew in his gut that she would not leave him now—not when there was a very real chance she carried his babe within her. And not when her people needed her. She was a lass who knew her duty.

Duty?

The word pierced him through. By God, he wanted to be more than some means to uphold her duty. In a blaze of comprehension he understood her frustration with his pathetic attempt at a proposal. No wonder she had stormed off to collect herself.

But if she hadn't departed for good, that left only one other possibility....

Fear gripped him as he admitted the very real alternative—that something had happened to her after she'd left him. And he'd been too caught up in his own frustrations, too blinded by the past to see what was right in front of him.

Love.

Damning the timing of a revelation he prayed did not come too late, he sprinted from the north tower back outside. As he called his brothers to him to organize a search for Rosalind, throughout the whole of England and Scotland, if necessary, he did not need to invoke the McNair motto of Family Above All to spur them to action. He knew Ian would track Rosalind faster than she could travel with naught but an hour's head start. Malcolm's English bride had won their hearts as surely as she had captured his own.

He only hoped he had the chance to tell her.

Rosalind awoke with her teeth jarring together painfully in an unceasing rhythm.

Forcing her jaw to remain still, she lifted her head slightly from its bouncing perch. Nausea roiled in her belly as she moved, a blinding pain in her head bringing everything back into focus. The argument with Malcolm. Her walk to the garden, where she'd been hit....

"Don't move," a feminine voice whispered harshly in her ear. "It won't hurt so much."

Confused, Rosalind remained as still as the perpetual jolting allowed. Slowly, she realized the jarring came from a horse's racing hooves, and that she was somehow secured in a saddle behind a warm body.

A warm, feminine body with a vaguely familiar voice.

"Who are you?" She could not imagine what woman would have had the strength to knock her out and drag her onto horseback.

"Shh," the impatient voice whispered back, familiar somehow. "'Tis Moira. We ride as Gregory's prisoners toward the Scottish king's encampment."

Rosalind's whole world slowed to the dull pace of her thudding heart. How on earth could Gregory have breached Beaumont's walls, which now stood stronger than ever before, with Malcolm overseeing their defense? And yet Rosalind could discern the hoofbeats of several other horses nearby, as if at least five men rode close to the mount she shared with the serving maid.

"You are a prisoner, too?" Rosalind simply could not piece together how Gregory's one ally at Beaumont would become his captive.

"I protested his scheme to abduct you."

Before Rosalind could ask more, a male voice from behind intruded on her thoughts. "Your hostage seems to be awake, Evandale."

Farther ahead, a man whistled and Rosalind felt their horse slow. Assuming there was no sense in pretending to be unconscious any longer, she lifted her head carefully to take in their surroundings for the first time.

"So she is." Gregory approached from the front of the small party, which totaled seven horses in all. A few of the men's faces seemed familiar from her brief expedition to Baliwick Keep. The others were strangers, but equally rough-looking. "We ride to commit grand deeds and leave a lasting impression on the Scots, Rosalind. I'm so glad you will be alert enough to take your revenge on the scourge of the north."

Recognizing the cliffs ahead as the same low mountains she sometimes spied to Beaumont's north on a clear day, she realized they were indeed headed into Scotland.

"It seems I've been seeking revenge on the wrong people for a long time." She forced herself to sit upright, grateful that their mount now stood still. It required every bit of strength she possessed to face the man who'd planned the murder of her whole family, and she did not blame Moira for shuddering violently as he neared. "Pray do not feel the need to include me in your plans."

"I fear you've been misinformed, lady, but I will have my retribution on your Scots despoiler before I am through." He reined in as his horse came flank to flank with hers. "Although I'll admit I'm surprised you would listen to the invader's words over mine. Perhaps you forget who will be the rightful lord of Beaumont?"

Cold fury sickened her at the thought of what this man had done to destroy her family. Her future. Her confidence. There had been a time when she would have railed at him for his evil deeds, giving no thought to anything save the need to fight back. But Malcolm had taught her more caution than that. Plus she had Moira's safety to consider, as well as her own.

No more would recklessness mark her actions. Too many people counted on her wisdom as their lady. The laird's lady. At last she was ready to embrace the destiny of the phoenix and heal the pain of her past.

"I have never forgotten my duty to Beaumont." In this, at least, she could be honest. Swallowing back her fears to arm herself with the only weapon she possessed, she sought knowledge and answers so she might go about formulating a strategy. A plan to save herself and the maid who sat quivering before her. "May I inquire exactly what sort of revenge you have in mind?"

An hour later, Rosalind half regretted her attempt to uncover the details of Gregory's despicable campaign against the Scots. Knowledge might be a tactical necessity, but it ate away at her as they rode closer to Robert the Bruce's hidden encampment and farther away from everyone she loved. Farther from Malcolm.

Heart aching with wanting him and with regret at not swearing her love to him the moment she'd realized her feelings, she bided her time as they traveled slowly, quietly, into hostile terrain. After tracking the Scots king's movements when he'd departed Beaumont, Gregory now planned to surprise Robert the Bruce with an attack. Gregory hoped that by delivering news of the Bruce's death, he would gain favor with Edward and the support he needed to reclaim Rosalind's keep. As for her, he planned to wed her once he was certain she did not carry another man's babe. But if she did, he'd simply tell the king it was his, and he'd let a midwife rid her of the child after they'd safely married.

Rosalind's womb had clenched achingly at his callous words, even as she knew she would never allow that to happen. Still, every detail of Gregory's malicious strategy had aggrieved her, but she had paid attention carefully, realizing Malcolm would need to know of the tactics once he arrived. But as the night stretched on endlessly, Rosalind began to wonder if he would find her missing soon enough to save his king. Would he think she'd left of her own volition this time? Surely he knew her too well by now.

When she could bear the silent darkness and the weight of her own fears no longer, she leaned close to Moira's ear and spoke as softly as she could.

"How did Gregory slip into Beaumont unnoticed?" Rosalind peered down at her belt as she waited for an answer, troubled by the loss of her mother's pomander at some point tonight.

Moira paused so long Rosalind feared she would not answer, but finally, the girl turned to murmur back. "When he helped rebuild the southern tower, he included a few loose stones in the walled garden, and also a few on one of the courtyard's outer walls, although I'm not sure where. You must check the whole structure for damage, my lady, for this one is slippery as a snake."

Rosalind would worry about her keep later. Right now her main concern was not endangering the Scots. If Malcolm did not arrive in time to stop Gregory, she would have to find a way to warn King Robert of the English threat. But how could she accomplish the feat while still a prisoner?

They reached the top of a hill under the cover of a thick stand of trees. Quickly, soundlessly, Gregory's men slid off their mounts to fall to their bellies. Gregory approached the captured women, first lashing Moira more tightly to the saddle and then pushing Rosalind to the ground. Had they arrived at their destination? Her heart raced within her chest as she glanced up at the moon, far advanced in its arc across the sky. It must be long past midnight. A couple of hours from dawn, she guessed.

"You will have a front row view of your vengeance, Rosalind," he whispered in her ear, his breath stale and his body rank with the scents of the road. He pushed her to the fringes of a small clearing, where he pushed her flat to the ground beneath him.

When she was able to lift her chin without arousing Gregory's notice, she peered through the trees. No campfire brightened the night, so it took a moment for her eyes to discern the dark forms lying in the clearing. Sleeping.

They were at their rest the same way her family had been when their home had been set on fire all around them. Had Gregory remained this close to the burning tower that night for a front row view? Had he heard their screams?

Tears burned her eyes, pain clawing through her chest. She would not allow Robert the Bruce to suffer thus. No man deserved to die so ignobly, and especially not a proud warrior Malcolm saw fit to follow into battle. But most of all, she had to save this small band of sleeping men because she had not been given a chance to save her mother. Her father. Her young brother, who'd already wielded a sword as deftly as men twice his age.

As she lay very still, her mind made up, she heard the musical lilt of the Scots brogue.

A sentinel on duty, perhaps?

This was her chance. Whoever watched over the king tonight, he would hear her easily if she called out to him. This was to be no honorable battle among warriors, but a treacherous massacre by a man no more a true and noble knight than the vermin that crawled in dark dungeons. As she counted the sleeping forms about the clearing, she knew the Scots were a greater force of men than the small group that ventured up the hill with Gregory.

The majority of her body was pressed between Gregory and the ground. Only her head and one shoulder were free of his weight. She prayed Gregory would not feel her large intake of breath as she prepared to shout.

"'Tis a trap!"

The words resounded in the still of the night before the steel blade of Gregory's knife pricked her neck, cutting off the sound.

* * *

Riding deeper into the rocky terrain of southern Scotland, Malcolm detected Rosalind's cry with his heart more clearly than with his ears. He could not mistake that voice he'd grown so familiar with over the last moon.

He would trust his heart this time instead of cool-headed strategy, he decided. If his love for her made him less cautious, he did not care.

He heard his brothers' shouts behind him as they urged their mounts faster. Ian had tracked Rosalind's captors easily, his task simplified once they'd spotted Rosalind's pomander on the ground in the middle of nowhere, affirming their course. They'd discerned that the path followed the same general direction Robert the Bruce had planned to take after departing Beaumont Keep. Treachery was afoot this night, and somehow Rosalind had landed in the thick of it.

Saints protect her until he could.

The sounds of battle emanated from the top of the rise, all precipitated by Rosalind's shouted warning. Had she endangered herself to alert Malcolm's king to their presence? No other scenario made sense to his racing thoughts.

Vaulting from his horse, he saw that a band of Scots swarmed a small group of ragged English knights. He noted the serving maid Moira cowering atop a frightened horse nearby. But Malcolm barely took note of any of this. He had his eye on one man alone. The man whose blade glinted in the moonlight beside Rosalind's pale neck.

Gregory Evandale.

Malcolm gulped back an empathetic pang as he forced himself to gauge his opponent rather than Rosalind's panicky wide eyes. Thank God for the full moon, which bathed the whole clearing in ghostly light as swords clashed, some men shouting in rage while others called out in terror. Evandale's grip on Rosalind was steady. Firm.

"Back off, McNair. You do not want the blood of your whore on your hands, English or not." Evandale looped a length of rope around their wrists, haphazardly tying his captive to him.

"Dinna hurt her. I am unarmed." Noting the slow trickle of red running down her slender white neck, Malcolm backed away, laying his sword on the ground. Never had he felt so helpless.

She had risked her lifeblood to save his people, and now he could only watch as a madman threatened her. His own throat seemed to dry up and close as if he were choking, his windpipe squeezed by guilt and recrimination.

Why hadn't he placed more faith in her? Trusted her with every bit of information he'd learned of Evandale's treachery the moment he'd discovered it? Malcolm owed Rosalind so much.

Her eyes communicated no blame. Only forgiveness and a love he wanted so damn badly his hands shook with the need to reach out and touch her.

Yet Gregory held her in front of him, cravenly shielding himself from potential attack with Rosalind's body. By now, most of Evandale's men had been either killed or captured. The king would have been brought to a safer location to regroup, Malcolm guessed. From the corner of his eye, he spied Jamie cinching the wrists of an unconscious man to a nearby tree.

"This scruffy lot will hardly bring a fine ransom, eh, brother?"

Receiving no response, Jamie must have looked up to see the encounter between Malcolm and his English foe, for his voice took on a more clipped tone.

"What do you want?" he called, interrupting the silent face-off.

Gregory glanced from one man to the other while Malcolm waited for any opportunity to approach.

"I want a horse." Evandale's forehead shone with sweat in the moonlight, and his voice had a desperate edge. "You do not wish her dead, do you, McNair? You have grown accustomed to having her in your bed, have you not?"

Malcolm stepped toward him, willing himself to move as slowly and steadily as possible so as not to startle his opponent. He had not lost a fight in ten years, and wasn't going to now, not with Rosalind's life at stake.

"Ye can have yer horse." He waved for Jamie, knowing his brother would aid him. And now that the battle around them had quieted, there would be more of Robert's men ready to help. Yet all the combined muscle of the Highlands could not save Rosalind if Evandale's knife went astray.

"Do not come any closer," Gregory warned, his

blade shifting slightly. "One more step and she is dead."

Nervous men did stupid things. Hellfire, he couldn't let this man's stupid move hurt the woman Malcolm loved.

"If she dies, ye will follow her in the next instant." Malcolm shook his head. "Nay, in the next instant ye shall pray for death, but it shall not be granted to ye. Ye will suffer long and slow if ye so much as nick her, so I suggest ye hold the lass a bit more gently."

"Then where's my horse?"

Jamie brought a mount forward, but Gregory did not take the reins immediately. He eyed the beast and Malcolm by turns, as if unsure how to mount while maintaining his hold on Rosalind.

If only the bastard did not hold the knife so tightly to her throat, damn his eyes. The Englishman would kill her if he were allowed to leave the encampment with her; Malcolm knew it deep in his bones. He had to keep Gregory here, and keep him talking.

"So ye will be the coward yet again, Evandale. I have learned ye're always eager to turn tail and run from a fight, never facing yer enemy directly."

"You are the first man to ever suggest I did not appreciate a good brawl, McNair. I am usually blamed for entering a fray too enthusiastically."

"Ach." Malcolm scoffed, sensing a potential weakness in his enemy—pride. He kept his finger on that sore spot, preparing to dig deep. "That wasna the case when ye set yer lord's house on fire in the dead of night. Does it nae chafe yer pride that Rosalind always railed about the act as a plot of sheer cowardice?"

He kept his tone deliberately light, as if challenging a man in a tavern boasting contest instead of wagering Rosalind's life on the outcome of their argument.

"It matters not, since you and I both know it was not fear that forced me to set fire to Beaumont, but the acquisition of power." Evandale nudged Rosalind closer to the horse with a rough shove, his breath a white cloud in the cold night air. "Besides, your countrymen do that sort of thing all the time."

"To garrison quarters and weapon supplies, mayhap, but nae to perfectly good keeps." Malcolm turned to the crowd of other Scots around them and gave a sly wink. "Especially nae to those keeps we are trying to gain for our own."

Laughter shook the clearing as the Scots took up the call to mockery, and Malcolm thanked God he could count on his men to follow where he led.

"Destroy it first and then take it," one man shouted. "A brilliant scheme."

"In three years he still hasna managed to wed the heiress," Jamie called above the din. "How long did it take a Scotsman to claim the lass?"

Malcolm thought he'd probably owe Jamie a few blows for the possible insult to Rosalind, but forgave him instantly as he realized the comment seemed to hit gold. Evandale leaned forward to sneer contemptuously at the group.

They'd struck a nerve.

"We will see who gains Beaumont in the end, you heathen pigs." He lifted his leg to the stirrup and hauled himself into the saddle, dragging Rosalind with him. "I've got the heiress now."

He moved only slightly, but it was enough to change the angle of the knife at Rosalind's throat.

As the last word died on Evandale's lips, Malcolm lunged for the arm with the knife, startling the horse into motion and inciting an uproar in the clearing.

Jamie attacked at nearly the same instant, and was already hanging on to man and beast on the other side when the frightened horse reared at the sudden weight and pull of four adults on its back. Jamie worked his blade furiously against the rope that bound Rosalind to her captor, the rearing of the horse thwarting his efforts at every turn.

The motion of the horse failed to faze Malcolm, who held on to Gregory's arm with the ferocity of a wild dog with a fresh kill in its mouth. But he could not control the movement of Evandale's arm as it flailed in reaction to the jolt of the horse and the attackers at two sides.

With brute strength, Malcolm kept Evandale's blade away from Rosalind, but as Jamie's knife freed her, she began to slide awkwardly from the horse. Malcolm reached for her with his other arm, afraid she would be trampled.

And in that moment of distracted focus, Evandale lunged, his blade striking her shoulder. Her eyes rolled back and then closed as if in a faint or—hellfire—the bastard had killed her.

Malcolm yanked Evandale from the horse the moment Jamie's arms steadied Rosalind's limp body.

Wrestling his quarry to the ground, Malcolm scarcely saw Gregory's face for the mental image of the jagged red wound gaping across Rosalind's chest. He pounded the Englishman's hand until his opponent released the bloody weapon, and only then did it occur to him how easily Evandale had let go.

The cheers of his men and even the picture of Rosalind's fatal wound faded from his mind as he again focused on his rival. Gregory Evandale lay dead at Malcolm's feet, his neck twisted in their fall from the horse.

Malcolm never relished the taking of a life, but this man's death left him especially empty inside. Rosalind's family had been avenged. Rosalind had been avenged, yet…

He had never failed so deeply if the woman he loved had been wounded as gravely as he feared. And he'd never had a chance to tell her. Regret and fear seemed to suck the lifeblood from him as it occurred to him he did not have the courage to gaze upon her right now if…

Holy hell. For the second time in his life, he'd failed to protect a woman he felt responsible for.

"Malcolm." Jamie's voice drew him back from dark places within. "I think she calls for ye."

He blinked rapidly, trying to focus on the words spoken to him and the person who spoke them.

"Hurry," Jamie pressed. "I dinna know if she is close to death."

Sweet Mother of Heaven, he meant Rosalind.

Malcolm rushed to where Jamie and Ian already fidgeted over her supine figure. Besides the long red gash that crossed her chest from her left shoulder to a hand's span beneath her right collarbone, she bore a purple bruise at her temple.

"I will hold her." If she was aware of anything before she passed out of this world, selfish or not, Malcolm wanted it to be him. Nudging his brothers aside, he placed his hand over the linen they'd laid against her bleeding wound.

Douglas McConnell, a grizzled Highlander with a scant knowledge of medicine, hurried over.

"Gently, McNair." He gripped Malcolm's forearm, forcing him to loosen his hold a bit. "A wound needs firm pressure, nae the whole force of yer sword arm."

"Think ye she may yet live?" A flame sparked within his chest.

Hope.

"I am nae sure, but she has no hope at all if ye squeeze the last of the poor lass's lifeblood from her chest. Someone get a fire going, real hot like."

Several men ran to do Douglas's bidding, while Malcolm knew he'd been gifted with that rarest of life's opportunities—a second chance.

"What can I do?" he asked, needing to do something—anything—to help her.

"She will die for sure if we move her. Can ye build a shelter around her without dropping anything on the poor lass or getting in my way? She needs a warm place to recover, if she has it in her, but we canna drag her through the woods. Her wound is too great."

"She has it in her," Malcolm assured him, new-found conviction pulsing in his veins as he relinquished her slowly, carefully, into Douglas McConnell's care. "I can build a damn keep about her, if ye will only hold her among the living."

Malcolm watched her sleep for long hours of the night and into the next dawn, thankful every time her chest rose faintly and fell again. She looked frail in the glow of the firelight. Her skin was even more pale than usual, her lips and cheeks devoid of their usual rosy hue.

Yet he was aware of a strange sense of dependence upon the slender figure that rested before him. Despite her small frame, she embodied strength in Malcolm's mind. She was loyal, she was brave, she was clever. Where else would he find a woman who could wield her own crossbow with the fierce accuracy of any knight *and* tenderly care for her people with the warmth of a woman's heart?

He was heartsore to imagine life without Rosalind Beaumont. No more lessons in farming. No more arguments in the garden. No more lovemaking in her rose-scented chamber.

He withdrew the small pomander, which he had carried since discovering it on their journey earlier. Fingering the carved images in the polished silver, he closed his eyes and prayed. Then, gently shifting the blankets at her waist, he clipped the pomander back onto her girdle, laying it in its rightful place to work whatever magic it might contain.

Chapter Eighteen

Days passed. Rosalind did not know how long it was since she'd been injured, but she had been vaguely aware of a frightening time in a strange forest, with an extraordinary assortment of Highlanders surrounding her bed. Maybe she'd dreamed it. But she was certain she'd at last come home to Beaumont, even if her condition had weakened and fevered dreams still plagued her.

She remained certain of her location because she could smell the roses. Malcolm would bring her to her mother's garden to sit and recover her strength, even though he had no idea why she needed to be here to regain her vigor. When she was well enough, she would explain it all. Reveal to him how she'd buried her parents and her brother in a far corner of the once-charred plot. Explain how she'd protected this site and tended it because the earth here had welcomed her family and flourished in honor of them.

And some days, like now, as she sat on her bench

beneath a cherry tree, she could almost imagine she visited with her family. No doubt the leftover fevers helped her retain the illusion. Truly, she enjoyed those days of rest and recovery and mild delirium. They were some of the happiest of Rosalind's life. Her mother greeted her with the open-armed welcome of a parent who has not seen her child for years. Her father spun her around in a whirling dance, telling her over and over how proud he was of his heir. She spent long days playing with her brother, who was just as she remembered him. But at last her mother urged her to return to Malcolm. To her destiny.

Family above all, Rosalind thought.

"We have only come to comfort you in your time of need, Daughter." Her father's voice echoed in her head. "But now there is much that needs to be done at Beaumont."

"I tried to stay loyal to our king, Father, truly I did, but—"

He held up his hand. "You are my heir, Rosalind. I trust *you* to decide where Beaumont should stand in these times of unrest. You will do what is best for our people and your family."

"Can you tell me what is the right thing, Father? I have struggled over it for so long…."

"The answer is within you, Rosalind. You have not grappled with your heart and soul all this time only to have me tell you what path to follow."

"I am in love with a Scot, Father. It was not his people who set the fire."

Shannon Beaumont stroked her daughter's fevered

brow with a cool and soothing hand. "Your young man has avenged our deaths. He is a brave and loyal warrior."

Her words faded as the Beaumont family retreated from Rosalind's sight. She felt a crushing pain in the area of her heart to see them leave. She cried out, but it was only a moment before another hand touched her. Soothed her.

Only this was not the cool, long-fingered hand of her mother. It was a warm, huge palm that covered her whole cheek.

A man's hand.

Her pain lessened considerably.

"Can ye hear me, lass?"

She smiled to perceive the lilt of Scotland in the voice. She warmed to its rich timbre, its comforting sound. Even as weariness overtook her, she trusted that she could sink into that sound, and into the hard warmth of the strong male beside her.

"I will import a hundred of the most rare rosebushes for ye if ye will but open yer eyes and heal."

She smiled at the thought of rosebushes.

"Ach! I see a grin play about those fair lips, lady. Ye can hear me, after all, and are just playacting at sleep. I see that I am having to buy yer affections to get any notice from ye. Who knew ye to be such a covetous creature, Rosalind Beaumont?"

Sighing peacefully as the warm hand stroked her hair, she breathed in the scents of sun and leather and wind as the man leaned over and kissed her brow.

Malcolm.

The thought of him sent a delicious shiver through

her body. He was here with her, taking care of her. Hadn't her mother said he was brave and loyal?

Rosalind knew her course of action now. She would marry Malcolm McNair, just as she had planned before Gregory made one last attempt to hurt her family. She loved this particular Scotsman with all her heart.

Vaguely aware of strong arms carrying her back to her bed, she fell into a deep, healing slumber, dreaming of a phoenix with brilliant wings outstretched.

"Malcolm?"

He could almost believe he dreamed her voice. It would not be the first time in the last five days that he imagined she called out to him. He had scarcely left her side in all the time she'd spent healing, stepping away for only moments at a time or when Gerta forced him out with her haranguing rants.

"Malcolm?"

Levering himself up onto an elbow where he lay atop her blankets, beside her on the large bed, he found her gaze clear and focused. Her cheeks were vaguely pink. Her brow felt cool and dry for the first time in five days.

She would live. Douglas McConnell had already confirmed as much when he'd given Malcolm permission to bring her home two days prior. Many times over the past few days Malcolm had thanked heaven he'd found a woman with so much strength and determination. Never again would he bemoan Rosalind's ambition. Only that unflagging will of hers could have kept her alive after what she'd been through.

"Aye, love? I am here." He squeezed her hand and

stroked her hair, gestures repeated countless times in the past days and nights.

"You are really here." Her voice rasped oddly from lack of use.

He passed her a cup of wine from the chest at her bedside. Gerta had delivered food and wine so frequently since he'd brought Rosalind home that Malcolm had taken to sneaking some of the food to the keep's cats. The old nurse had near fretted herself sick when she'd seen her mistress's wounded body.

"Aye, and where else would I be with ye teetering near the edge of death?" He watched her drink, gratitude for her life swelling inside him. He would not take this chance with her for granted.

Would never take *her* for granted.

Nay, she would soon become part of his family, and he would place her needs above his own, in keeping with the McNair creed. And he would do so not out of any sense of duty, but out of love.

"I am better." The scratchy quality had left her voice, her tones as soft and mellifluous now as he remembered. "*Much* better."

"Is that so?" He wondered if she had many memories from her wound and the recovery. He'd tried so hard to make some of it pleasant, with visits to the garden she loved. But he knew she'd been in pain much of the time. "Yer wound doesna hurt?"

She lifted her body a fraction of an inch and promptly winced. "Perhaps still a bit sore."

"Dinna do too much now that ye are fully conscious at last." Steadying her on the pillows, he helped prop her up a bit higher. He stroked her hair from her face, savoring the warmth in her gaze. "But ye're feeling better in other ways?"

Rosalind closed her eyes at the sensation of Malcolm's hands upon her. His touch comforted her, aye, but there was more to it than that. Despite her physical weakness, a rogue twinge of desire surprised her. Delighted her. But she would tell him that later, after they'd settled so many other things between them.

"Strangely enough, I feel as though I've come to the end of a long journey. I did not understand much of what happened after you fought with Gregory on horseback, but I was alert enough to realize he died." Malcolm would have interrupted, but she did not wish to speak of her captor any longer than necessary. Placing her fingers lightly across his lips, she shushed him. "He would have killed Moira and me both eventually." Her hands skimmed her flat belly as she remembered what else he'd threatened. "And he vowed to take the life of any child I carried if I was expecting."

Malcolm's voice dropped to a scant whisper as he brushed his fingers along her arm. "Are ye?"

"I don't think so." Peering up at him, she could almost believe she spied something new in his gaze. Some tenderness she'd never noticed before. "But I cannot be sure. Just the idea that he would go to such lengths to achieve his ends..." She shuddered at the memory. "I only wanted you to know I don't blame you for killing him."

"He broke his neck in a fall from the horse." Malcolm twined a strand of her hair about his finger, staring down at the pale lock. "I have thought many times since that night how fortunate I am that it wasna ye who fell instead."

She detected the pain in his voice. The recrimination. Two emotions she knew well. "You did everything you could to save me. My last solid memory before the pain set in was of you steadying me after Gregory slashed at my chest. If not for your arm around me then, I surely would have fallen. I could have broken my neck or been trampled."

"It's a bloody miracle we survived, is it nae?" He met her gaze then, his blue eyes definitely full of tenderness. She had not been certain before, but now she could see the love shining there.

"Aye." Her heart pounded in joyful acknowledgment of what he'd said—and didn't say. Even if her battle-weary warrior could never speak the words her heart craved, she would bask in the warmth of his eyes, where his love was deliciously obvious. "A miracle."

She would have liked a few more moments alone to follow that thought, but their conversation was interrupted by Gerta's appearance in the entryway to Rosalind's solar. Gerta took one look inside the chamber and then turned back to shout down the corridor.

"Our lady is awake!"

The news seemed to echo through the whole of the stone keep, bouncing off the walls from one server to another until a great cheer went up in the hall at the base of the stairs.

"Thank the dear Lord you are well, my lady." Gerta

bustled about the room, checking the fire and Rosalind's brow, and patting her hand. "You had us all so worried. Your young laird here, most of all."

Malcolm did not deny it, a fact that warmed Rosalind's heart even more.

"I am surely well only because of your care." Her cheeks heated under Malcolm's stare. "I owe you both many thanks."

By then, footsteps clunked in the corridor, followed quickly by the appearance of a handful of her household staff peering in her doorway to wish her well. Ian and Jamie McNair came crowding in behind them.

Malcolm's brothers shoved their way inside in a mutual raid on her domain. Ian reached her first.

"Praise the saints." He clapped Malcolm on the shoulder, while Jamie laid a gentle kiss on Rosalind's fingers. "Welcome back."

Jamie bowed deeply. "Aye, this place is sadly lacking without ye. Yer future laird doesna possess the same gracious hospitality as ye."

Although she smiled, tears welled in her eyes as she gazed up at the McNair men, a stalwart wall of muscle to protect her from the rest of the world. Ian and Jamie were the brothers of her heart. And Malcolm was so much more.

"Rest well," Ian told her, pushing Jamie out of the chamber along with a handful of maids and other stragglers. He turned to wink at Malcolm before leaving. "And take yer time about it."

Gerta scurried out after them, closing the door with a soft thud.

Rosalind thought she would never tire of being left alone with Beaumont's new laird. She had so much to look forward to once she recovered fully.

"Ye have no idea how grateful my king is to ye for what ye did to save him and his men that night, Rosalind." Malcolm poured them both more wine, his movements as careful and measured as his words. "I think ye may be an honorary Scot in the Bruce's book, whether ye will it or nae."

"Me?" She smiled and took another long drink. "I do not think I have the lilt for a Highland lass." Her smile faded as she thought of her shout into the darkness that night, an act some of her countrymen would consider treason. "I simply could not allow a massacre. My father was given no chance to fight, Malcolm, and I could not rob another noble knight of that opportunity."

"Ye showed mercy when it was called for. I imagine yer sire would be proud." He set aside his wine again, and then hers. "I am proud of ye, too."

"Really?" The warmth curling through her had little to do with the wine and everything to do with Malcolm.

"More than ye can know." He touched the pomander that she was surprised to see dangling from the chain at her waist. Had he put her lost charm there? "I regret not telling ye of Evandale's treachery sooner. Ye had every right to the knowledge. My only excuse— and it isna an adequate one—is that I have long commanded the Bruce's troops. I only concerned myself with preventing Evandale's return and nae yer needs."

"He rebuilt some of the walls with loose rocks." She'd learned that much on her own at least. "We must check every inch of the outer walls, and the garden walls as well."

"Aye." Malcolm knew already. Of course he knew. But he listened to her suggestion anyway, even though he'd surely already assigned men to the task.

She fell in love a little more.

"But right now, I am nae concerned with Evandale or defenses or how much Robert the Bruce sings yer praises."

"No?"

"Nae." He pulled her to him gently. Carefully. "I love ye, woman, more than ye can guess."

Words evaded her at his admission, so unexpected and so welcome. She could only blink in mute response, her mind surely not comprehending him properly.

But then his hands were all over her, caressing her shoulders, skimming down her arms and sliding over her back. "I love ye, lass, so much I thought I died inside when I saw Gregory's knife sink into ye. It nearly killed me to think of ye gone from me."

"Truly?" Her arms were weak as she lifted them, yet she found enough strength to wrap them around her warrior.

"Aye." Vehemence filled his voice as he released her enough to peer down at her. "Ye must swear ye'll never leave me. I dinna think I could bear it."

"I swear it, my lord, since I love you with all the fierceness of my heart." She trailed her fingers over the hard planes of his face, tracing the rough edge of his jaw, the sensuous curve of his mouth with her finger. "And I vow I will fight *for* you as passionately as I once fought against you for the sake of my home."

A smile curved his lips. "That is a promise of formidable strength."

She laughed contentedly, realizing the warm, teasing voice from her feverish dreams had been all too real. Malcolm had talked to her often in the hazy days of her fever, but she had scarcely dared to believe some of his promises.

Remembering one in particular, she paused.

"Did you really say you would import a hundred rosebushes for me?"

"Ach. Ye did indeed hear me then. Yes, my greedy one, I did say that. But I dinna care how many roses I have to find for ye, as long as ye will tell me more of this love ye have for me." He kissed the palm of her hand in a slow, deliberate gesture, his eyes never leaving hers. "Tell me of that."

"Malcolm." She closed her eyes as he drew lightly on each fingertip, and she suddenly remembered that the very first reason he'd wanted to marry her still applied. There would be so much pleasure between them.

"Tell me." He stroked lazy circles up her arm before dipping underneath the blankets to curve a hand about her hip.

"I do not know how I came to love a heathen Scot." She sucked in a breath as his fingertips brushed along her thigh. "But I can assure you that I am powerless to stop myself."

"I'd better cease before I am powerless to stop myself, as well." He kissed her long and deeply, the taste of him arousing her for more intimate touches. "But I will be content as long as ye promise me a wedding, lass."

"I promise." She nipped his lower lip and wriggled closer to him. "And pray, do not halt on my account, my lord."

"Ye only just recovered." He closed his eyes as she tugged at the ties of his tunic and laid kisses along his chest. "I wouldna hurt ye after ye've worked so hard to regain yer health. Ye ken?"

"Please." Shoving aside the linens, she pressed herself to him without the barrier of the sheets. After her fearful trek into the night with Gregory and her bout with injury, she wanted nothing so much as to join with Malcolm again, to be secure in her love for him, and the knowledge that her love was returned.

He hesitated for a moment, as if he feared disturbing her newly healed wound. Sensing his dilemma, she slid her arms about his neck and drew him down over her.

"We will be careful. And I have great need of you." She kissed him lightly, delighting in his resulting groan. "Ye ken?"

Powerless in the face of such logic, Malcolm went about healing the rest of Rosalind's wounds, demonstrating his love in ways that his words had not begun to describe.

Epilogue

~~~~~~~~~~~~~~~~~~~~~~~~~

August 1309

The unmistakable hiss of an arrow whizzing through the sky reached Malcolm's ears, and he followed the arc of his wife's shot with amazed eyes as they stood atop the crenellated parapets of Beaumont Keep.

The sun shone brightly upon them, as well as the fields ripe to bursting with another good harvest. He smiled as Rosalind lowered her crossbow, an unmistakable glint of pride in her gray eyes as she turned to peer at him.

"I'll have you know that motherhood has not compromised my aim, heathen." She winked cheekily, the last two incredible years together having given her a fresh happiness that benefited everyone around her. Malcolm most of all.

"I never suggested it had for a moment, lass." He

slid his arms around her, grateful for a few moments to have her all to himself while Gerta watched over their new babe, Keenan, and their toddling firstborn, William. "Mayhap it has improved yer shot, if anything. I dinna think I would have ever breached yer walls if ye had launched that arrow with such aim back then."

"Really?" Leaning against the wall, she sent him a mock glare. "Then why did you suggest we come up here so we could practice my shot?"

"Did ye not guess?" He stepped closer, bracketing her body with his arms, savoring the rose scent of her that he would never tire of if he lived to be a thousand. "Maybe I just wanted an excuse to get ye alone."

He cradled her cheek with his palm, his eyes roving over her hungrily. Her green-yellow gown shimmered with the precise hue of newly unfurled spring leaves, the voluminous folds and rich color conveying wealth. A golden girdle sparkled around her hips in the sinking sunlight.

And her hair…

It still outshone her golden adornments, floating in a halo about her head and shoulders, then rippling clear down to her waist. Merciful saints, but he loved this woman.

And while her beauty pleased him, mostly what he loved was her strength. Her fearless defense of those she loved, her untiring willingness to sing William all his favorite lullabies at night. Her insistence on riding by Malcolm's side when he toured the perimeter of their lands. Truly, she was the strongest woman he'd ever known.

"Well, Malcolm McNair…" She peered around their breezy tower perch, taking in the vast expanse of Beaumont below them and then their private stone enclosure high above. "It seems you have gotten your wish and we are very much alone. Just what did you have in mind?"

"Come with me." He pulled her farther along the wall, up over the gatehouse toward the south tower, where the parapet overlooked the garden she'd expanded in the last two years. Roses climbed the walls beneath them and the floral scents from her private sanctuary, the resting place of her family, drifted on the warm breeze. "I brought out a few items we might need…."

He watched her gaze fall upon the nest of blankets he'd arranged there, a heap of furs and linens that would keep them well insulated from the rock walls all around.

"You wicked, wicked man." Smiling as she declared him so, he noticed her pronouncement didn't keep her from twining her arms about his neck. "After all this time you still have pleasure on your mind."

Welcoming the press of her soft curves against him, he tugged her down into the blankets to enjoy his bride.

"Aye, but I married ye for so much more than that, wife." His heart still clenched sometimes as he thought of how close he'd once come to losing her.

"I love you, Malcolm McNair." She breathed the sentiment over his lips as she kissed him, her honeyed lips the sweetest confection he'd ever tasted.

"I love ye even more, lass." Sliding her gown away from her shoulders, he rained kisses over old scars and soft skin, savoring every inch of her. "Now ye only have to let me show ye how much."

* * * * *

Harlequin® Historical
Historical Romantic Adventure!

THREE RUGGED WESTERN MEN
THREE COURAGEOUS LADIES
THREE FESTIVE TALES TO WARM
THE HEART THIS CHRISTMAS!

ON SALE OCTOBER 2005

ROCKY MOUNTAIN CHRISTMAS
by Jillian Hart

Summoned on a dangerously snowy night to deal with two stowaways, Sheriff Mac McKaslin discovers they are none other than a homeless young widow—Carrie Montgomery—and her baby. But will the sheriff send them out into the cold...or find a warm place for them in his heart?

THE CHRISTMAS GIFTS
by Kate Bridges

When Sergeant James Fielder arrives with a baby on his sled, he turns to Maggie Greerson for help. This special interlude allows Maggie to fulfill her secret dream of having a child— and explore the attraction that has always drawn her to James....

THE CHRISTMAS CHARM
by Mary Burton

Determined to prevent her younger sister from marrying the wrong man, widow Colleen Garland enlists the help of her onetime love Keith Garrett. Will their rescue mission finally lead them on the road to true love?

BRENDA JOYCE

On the evening of her first masquerade, shy Elizabeth Anne
Fitzgerald is stunned by Tyrell de Warenne's whispered suggestion
of a midnight rendezvous in the gardens. Lizzie has secretly
worshiped the unattainable lord for years. When fortune
takes a maddening turn, she is prevented from meeting Tyrell.
But Lizzie has not seen the last of him....

Tyrell de Warenne is shocked when, two years later, Lizzie
arrives on his doorstep with a child she claims is his. He
remembers her well—and knows that he could not possibly
be the father. Is Elizabeth Anne Fitzgerald a woman of
experience, or the gentle innocent she seems?

The
MASQUERADE